Praise for

WHAT'S LEFT *of* *the* NIGHT

"In most lives there are no crucial moments, only representative ones. *What's Left of the Night* illuminates three days in 1897 when Constantine Cavafy began to glimpse what would be his destiny (his voice and his subject) as a major poet. Sotiropoulos notices every encounter and records every intuition with a lyrical, impressionistic style of her own. A perfect book."

—EDMUND WHITE,
author of *A Boy's Own Story* and *Genet: A Biography*

"This elegant translation by Karen Emmerich of a provocative account of C.P. Cavafy's visit to Paris, based on published sources and archival work combined with novelist Ersi Sotiropoulos's rich imagination, illuminates an artist in ways that will please both those already familiar with Cavafy and those discovering this great poet of the past century."

—EDMUND KEELEY,
author of *Cavafy's Alexandria* and translator,
with Philip Sherrard, of *C. P. Cavafy: Collected Poems*

"Splendid ... limpid and passionate ... fluid and musical, Ersi Sotiropoulos's prose says it perfectly ... You can read this beautiful book by Ersi Sotiropoulos as an account of three key days in the life of Constantine Cavafy. You can read it as a passionate introduction to his work ... but you can also see it on a more metaphorical level. That of a reflection about art. How is it born? Where does it come from?"

—*LE MONDE*

"Ersi Sotiropoulos fathoms with acuity the birth of her hero's unique voice ... In language marked by chiaroscuro, sobs and sublime anger, she suggests that the gloomy darkness of real life is often the breeding ground of a great oeuvre."

—*MAGAZINE LITTÉRAIRE*

"Sensual, carnal and profound, this novel manages to render through its own rhythm the scansion of Greek verse, thereby transporting us along on the wanderings of one of the greatest poets in the history of world literature. Not to be missed."

—*LES CHRONIQUES CULTURELLES* \

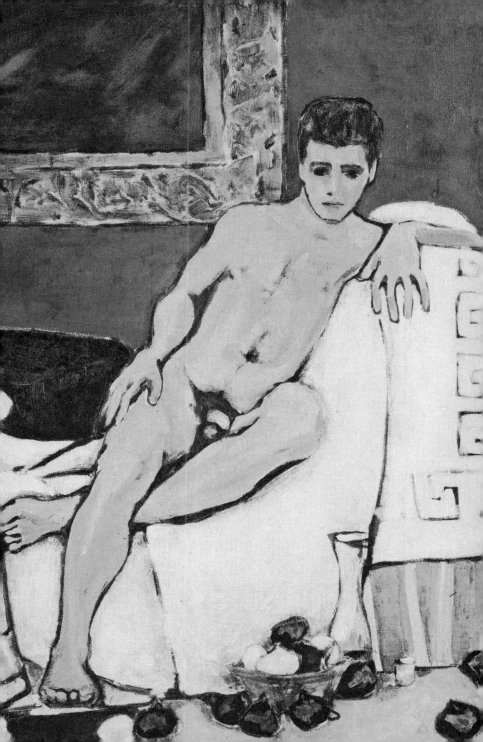

WHAT'S LEFT *of* the NIGHT

ERSI SOTIROPOULOS

Translated from the Greek by Karen Emmerich

NEW VESSEL PRESS
NEW YORK

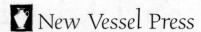

New Vessel Press

www.newvesselpress.com

First published in Greek by Patakis in 2015 as TI MENEI AΠO TH N Y XTA
Copyright © 2015 Ersi Sotiropoulos
By arrangement with Walkabout Literary Agency
Translation Copyright © 2018 Karen Emmerich

Support for the translation of this book was generously supplied by the Kostas and
Eleni Ouranis Foundation, under the auspices of the Academy of Athens.

Library of Congress Cataloging-in-Publication Data
Sotiropoulos, Ersi
[TI MENEI AΠO TH N Y XTA. Greek]
What's Left of the Night/ Ersi Sotiropoulos; translation by Karen Emmerich.
p. cm.
ISBN 978-1-939931-61-0
Library of Congress Control Number 2018940331
I. Greece—Fiction

Someone calls to me from Seir,
"Watchman, what is left of the night?
What is left of the night?"

ISAIAH 21:11

For P (v + t)

Eyes closed, I turned toward you in bed. I stretched a hand through the half-light to touch your shoulder. That exquisite curve, the pale skin, paler against the dirty sheet. Nothing written on skin can be erased, I told myself. Five years ago, at a similar hour, you stirred in your sleep and your thigh brushed against me. I was still wearing my shirt. My hand slid over your chest, which was hairless and tawny with an undertone of ochre. I remember it strong, hairless, bright. The line of your mouth, that pink, open circle, and the gleam of a tooth, barely visible. A bit of dried saliva. I traced your lips with my fingers. Then my hand crept lower, lower still. You breathed, snoring slightly. In your sleep you rolled over and wrapped your arms around me. You murmured a word I didn't know. Perhaps you were thirsty. My hand opened and closed ...

A shudder swept over the empty bed. I'd left the window open and the curtains fluttered in the Parisian breeze. It was time I abandoned these rêveries. John would be waiting in the lobby.

The earth still seemed flat then, and night fell all at once until the end of the world, where someone hunched in the light of a lamp would be able to see, centuries later, a red sun setting over ruins, would be able to see, beyond seas and ruined harbors, countries lost in time living in the glow of triumph, in the slow agony of defeat. History repeats itself, he thought, though he wasn't sure whether it really was repetition. His talent and persistence alone would allow him to see. Gripping his pen, he listened. Sounds, lights, smells, it all came flooding back. It was night once more on the flat earth. Voices reached his ears. A strain of cheap music from Attarin where the shops were open late, the sound of a barrel organ whose saccharine melody swelled and overflowed and climbed the muddy stairs. In the rooms upstairs limbs mingled on threadbare sheets. For half an hour of perfect pleasure, half an hour of absolute, sensual pleasure. Limbs, lips, eyelids on the squalid bed, kisses, gasping mouths. Then they would leave separately like fugitives, knowing this half an hour would haunt the rest of their lives, knowing they would return to seek it again. But now all they wanted was for the night to swallow them up, and as each hurried down the stairs that unbearable tinkle of music greeted him once more, a wobbly chime that mocked the oppressive thud of his heart. The street outside was always deserted, and the footsteps of an invisible shadow would echo in the distance, then fade. He'd stand for a moment in the doorway, then button his coat and walk quickly away, hugging the wall, head bent, collar raised. And sometimes it happened, it had in fact happened, that his eyes would meet the eyes of another man skidding like a rat through the darkness, some nervous, well-dressed man coming from the other direction, heading hypnotized toward those same stairs, that same room, to roll over those same stained sheets.

And if the lovers don't respond to your touch? he thought. If they're warm, soft-skinned statues that receive all caresses with the indifference of works of art? That Platonic idea enticed him, but only to a point. The object of desire was so distant, so close. Lips, limbs, bodies. Lips, gasping mouths. That was what he should write about. So close, so distant. That was the purpose of art, to abolish distance.

He recalled the figure of a youth from years ago. Had it been in Constantinople? Yeniköy? A beardless youth working as an ironmonger's apprentice, and as the boy bent half naked over the anvil, sparks flying onto his glistening chest, he saw his face lit heroically, imagined him crowned with vines and bay leaves. They hadn't spoken, and he never saw him again. Who would write about him? Who would heave him up out of the oblivion of History?

Years later, someone hunched in the light of a lamp would be able to see a red sun setting over mythical cities, would see burning grass through rusted iron, where once a marble fountain spurted water and the last droplets ran dry in the evening light. He would see the crimson rays shining on the young body of the apprentice in Yeniköy, fleetingly illuminating a possibility, yes, a possibility that assumed substance, an almost material substance, as that same youth now weaved between the columns of an ancient agora among the crowds of Antioch or Seleucia, and many were they who praised his beauty.

That "years later" is now, he thought. He alone could see. Only he wasn't yet ready. His impatience chafed at him, and contrived miserable, graceless poems, which he tore up in self-reproach. And then there was that clunky pastiche ... A heap of adjectives and too-fine turns of phrase, the churning runoff of a lyricism he hated but didn't know how to leave behind. How can I shake free of that sentimental burden? he wondered. Often during the day he felt useless, irresolute, a failure. The problem was Alexandria, the city stifled him. His provincial life, his circle of silly people with their unshakable self-confidence, the feluccas and fellahin, the landscape like a cobwebbed stencil whose heavy humidity sank into your bones—it all weakened his nerves. And often he determined, without really believing it, that he needed to erase the Alexandria within him if he really wanted to write.

But now he was in a foreign city that charmed and repelled him in equal measure, a cosmopolitan capital that glittered with refinement, whose smallest corner seemed large and important. He needed to resist his bad mood and find a way to enjoy these final few days of the trip. No more wavering, he thought, I'll make a daily schedule and stick to it. He reflexively straightened his tie and descended the three steps into the hotel lobby.

"Monsieur Cavafy!" he heard someone call.

The large hall was empty, its central chandelier lit above a marble floor that shone like the surface of a lake. The aged concierge was moving slowly in his direction.

"Monsieur Cavafy, your brother was waiting for you. He left just a few moments ago for Café de la Paix."

It was a warm summer evening, the temperature around 80 degrees Fahrenheit. Mild weather with a salutary wind. Perfect for the light redingote he was wearing. A good thing he hadn't decided on his heavy linen jacket, he thought, a good thing indeed, and quickened his pace. But as he walked swiftly, following the flow along the boulevard, where coachmen trundled toward the Opéra brandishing their whips, he felt the moroseness that plagued him coming back and knew that sooner or later the familiar unease would descend upon him again.

"Costis, I finished it," John called as soon as he caught sight of him.

He appeared to be in a magnificent mood. He was holding the manuscript in his hand and waving it in the air like a trophy.

The waiter set two steaming cups of chocolate on the table.

"Thank you for thinking of me," he said, though he would have preferred a cold tea.

"Well?" John asked with a wide smile.

"I'm late. I must have fallen asleep."

"I'm sure it's done you good."

He noticed an old woman coming toward them, hand outstretched, dragging one leg. Her hair was matted and every so often she stumbled.

"Give her something. I can't bear to look at her."

The old woman came over to their table, casting a gluttonous glance at the plate of petit fours.

"Give her something," he said again. He glanced at the manuscript, now rolled into a tube in his brother's hand. He could make out a few letters, slightly slanted with the tails of the *p*'s and the *y*'s curving elaborately upward.

John stood and dropped a few coins into the woman's hand.

"Dieu vous bénisse," she said. Some of her teeth were missing.

"*Dieu* doesn't seem to have blessed you, poor thing."

She dragged herself like a bundle of rags to the neighboring table and stretched out her hand beseechingly.

"But why?" John wondered. "Why should we accept squalor when it's depicted in a painting, even praise its aesthetic value? Whereas in real life we reject it. That woman could be beautiful. Everything can be beautiful. It depends on one's point of view—or, to be more precise, on the mental disposition of the viewer—"

"We can't call just anything beautiful," he said, cutting his brother off.

"Of course, anything that makes us feel, why not?"

"Even an animal? That old woman has the beauty of a sow in mud."

"There isn't just one kind of beauty," John began, then fell silent. As always when he tried to find the precise words to express an idea, he got tangled up in his own train of thought. He sipped his chocolate, then stirred it slowly with the little spoon. "Why must you be so absolute," he said, as if it weren't a question. "Sometimes I wonder … It's quite unfair, in the final analysis." He wasn't looking at him, as if he might be addressing some random passerby in the street, or all of Paris.

"Let me read it," he said, and reached out a hand to take the manuscript.

This was their free afternoon. They had agreed over lunch at Le Procope to take this chance to rest and reflect, to recall certain moments from the month and a half they'd been traveling, to dust off forgotten details. They both enjoyed comparing their accounts of things and they did so often, savoring that moment when the simplest incident took on a strange quality, an almost unexpected turn as the words to describe it were shaped and rounded in the other's mouth. At this point there was a whole host of events for them to remember and laugh over, getting a foretaste of the responses their stories would evoke when they were back in Alexandria, laughing at the fiascoes of their trip, like their aunt's flatulence at dinner in Holland Park, not one, not two, but three superb, resounding farts in quick succession; the others at the table had coughed to cover the sound, but even that didn't solve the problem since an unbearable stench began to spread, and one by one they rose from the table as their aunt in her black, collared pelerine kept protesting, But where are you going, my dears, I hope the perch hasn't upset you, it must have been the perch—and ever since, whenever anything odd or untoward happened, they would say to each other, "It must have been the perch."

Mother will love the story about the fart, she'll make us tell it over and over, he thought. It must have been the perch, he repeated inwardly and almost laughed aloud. Out the corner of his eye he saw John watching him and waiting.

"I like it," he said and gave a dry cough. "It's a very solid poem. I'd like to read it again."

His tone of voice struck him as false. And why the devil had he coughed? They were always perfectly frank with each other, or at least so he believed, only today he had a feeling he should watch his words. It was no small thing, what he'd let slip yesterday. In the middle of dinner as they bent over their crispy squab with peas, chatting lightly about some literary subject that he could no longer remember, he'd mentioned *en passant*: "There isn't room for two poets in one family." He'd regretted it immediately. At first John pretended not to hear, didn't respond. But a few moments later he raised his glass, saying: "In that case I suppose I'll have to make way. Cheers ... *à ta santé!*"

His efforts to mend the breach kept them talking late into the night, and he'd been the one to suggest that his brother rewrite an old poem and change its setting to the fire at the Bazar de la Charité, from which Paris was still reeling. The occasion for the earlier version had been a snippet of conversation a friend of John's overheard at an art opening in Alexandria. A Greek society lady, the wife of a successful merchant—the friend hadn't given her name—was gazing at a painting of a setting sun smeared with purples and reds, and leaned on the shoulder of the man beside her, a well-known figure in the Greek community, likewise married—the friend hadn't given his name, either—and whispered with a heavy sigh: "I'd prefer to set in your arms." He had found it insipid, the metaphor or allegory, whatever it was, but John laughed and jotted it down. He later wrote a poem about the bombing of Alexandria in 1882 and the conflagration that followed. In the poem, the genteel lady's words served as an ironic counterpoint to the catastrophe and the vandalism that subsequently swept the city. The composition was weak and unnecessarily overblown, he'd observed to his brother. The phrase in question was absent from the present version of the poem, but an equally distasteful "sunset of friendship and feelings" had crept in. Just listen to that, sunset of friendship and feelings!

"Did you notice the second stanza?" John asked. "I'll read it to you in Greek, I translated it and the rhyme works better." He twirled his mustache before beginning the recitation:

Charred are the corsets and crinolines
ashes the silken sash,
burned are the skirts of which to now
lavender freshened the stash.

"I wanted," he continued, "to emphasize the fact that the fire at the Bazar concerns only the aristocracy. What does it matter that a few dozen servant women died in the fire? The Countess Mimmerel burned, and the Marquise of Isle. The empress's sister burned, too. That's what counts. A whole village in Brittany could have burned and there wouldn't be the same outpouring of national mourning. Do you see?"

"I agree, though I don't quite see the difference. Drama is drama."

"That doesn't mean, of course, that I was trying to write a social poem."

A failed poem, he thought. He remembered the first few days after they arrived in Paris from Marseille, when the region still smelled of sulfur and all the hotels were passing out damp towels to the ladies. And in fact the Bazar continued to burn for days, all the lace and fine linen piled inside crackling in a slow death. It had become the top attraction in Paris, people came in from all the *faubourgs* to gape at the charred carcass.

"It was May 4, am I right?"

"I think so. We heard about it on the train, remember?"

At the corner of Boulevard des Capucines there was a cloud of white smoke and a crowd of coachmen, shouting. Apparently a pipe had burst. A black figure emerged from the smoke and came toward them.

"Look," he said. "Your ethereal Aphrodite is headed our way again, looking even more dazed than before."

John turned to see. The beggar woman walked past on the sidewalk, staggering and bumping against the tables. A waiter came rushing out of Café de la Paix and tried to usher her away, first shouting, then shoving. The old woman fell in a heap into the street, rolled onto her back, and started talking to the sky.

"You degrade your art," John said, his tone polite but unyielding. He unrolled the paper with the poem on it and leaned back in his chair, pretending to read.

It must have been the perch, that's what he'd like to say to Johnny now. Their aunt's words suited him perfectly today. Only he didn't know how his brother would take it. He could be quite sensitive. Then again it might make him laugh. He was about to utter the phrase when a large head with sheep-like curls and wide-open, perfectly blue eyes appeared before him.

The sheep's head began to speak right away in a meek, powdered voice, his eyes moving between the two brothers.

"My dears, my dears … How small the world is, no?"

"Truly Lilliputian! What a pleasant surprise!" John said, rising to his feet to greet the stranger warmly.

"I saw you from the stairs of the Opéra and said to myself, can it be? I ran as fast as I could. Oh my dear, my precious friends."

"Constantine," John said, "meet the dear Nikos Mardaras."

The stranger's handshake was strong enough to pull the hand off his arm.

"So, you've returned to Paris? What luck, what a fortunate coincidence."

Nikos Mardaras explained that he had been informed of the brothers' arrival quite awhile ago, got the name of their hotel from common acquaintances in Marseille, and came in search of them as soon as he could, but at the Saint-Pétersbourg he learned that they'd just left for England. Shaking his curly locks, he inquired about the details of their stay in Paris, where they had dined, whom they had encountered, chiefly concerned as to whether they had visited the proper places, oh, you went yesterday to the Comédie Française, and also saw this year's Salon, very good, he said approvingly, pinning first one and then the other with his gaze as if two pieces of bait hung before him and he wasn't sure which to choose. John, who seemed rejuvenated by the unexpected meeting, happily answered this stream of questions, and Constantine was surprised to hear him say it was a shame they had run into one another so late, now that their stay in Paris was drawing to a close, they would only be there for two more days, the final two days of this extended trip, it was truly a shame.

He himself wasn't entirely sure whether he was bothered by Mardaras's intrusion. For a few minutes he studied him silently, with curiosity. Certainly his head was his most notable feature. The thick hair, unruly, a washed-out blond like hay from a pillow. His mustache was also thick, light brown. The wide chest, somewhat *pompé*, disproportionate to the rest of his body. As he sat across the table twining his short calves carefully around his narrow cane, he looked like a big-eyed ewe out on a morning visit. He was dressed to the nines, though on second glance his redingote seemed worn, the fabric on his shirtfront shone, and the orchid in his boutonniere had begun to wilt, it must have been at least two days old. The name Mardaras felt somehow familiar, and he tried to remember where he had heard it before.

"I hear you practice the fine art of poetry with great success," Mardaras said, as if swallowing a sweet.

He was addressing himself to Constantine.

"John is the poet in the family," he said, looking at this brother. Seeing John's expression, he wished he hadn't spoken. That easy praise was the wrong move.

"Of course, of course, our dear John also," Mardaras hastened to agree.

His interest in the brothers seemed to have been exhausted, at least temporarily. Already his gaze ran to the surrounding tables, trying to identify some familiar face.

"Do excuse me for a moment," Mardaras said, jumping up from his chair.

"Who on earth is he?" he quickly asked John, who had no time to answer before Mardaras leaped back to their side.

"False alarm!" he cried in English, then burst out laughing.

He seemed to burn with the desire to gossip. Emitting tiny roars, he told them how a very famous society woman had set her sights on him, and he thought he'd recognized a friend of hers at a nearby table and hastened to pay his respects so there would be no misunderstanding, ha-ha, anyhow it was just a temporary flirtation, a little emotional excitement, nothing serious, he concluded with satisfaction.

People came and went, smartly dressed ladies with white lace umbrellas dragging well-dressed children in their wake, followed by governesses loaded with purchases from Galeries Lafayette, while Mardaras sat stiffly in his chair and commented now and then on what they were wearing, how this year's corsets emphasized the bust which stuck out appetizingly, like a basket of fruit, or how crinolines seemed to have been abolished entirely, only women from the provinces still wore them, and perhaps a few foreign barbarians, since of course there was no doubt that French fashion was at the forefront internationally; with a single stroke of the brush the French could change the female silhouette, certainly the English knew as much even if they wouldn't admit it, but what can we do, my dear friends, civilization stops at the English Channel, forgive me, I don't mean to insult your fondness for old Albion. He mentioned innumerable poets, painters, and men of the world, lingering on one young writer in particular, Marcel Proust. The name was

unfamiliar to him. Apparently Anatole France was his cham-
pion, and this Proust had begun to have some success. Mardaras
sang the praises of a poet, too, who was being talked about more
and more by those in the know. That name, too, was unknown
to him. Both of them were quite worldly, invited to all the best
salons.

Soon afterward, Mardaras dashed toward another table, and
John leaned over to admit that he didn't know him very well at
all. They'd met only once in Cairo, at an event for some visiting
French archaeologists, a bit of an odd group, mostly amateurs,
the details escaped him now. What he did remember was that
Mardaras had been living in Paris for years thanks to an inheritance from an uncle.

"I see he's made an impression on you."

"That's a bit of an exaggeration. But I thought we might
dine with him tomorrow. He seems to know everyone in Paris.
And he's quite entertaining."

"Entertaining? Are you serious?"

"Well, he can be tiresome, too, I suppose."

"More like unbearable," he said, imitating Mardaras's way
of sitting upright in his chair with his eyes wide and his calves
crossed around his cane.

John laughed.

"You're a perfect caricature. At any rate, it's worth the sacrifice. He can introduce us to famous artists, people we otherwise
wouldn't have an opportunity to meet. I've heard he's a friend of
Jean Moréas. Something between friend and unpaid secretary."

The name Jean Moréas produced a vague discomfort of the
kind he wanted to avoid during these last few days of the trip.

He wondered whether John knew that he had sent two poems to Moréas's address in Paris, "Walls" and "The Horses of Achilles." John must know, he always informed him of his actions. He'd posted the envelope two months earlier but never received a reply. Meanwhile, Mardaras returned to their table and before he even sat down started telling them that the most wonderful, the most exquisite thing anyone could imagine had just happened, something unexpected, unhoped for, divine.

"A bit of information worth a million francs," he declared triumphantly.

"Do you dabble in the stock market?" John asked.

"Oh, nothing like that," Mardaras answered.

For a while he said nothing. Furrowing his brows and pursing his lips, he assumed the expression of a man struggling against the temptation to reveal something truly fascinating.

"I can't speak of it, it's top secret," he finally said.

What a clown, he thought. He wants us to beg before he'll serve up another bit of nonsense. Poor John was so naïve, hanging on his every word. What concerned him most of all at that moment were the poems he'd sent to Moréas. When precisely had he posted the envelope? He couldn't remember. Perhaps Moréas had already answered him during the time he'd been away and the response was waiting for him in Alexandria. That, unfortunately, was unlikely. His mother or brother Paul checked his correspondence daily and would have informed him. They always informed him.

"The government will likely fall," he heard Mardaras say.

"Thanks to that confidential bit of information you just received?"

"My apologies, I'm leaping from one subject to the next! It's my greatest flaw," Mardaras said. "That confidence was of a personal nature, how should I put it … entirely personal. It belongs to the realm of *plaisir*, of amusement. This, on the other hand, has to do with the Affair."

"We were speaking of the Affair," John said, and winked at him.

"What affair?"

"The Affair, my dear, the Dreyfus Affair! All Paris is up in arms about it, divided into two factions. Dreyfus, the Jewish artillery officer exiled on the charge of treason. Evidence was obtained, proof that he sold military secrets to the Germans, but now a host of indignant voices are questioning that evidence."

"We've heard about the case from the newspapers in Alexandria," he said flatly.

"Oh, of course, the Alexandrian newspapers. Perhaps you aren't aware, though, of what enormous proportions the issue has assumed in these parts. Brothers-in-arms won't even wish one another a good day. Couples communicate via written notes. The government will surely fall, my dear Constantine, I guarantee it."

"What position does Anatole France take on the matter?" he asked.

The question found Mardaras unprepared.

"I don't think there can be any doubt of Anatole France's stance," John said. "His opinions are already known to us. As you certainly recall, he explained the roots of anti-Semitism in a story of his, 'The Procurator of Judea.'"

"And what is your position?" he asked.

That'll show you, he thought. Mardaras, of course, had no opinion. He tossed his sheep-like head, opened his mouth to stammer something, then closed it again.

The conversation quickly moved on to another subject: *le Tout-Paris*. Mardaras explained its meaning to John, a unique meaning, he stressed, because le Tout-Paris was unlike the corresponding elites of Athens and other capitals. The aristocracy and the upper classes in Paris truly embraced the arts, and it wasn't unheard of for a poet of a lower social background to become highly sought after almost overnight, invited to the best salons—provided, of course, that he had talent and the proper introductions.

"You mean something like a court jester," he said.

"Not in the least!" Mardaras objected. "These are true, first-class artists. I can list names, if you like."

"And yet," he interjected, "in order for this artist of yours to become well-liked, he'll necessarily make concessions, concessions that will damage his art."

"Allow me to mention a few individuals to help you form an opinion."

"What use would names be? How is your poet any different from those flatterers chasing after the naked king, praising his attire?"

He'd spoken all in one breath and was surprised at himself for having fallen into a confrontation with this idiot.

"What naked king?" said John. "I think we've strayed from our subject."

"I'd like to note, though," Mardaras said, regaining his energy, "something that Moréas always says. It seems in line with your own opinions. Moréas believes that in our day, an artist's talent carries less weight than his ability to attach himself to the proper circles."

He pretended not to have heard. How could Moréas have entrusted his affairs to a man like Mardaras? An unpaid secretary. Unpaid, that explained it.

He glanced at John and rose from his seat.

He said he felt stiff, was going for a walk. Just a short one, he wouldn't be long. He wove between the tables, his broad steps quickly putting distance between himself and the others. At the corner of Rue des Capucines he stood for a moment with his hands in the pockets of his vest. He thought about walking to the Bazar, to see what remained of its carcass. But that would take quite awhile, he would be gone too long. Unconsciously, his steps took him in the opposite direction. What a clown, he thought. What a braggart. He must have dropped at least fifty names in half an hour. Mardaras's presence had ruined his mood. Yet he also knew his reaction was disproportionate, and that annoyed him even more. In some other situation he would have been content to smile at those banalities, waiting until he and John were alone and could let loose their wit. What was wrong with him? Why had he become so sensitive? He slipped deftly between passersby, not caring where he was headed.

He soon began to feel better. The current of the crowd flowed in the direction of the grand boulevards, over wide sidewalks dotted with cafés, beneath awnings and into arcades where strangers' silhouettes fleetingly took shape, then vanished again. A blind river pulled him into its current. He inhaled deeply and followed that vibrant ripple into the hum and dust. Crowds overflowed the intersections, lingered at shop windows before indolently setting off again beside stylish coaches and one-horse buggies that clattered away into the lilac light. Newspaper boys on street corners bellowed out the latest news. Where the road met Rue des Pyramides he stopped and stood as if hypnotized. Faces rushed toward him, shattering as they passed. The traffic became an utter crush at Rue de Rivoli, where the arches of the Louvre loomed like a domed seawall. Groups of friends disappeared down side streets. Their stroll would no doubt take them, later on, to more remote districts, off the beaten path. Secret, ill-famed neighborhoods. Shadowy doorways and basement rooms, he thought, feeling a flutter within.

A mob of musicians was just ahead of him, lurching this way and that, laughing and shouting drunkenly. One of them was dragging a monkey by the hand, dressed like a soldier with a little cap. He increased his speed so as to overtake them. Light flooded the paving stones, spread over the façades of the buildings, trailed over the silvery roofs—a fluid, shadowless light. As he walked, the lines of a poem he was writing came to mind. Every so often he would pick it up, poke and prod, then let it be. He had looked back at it recently and had been satisfied. Very satisfied. It didn't happen often. The musicality was flawless, the rhyme effective.

> *The city will follow you. The roads you wander will be*
> *The same. And in the same quarters you'll grow old, and see*

Such luminous, flowing lines. He repeated them to himself several times and then the entire poem, savoring each word, each turn from line to line. Yet something wasn't right. He wasn't sure what. He reviewed the poem once more in his mind, as if he were seeing it written on the page, and once more admired the meter and sound, which would intensify the reader's response. It was flawless. His best poem yet. A gentle breeze was blowing and seemed to be guiding him as he turned to head back along Avenue de l'Opéra. *The city will follow you*, he said to himself. Then he picked up the thread at the start of the second stanza, *You won't find other places, you won't find other seas*, and he must have been grinning to himself, laughing like a fool, he could tell from the surprised glance of a passerby.

But on the corner of Rue de la Paix he was again ringed by doubts. Something felt off toward the end of the first stanza, something bothered him. It was that "as they despise me," and the "learned to be" directly below.

> *I despise these people as they despise me*
> *Here where for half my life I have learned to be*

Me, be. He'd overdone it with that rhyme, it was too much. How oppressive rhyme was. He had worked on that poem for so long, and now he'd have to begin again. He certainly couldn't throw it out. It had a certain strength. The concept was exceptional. He began to recite the poem slowly, trying to keep an image of the lines on the page alive in his mind. Only now could he see where the poem hobbled. It wasn't just the me / be, or the be / see. The poem's horizon was too closed. It was about Alexandria. About someone who has wasted his life there, between the Corniche and the Quartier Grec, and longs to escape, to travel to some

other city, to be moved in new ways. Alexandria sucked the life
from him, drained him dry. And yet any city could give rise to
those same emotions, even Paris. You blame the city where you
were born for your failures, no matter where that is, thinking
the city is what constricted you, buried you alive. You walk its
streets feeling trapped, imprisoned. He stopped in the middle
of the street and watched a middle-aged man in a top hat walk
by hunched over, sunk in thought. Take this well-dressed man,
a resident of Paris. What luck, what bliss, most people would
think. But his life, too, is hemmed in on all sides. He moves in
circles between this boulevard and that avenue, this marquise's
salon and that courtesan's boudoir. He sees the same images and
scenes time and again until they make him sick. He, too, must
long for other horizons, other views.

"I thought you'd forgotten me," John said.

He had returned to Café de la Paix determined not to cross
swords again with Mardaras, to be as friendly as he could. He
found John waiting alone. Mardaras had left a short while ago
for some important appointment and wasn't sure whether he'd
be free in time for them to lunch together the following afternoon. But he could certainly meet them in the evening. He had,
in fact, suggested that they come and visit Jean Moréas's house.
It had an excellent library, there wasn't another like it in all of
Paris, full of rare volumes and all the latest works. John didn't
think they should pass up the opportunity.

Perhaps it'll clear things up, he told himself, though he wasn't
sure he was pleased at the prospect of meeting Moréas. In fact, the
more he considered it, the greater his unease grew. Two months
earlier he would have been eager for a visit of this sort. He would

have rehearsed what he'd say, carefully selected the topics toward which he'd try to steer the conversation. Yet no matter how much he toyed with the dates in his mind, there could be no doubt that Moréas had received his envelope. And had ignored him. Even if he hadn't liked the poems, he could have responded, dashed off a line or two thanking him for his trouble.

How insecure he was. A pretentious coward. He must fight against it, must fight.

"Fine, let's go. No sense wasting your energy trying to convince me," he told his brother.

The light was failing. They got up to leave. A lamplighter, a battered-looking man carrying a ladder and a long rod, was lighting the lamps on the corners of the streets. He climbed the rickety ladder, felt around with his hands for the wick, then blew with all his might, puffing up his cheeks. The blue flame flickered and went out. The man blew again and again until his lungs had to be close to bursting.

Horse-drawn buggies passed by, laden down. The traffic was subsiding, or rather, a sort of changing of the guard was taking place. The fancy toilettes, top hats, and gold watch fobs had all but vanished, as le Tout-Paris returned to its mansions to dress for the theater or other evening engagements, while a new crowd, dirty, unkempt, wearing caps and loosened belts, shouting and carrying baskets, appeared out of the side streets. John walked beside him, chattering about Moréas's library, how eager he was to see the books that had shaped the great poet's tastes, to discover which writers had influenced him—after all, he wasn't just any poet, but a leading cultural figure who had inspired many literary movements, perhaps one of a handful of individuals in Paris whose opinions truly mattered, and what a great opportunity it was for them to be able to study his library in peace.

"Oh, didn't I tell you? Moréas is in Greece at the moment," he heard John say.

So he was away. At last, some good news. It was likely, then, that Moréas had left before the envelope arrived. The information came as a relief.

"Has he been gone long?" he asked.

"I don't know, exactly. Mardaras has the keys to his apartment and goes by once a week to check on his correspondence."

"I sent him two poems."

"I remember, of course. 'Walls' and 'The Horses of Achilles.' You and I looked them over one last time before you sent them off. I think he's been gone a month or two. We can check with Mardaras. You didn't get a response, did you?"

"I would have told you," he murmured, then hastened to change the subject.

At the entrance to an arcade John stopped to haggle over a woman's shawl. The stall was piled with cheap fabric, bolts and remnants, kerchiefs whose colors screamed. Seeing his expression, John assured him it wasn't for their mother. It was for Rozina, the maid.

A gift for Rozina? He had difficulty believing it.

Then he noticed a thin child with curly brown hair sitting on the sidewalk beside a cage of pigeons. He had a stick in his hand and kept sliding it between the bars, staring at the birds. His legs were bare, covered in scrapes and bruises, the soles of his feet torn, and he had a deep gash of dried blood on his neck. People passed by, and a few stopped to talk to the boy. He, too, approached. The boy raised his head and looked at him with enormous black eyes. Exquisite, melancholy eyes. Then he bent back down over the cage and shook the stick lightly as if trying to pet the birds.

John paid and put the packet under his arm, and they set off once more.

"You'll never guess what Mardaras's secret was," he said as they turned onto the street where their hotel was.

John turned and looked at him expectantly.

"I'm counting on your discretion," he continued. He was joking, of course.

"I'm all ears."

"It's the kind of secret that passes from mouth to mouth. But only among a select group of mouths." He mimicked Mardaras's style. "It's quite exquisite, dare I say astonishing, unhoped for, divine."

"Why didn't he tell us both while I was there?"

"Perhaps you didn't seem sufficiently trustworthy? He said something else about you after you left, too. What word did he use, oversensitive? Choleric? No." John gave him a sideways look. "Thin-skinned, that's how he described you."

Thin-skinned ...

John told him that Mardaras's secret was the Ark. Tucked away on the outskirts of Paris, out by the fortifications. Once a great landowner's villa, it was now frequented not only by artists, politicians, and aristocrats, but also by young wagoners with muscular arms, even the occasional pretty servant favored by her employer. Apparently there were orgies. You could experience the loftiest of pleasures there, and the most depraved.

For years he believed his family could be an advantage for his writing, just as important as his talent or the things he read. A cosmopolitan family was a trump card for a poet. His ancestors had been swept up in the whirlwinds of history. Constantinople, London, Liverpool, Alexandria. Fortunes had been made and lost. Diamonds and pearls had been sold off in a single night. Beautiful houses, servants, and grand parties had been forfeited, not once but many times, like a theater set that vanishes when the curtain falls, replaced by a naked room with cracked walls and a bucket to catch the water dripping from the ceiling. How miserable our last house in England was, he thought. The drafty rooms, the milkman's prolonged whistle as night fell, the bone-chilling damp that moistened the sheets, tasteless green peas and eggs every night, eggs, eggs, always eggs. He knew the family had been ruined but was too young to understand what that meant. Everything around him was changing, yet no one spoke of it. There was no name for what was happening to them. Hints and innuendoes, misunderstandings, arguments—and then everyone sitting around the dinner table as if nothing had happened. *La face, surtout sauver la face.* That's what mattered, to keep up appearances. To hold their heads high, so no one in Alexandria would find out. Until the Fat One started kissing piss-stained skirts, writing tearstained letters to her sisters—he read them in secret—seeking a position for one brother, a bride with a dowry for another, launching a last-ditch effort to move them all to Marseille, her maddest scheme of all! And doors closing on them one after another. She would drag him with her on those visits. Of course she presented herself as a lady of the world, never asked for help, just waited for others to offer it. But why would they *offer* her anything at all? What could she possibly offer in return?

Thus they made their way back to Constantinople as beggars. Revolting Yeniköy. By then he was grown, though, and had a life of his own.

Beside that wretchedness, the myth of lost splendors. A myth that happened to be true. Cavafy & Co., which had nine branches at its height, and offices in Liverpool and London, Minya, Kafr El-Zayat. The great respect in which viceroy Isma'il Pasha held his father. The grand houses where they lived, first Maison Zizinia, then the two-story manor house on Rue Sherif Pasha—and the sour English nursemaid who ate butter only from cow's milk in the morning lest her liver suffer, the Italian chauffeur who helped himself to their oil. Seven brothers, lined up in descending order, decked out in sailor suits. The social calls of various dignitaries visiting from Athens, the metropole. The salons the Fat One held every Friday. He would assemble his train set in the hall and eavesdrop on their conversations. His father had given him a very realistic train, with four red carriages, an engine, and tracks. Its chimney spewed little rings of white steam as it ran whistling over the rug, its luggage compartment full of ants, or sometimes lizards he brought in from the garden. Ants? Had that train ever really existed? Or had he merely imagined it? It was a fantasy, like so much else. There was no red train in the hallway. He'd hidden behind the buffet, spying. If they saw him they would send him to his room. Teaspoons clattered, the maid hurried by with a tray of sweets, headed for the drawing room. Inside, conversation flowed as if on cotton, interrupted by small cries of admiration over one woman's silk gloves, another's diamond earrings, which had just arrived from Antwerp, as the maid appeared a second time with a tray of liqueur, fans fluttered, from out in the street came the water seller's hoarse cry and the distant whistles of ships headed for the Suez Canal.

Undoubtedly a family of this sort, with roots all over the world—which may, he often thought, be the same as not having roots anywhere—was an advantage for an artist. It wasn't the narrow Greek world, lives spent in coffeehouses, arguing about Trikoupis's latest, or what Prime Minister Diligiannis said. Or rather, it was that world, to be sure, but also the English, French, Turkish, Egyptian, and others still. As if the Hellenistic tradition were continuing through them. At some point, he thought, I should devote some time to our genealogy, sit down and trace the family tree, more thoroughly than the partial efforts I've made thus far. All those periods of exile, all the achievements, and the misfortunes, too. He often recalled all this, and sometimes it seemed that the legendary trajectory of Alexander the Great's descendants, full of expulsions, displacement, glorious conquests, and defeats, above all those humiliating defeats, might paradoxically be reflected in the wanderings, in a far later era, of this other family, his own.

And he knew they loved him, they loved him very much, he didn't want to be ungrateful. Particularly his mother and John. Of his six brothers, John had always offered the most steadfast support. John translated his poems, even though he would torment him for days, even weeks, over the rendering of a single word. He was the baby of the family, the favorite. They all indulged him. Then again, he considered, I don't ask much of them. He had never expressed any unreasonable demands. Even when he was a boy. For thirty-four years his steps had faithfully followed the ups and downs of the family. Particularly the downs. He remembered the wooden rocking horse he once saw at his cousin's house in London. Brown with white spots and a real leather saddle. His cousin rocked wildly, emitting shrill cries, not giving him a turn. He waited patiently. At some point he'll tire of it and get off, that was his thinking. There was a painting in the drawing room of a man standing alone on a beach staring out at sea. A fishing boat passed in the distance, appearing motionless in the gray-green waters. With his back to the wall, he gazed at the subdued colors, the faint details, the deserted shoreline, the solitary figure of the man, the caique that sometimes seemed to be leaning slightly to one side, and waited. He looked at the painting and thought how people must think of him as an orphan now. A beggar boy with rich relatives. He repeated those thoughts to himself as if they were about someone else. His cousin's shrieks grew louder. He didn't cry, didn't beg the Fat One to buy him a rocking horse, as another child might have done. Nor did he give any indication of how much he longed to ride. For thirty-four years. For all that time I've been a weight on their backs, and they've been a weight on mine, too, he thought.

But there were also days like today. Days when he'd prefer to have nothing to do with them. For them to release him from their love, to let him free. John had disappointed him this evening. How could he be flattered by Mardaras's attentions? How could he sit there with his mouth hanging open, listening to that fop and laughing at his failed jokes?

"You're parroting Mardaras," he'd said, and believed it.

He hadn't been able to stop himself. Now he regretted it.

It must have been past three. He'd fallen into bed with his clothes still on. It had been a struggle to climb the two flights of stairs and drag himself to his room. The window was ajar, the sounds of the night reached him weakly, like muffled sobs. He remembered how John used to sign his letters during the Constantinople days, "yours always, with love," and was flooded with guilt.

And that unfortunate phrase he'd tossed out yesterday at the restaurant: "There isn't room for two poets in one family." Where had that come from? There was no way to take back a thing like that, or to repair the damage. And it was all the more inexcusable for having been tossed off *en passant*, something he believed but didn't mean. He didn't mean it to refer to them.

His head spun. Perhaps he'd had too much to drink. That orange liqueur at Moréas's house, it had destroyed him. What an awful night.

It had been obvious from the start how the night would unfold, when he went down and found them waiting together in the hotel lobby. That double smile welcoming him.

He felt his annoyance growing the entire way to Moréas's apartment. He should have refused this outing. Perhaps he could make some excuse while there was still time and take his leave, return to the hotel. From the Pont Neuf he looked down at the waters of the Seine. Motionless. A stagnant, filthy swamp. The boulevard unfolded before them dark and ominous, the tired horses with their dirty manes trotted clattering over the pavement as he sat there silently, gloves in hand, instead of finding an excuse, stopping the carriage, and jumping out. Pale streetlights slipped by, geometrical flower beds, identical stands of trees. In the distance, the mouth of the Jardin du Luxembourg yawned in the darkness behind its iron fence with the golden spears.

The coachman must have been drunk, they seemed to be circling past the same places twice. John and Mardaras weren't paying attention, they were deep in discussion about the Dreyfus Affair. He had no desire to get mixed up in their conversation. He knew the topic and had opinions about it. What interested him wasn't whether Dreyfus was guilty or innocent. That, sooner or later, would emerge. Or perhaps they would never find out and the young officer would simply rot to death on Devil's Island, in Guiana. What interested him was the mechanism, the fabric of the conspiracy, if there was in fact a conspiracy. The role not of the protagonists but of those who worked in the wings, all those supernumeraries. And of course the business of "one against all" or "all against one" when the scandal broke had been enthralling to watch. If Dreyfus were to be proven innocent, he thought, the affair might lose its charm. At least from a literary perspective.

The coachman was surely drunk. They'd left Boulevard du Montparnasse behind and were once again trundling over the same stretches of Boulevard Saint-Germain, Rue Bonaparte, Rue des Écoles, all dimly lit. Passersby hurried past with their walking sticks, on their way to catch some bit of entertainment. They turned again onto Boulevard du Montparnasse. A few cafés were still open. Then a broad avenue, dark and anonymous with leaden glints, interrupted at some point by a colossal statue of a lion enthroned on a bronze base.

"Are we going in circles?" he asked.

"We told the coachman to take us around twice, so we could enjoy the Parisian evening."

They hadn't asked his opinion. They were having a fine time without him.

Clop clop. Two more blocks.

At last they arrived.

Mardaras jumped out first. In the dim light, John leaned toward him and touched his shoulder.

"Nikos told me that Moréas admires your poetry, that he's often praised your work."

John had spoken very softly. He barely saw his brother's lips move.

Mardaras pushed open a heavy double door whose bronze knocker was shaped like Medusa's head, then struck a match to light their way. They proceeded down a long corridor with storerooms on either side. Farther on it narrowed, probably culminating in some sort of garden because he could faintly make out foliage and the shadows of trees. To their left was a plaster concavity like an arch, leading to a staircase whose steps were wide and worn.

They followed Mardaras, who led the way, tapping his cane on each stair, lighting matches and tossing them away as they burned down to his fingers. On the second floor a bundle of clothes stirred on the landing as they passed.

"It's me, Marie," Mardaras said.

A pockmarked face with thick lips peeked out from between the clothes.

"Should I light your way, sir?"

"It's fine, we're almost there."

The bundle rose to its knees. She was practically a child, twelve or thirteen years old. She gave them a hollow look and collapsed again to the floor.

"Sweet dreams," John said, and laughed.

They continued to climb.

Mardaras told them the girl was the maid of the mistress of the Undersecretary of Water Management, who was married to an heiress with a massive fortune from diamond mines in Africa, who herself had a lover of her own, and so on. But why was the maid sleeping on the stairs? So she would hear the milkman passing by before dawn. If they left the pan in the entryway the cats would get at it, he explained, chuckling at the self-evident answer.

"And this is where Madame so-and-so lives" Mardaras announced on the third floor, filling in the name. "Her first marriage was to a prosperous art dealer, her second to an adventurer, and now she's the mistress of the Marquis de so-and-so, who is married to, etc., etc."

They paused behind the sheep's head on the fourth floor, waiting for him to unlock the door. The apartment was dark, dusty, orderly. Heavy furniture, velvet curtains, chairs with carved wooden legs scattered here and there. A few paintings, mostly seascapes. A Bokhara rug of deep red. Mardaras paraded from room to room as if the apartment were his own. He lit the candles and lamps, invited them to sit, then vanished.

Moréas's library occupied an entire wall. Shelves from floor to ceiling. A bust of the goddess Athena stuck out like a sullen-faced cult figure, lodged between volumes of the Littré dictionary. The books were arranged in alphabetical order. Poetry, poetry, poetry. Only French novels. At least at first glance, there seemed to be no historical volumes. Or philosophy. Or English literature. John had settled onto a stool and was pulling the books off the shelves one by one. He regarded them almost with awe before putting them back in place.

Mardaras's voice rang out from another room:

"Sit down, please sit, what would you like to drink?"

Two stacks of Greek newspapers sat on the floor. A second, smaller bookcase covered in glass stood by the front door. It primarily contained journals and a few law books. On the wall, a Byzantine icon in a silver frame. *In the darkness and shadow of death* ... the letters were worn away. He looked at the icon and wondered how Moréas could have praised his poetry without having read it. Unless the envelope had reached him, but he had to leave for Greece and hadn't had time to respond. Unless ... There was another possibility, too: that one of the periodicals in which his poetry was occasionally published had fallen into his hands. It was likely, quite likely.

Mardaras served liqueur. It was Moréas's favorite, he said, telling them what it was called. It was orange in color. Dry, rather tart.

"Are you a symbolist?" Mardaras asked.

Where had that question come from? He was in no mood to answer.

"I don't like -isms," he said.

He thought the conversation would end there but hadn't reckoned on Mardaras or on John, either, whose face lit up as if he were in his element. For John the symbolists, like the Parnassians, whose poetry he respected, also represented something outside the bounds of art; it wasn't easy for him to explain, but he was curious as to whether such literary trends were a matter of *necessity*, whether in other words they arose because society was advancing and progressing, or whether they were mere exercises in style, an aesthetic choice, a trend. He would be interested to hear Mardaras's views on the subject.

Five minutes later:

"Do you believe in art for art's sake?"

Mardaras was addressing him again.

"I believe in life for art's sake," he answered without giving it much thought.

But Mardaras no longer bothered him. At least not at that particular moment. That blithe sheep's head seemed entirely innocuous. He drank two more glasses of liqueur. His mood was much improved. The alcohol had helped.

He stood up to browse the library. He wondered if he would find a volume by that young writer Marcel Proust, wasn't that his name? The one Anatole France was championing. He knew the work of Anatole France well, had a particular regard for him and was curious to find out more about this writer he was promoting. As for that other promising poet, he couldn't recall his name.

He bent down and looked at the titles, but didn't feel like searching.

Behind him John and Mardaras continued the conversation.

The word Ark caught his ear. Likely that was where Mardaras would heading after this and from the tone of his brother's voice he could tell the topic had excited his imagination. "The place is guarded on all sides," Mardaras was saying. He would be taken there by a trusted coachman, sent by the Ark to collect him.

He stopped listening.

He dragged a finger along the books, their dusty spines, the embossed gold letters. Where the bookshelf ended, the sitting room narrowed into a sort of alcove where a gas lamp cast a raw, gray light, a smaller room with a low, sloping ceiling like you might find in an attic. There stood Moréas's desk. All but bare, with a double candelabra and a stack of blank paper. Inkstand, letter opener, blotting paper, all perfectly aligned. In one corner a dozen or so letters, neatly stacked. And then he saw it. The envelope of his poems.

He approached quickly. He saw his own handwriting: *Monsieur Jean Moréas, rue … Paris, France.* Above the address someone had noted in pencil:

Weak expression Poor artistry

In red pencil. He seemed to remember the moment, the precise moment before he left the house for the French post office in Alexandria, a warm day, unseasonably warm, and his hand was sticky with sweat. He had smudged the first envelope and thrown it away. That was the second one. He remembered what had happened earlier, too, because he hadn't known which poems to send to Moréas, had changed the contents of the envelope several times, undecided to the last.

He nudged the envelope with one finger. For some reason he couldn't bear to touch it.

His poems were in there.

He went back to the sitting room. Mardaras had tossed out some sudden question, and was now looking at them both with wide eyes. John is the first bit of bait, and I'm the second, he thought. He hadn't heard the question. All he wanted was to take his brother aside and tell him about Moréas's note.

Symbolisms, romanticisms, Parnassianisms. The conversation curled like a snake around the same topics, coiling tightly, unfurling, swelling up once more. John, free of his usual shyness, was pacing up and down, gesturing and saying: "But if we accept the one, then we're obliged to accept the other." The one and the other. Which one and which other? *Weak expression Poor artistry.* Something was pressing on his chest. He needed to get outside, to walk.

Ten more minutes. Fortunately Mardaras, unable to concentrate for long on any topic, was preparing to leave. All three men headed for the door. Then, just before they parted ways, that irritating conversation began, which delayed them even more—and which he wished had never happened, as it proved the undoing of an already abominable evening.

He must have fallen asleep. There'd been a dream, but he'd forgotten it. He remembered only the dazzling colors, appearing and then fading, one after the next. Like a scene from Alexandria in ochre and red. Not a real landscape, a painted one.

He stood up and undressed. He laid his clothes on the chair and went back to bed. The temperature must have dropped, it was chilly now and he covered himself with the cotton blanket.

He fell asleep again. He was in some public building, in a corridor. It was dark. There was a sign saying WOMEN'S TOILET on one door and beside it, dimly lit, another that read BOYS' TOILET. The word BOYS' seemed strange to him, but he couldn't wait. He went in and shut the door. Then a terrible shape appeared in the porthole window. The yellow face of a man with no hair at all began to shout that they were closing and he needed to mop. He'd only be a moment, he protested. Besides, he lied, he was the manager's son. His need to relieve himself was a torment, and the face he saw in the window was now his own, aged and bony, peering at him sternly. Then he found himself before a closed door. He was very young and kept knocking on the door for someone to open it. His parents and brothers were inside. He shouted, kicked at the door. Inside, they kept entirely silent so he wouldn't hear. He couldn't understand why they didn't want to open the door and let him in.

When he woke, he remembered his dream very vividly. He opened his eyes and the first thing he saw was the outline of his clothes on the chair, illuminated by the dim light filtering through the window. The collar on his shirt stood up stiffly, the sleeves puffed as if his body were still inside. If I die now, he thought, my clothes will remain there on the chair.

For a while he felt as if he were on a train. The wagon swayed back and forth on the tracks with a soothing motion. He closed his eyes. Then they sprang open again. The events of the evening, culminating in his glimpse of Moréas's note, spun in his mind like a whirlwind, a series of unpleasant thoughts, one after the other, or one giving rise to the next as if they were logically related, the most insignificant detail leading to something truly distressing, irreversible, and together they conspired to crush his morale and torment him.

Something truly distressing, irreparable. If he was entirely honest with himself, he knew Moréas's note was a literary condemnation. Not because he knew le Tout-Paris, or because le Tout-Paris knew him, or he even because, as John would say, he was a figure who had inspired literary movements, but because he had experience. Countless young poets must have sent him their poems. And he must have responded to so many, to thank them, to encourage them in those first steps. In his own case, he hadn't bothered to send even the most perfunctory note.

Weak expression Poor artistry

And if Moréas was right?

• • •

He needed to get some sleep. Tomorrow he would be utterly exhausted, dragging himself along behind John. He tried to recall once more that sensation of being on a train. He lay in the compartment, his limbs slightly numb. His head rested gently on the down pillow. The wheels hammered against the rails with a hypnotizing sound. The train sped through the night, cutting through plains, over hills, low mountains. White steam gushed from the chimney and was whisked backward. The whole land-scape was whisked backward. Fields, wooded expanses, thick stands of trees. He propped himself up and leaned over to look at John, who was sleeping in the bunk below, his forehead calm and smooth. In a few hours they would be arriving in Paris. The prospect made him tense. This was a true leisure trip. The first of his life. Hotels, restaurants, theaters. A few years ago he couldn't even have dreamed of such a thing. Paris. A city he knew only from books and others' descriptions. The City of Lights. His heart pounded wildly.

He started upright in bed, put a hand to his chest. His heart raced. He sat frozen, completely still. Again he noticed the clothes on the chair before him. Years may pass, he thought, and nothing will remain of me, my bones will dissolve, but my clothes will still be lying there on the chair. Still lying there on the chair!

He sat hunched on the sheets, one hand clutching his heart. As if through a lens he saw himself in the middle of the room, seated on the bed, eyes wide open in the dark. Nightdress rumpled, body curved like a butcher's hook, breathing irregular. It's nothing, he told himself. Perhaps he had a slight fever, but it was nothing serious. Perhaps he'd caught a cold on his walk that afternoon. He slowly slid his legs from under the covers, the soles of his feet skidding over the cold floor. He lifted the chair with both hands and stood there barefoot for a moment like a fool, holding the chair in the air with his clothes hanging off it. He carried it to the other end of the room and set it down between the door and the dresser. It was a dark corner, and with the chair nestled into that space he wouldn't be able to see it from the bed. He went back and lay down again.

He remembered a passing acquaintance who had been traveling on the same train to Paris. He'd come to their compartment to say hello shortly before the train was due to arrive. When the man appeared, he and John had been tallying up their expenditures. As always, there had been a slight spat because his brother's wastefulness annoyed him, and when he raised his head and saw this portly, middle-aged man with drooping lids and a sleepy expression, his first thought was that the man looked like the sort of person who might fall asleep with a cigarette still burning in his hand. The funny thing was, this potential arsonist was the one who told them about the fire at the Bazar. He sat down and made himself comfortable for quite some time, as the landscape sped past outside the train window. It was an unchanging landscape. Every so often some detail would leap out, a donkey, a cottage, a villager holding a canteen. Another donkey, this time the villager by its side drinking from the canteen. Scarecrows crowned with blond tassels slipped backward. Stables, thatched roofs, outbuildings all disappeared one after the other beneath a low, colorless sky. John and the acquaintance whose name he couldn't recall were discussing the latest gossip from Alexandria, who had married, who had died.

The journey had been monotonous from the start and now, in hindsight, his impatience seemed extreme. The little excitements of a provincial man winding himself up, preparing for a miracle while inside he is deeply bored. Knowing all the while just how bored he is.

This acquaintance had a facial tic that occasionally twisted his mouth. He hadn't noticed it at first. When their impending arrival was announced, the man leaped to his feet to return to his compartment. His face twisted into a grimace as if he were choking. The transformation lasted only a second, after which his face again assumed the bored expression of a man who might fall asleep holding a lit cigarette. "Be careful," he told them, "Paris isn't for everyone, it can even bring about neurasthenia in some."

What a thing to say. Alexandrian nonsense that confirmed the provincialism of a city that rejected anything different. Anything outside its own leisurely rhythms, the evening strolls through Ramleh, and the three basic topics of conversation—the price of cotton on the exchange, who had and hadn't been invited to the viceroy's last gathering, and how to find a good cook— was dangerous, worthy of condemnation. New experiences could damage one's health. In London one risked melancholy, in Paris one's nerves might suffer. Though perhaps the conversation at Moréas's home that evening had indeed been an example of neurasthenia. Three deaf men talking. Finally they had risen and the evening had ended, each thinking his own thoughts. As they headed toward the door someone said something about the war over Crete. That was why Moréas had gone to Greece, though it wasn't clear whether he was there as a journalist or to join the fighting at the front. Who had initiated that conversation? John, who else. Mardaras had other plans for the rest of his evening, and seemed to be in a hurry.

They returned to the sitting room and settled back down into the armchairs. They all knew people who had been to the front, who had been wounded, even killed. His friend Rodokanakis had been wounded in the arm and forced to return to Alexandria.

"An unfortunate war," John sighed.

"A stupid one," he countered.

The others looked at him.

He explained his point of view. The outcome of the war had been apparent from the start. It was entirely irresponsible of the politicians to get the country involved. Prime Minister Diligiannis had given in to demagogic impulses, if not his own then those of others around him. Thermopylae and Smolenskis, to be sure ... What grand symbolism. Poor nation, now they would be in debt for all time.

"I understand the emotional drubbing the Greek people have suffered, but admit it, the outcome was entirely predictable," he said at last.

John turned toward Mardaras, waiting for him to respond. Was it merely a gesture of politeness, or did he think the other's opinion counted that much? He didn't want to believe the latter, though the way the conversation had unfolded seemed to confirm it. He poured some liqueur in his glass without waiting for Mardaras to serve him.

For a moment they were silent, exchanging glances. The scene was both comical and preposterous. John looked at Mardaras, Mardaras at John, and he looked at his glass, which was already empty.

"We should be going," he said and stood.

It was already late.

As if emerging from lethargy, Mardaras went to pick up his cane, then came back and sat down again.

"Just a minute," he said. "What you're saying is outrageous."

John smiled.

"Constantine does like to be original," he said. As if it were a compliment.

The conversation became heated. Mardaras's positions, which weren't positions so much as opinions borrowed from here or there, a confusion of nationalist prattle and romantic elation, seemed to him so shortsighted, so unsubstantiated, that for half an hour he forgot all about Moréas's note. John seemed to be following from a distance, though by keeping out of the conversation he was, in a way, supporting Mardaras. He couldn't figure out why his brother had adopted this neutral stance, since John knew his thoughts on the war perfectly well, they had discussed it so many times. While they didn't entirely agree, they at least shared the same general point of view, and both were worried about the consequences for the Greek state of this imprudent intervention in Crete.

"We're talking on different scales," said Mardaras, who clearly wanted to end the conversation, probably so he could make his way to the Ark. "You're speaking pragmatically, like a banker calculating losses and gains, while I'm referring to the Greek spirit."

"What do you mean by the Greek spirit? Are you speaking metaphysically?"

"Not at all. I mean the spirit that rose up against the Turks in 1821. The spirit that nourished so many artists and public figures. The spirit of Dionysios Solomos, the spirit that stirred him to write our national anthem. That very same spirit is what inspired our intervention in Crete."

"Solomos watched it all from his manor house on Zakynthos, while the besieged in Missolonghi were eating rats, or rather the rats were eating them."

He had probably taken things too far.

"Dionysios Solomos suffered in spirit even more than he would have had he been there in person among the besieged."

"This spirit of yours, it seems to me, has led the country into bankruptcy."

"You're far too ironic. History will prove you wrong."

History will prove it. Yet another empty phrase.

John intervened, his voice calm.

"Nikos, you're right, it's a matter of different scales or perhaps different spheres of the human condition, but I know Constantine's views very well, we've discussed the topic many times, and while it may sound rather harsh, it does have a firm foundation in history. At the end of the day, your motivations aren't that dissimilar. He, too, is moved by his love of Greece."

What on earth did love have to do with it? In his attempt to bridge their positions, John had leaped to the other bank of the river, had crossed into Mardaras's territory and joined the enemy's side.

He didn't recall what else had been said. He was too irritated to follow. But when reference was made to the previous year's Olympic Games in Athens, and the others' mouths spewed exaggerated praise of this national feat, he couldn't keep from commenting. Yet even as he spoke, he realized that he was stretching the thread of his thought to its limit, that in other circumstances, while his opinions would have been the same, he would have expressed them differently, more obliquely, with less malice. He was aware that his combative mood was probably a reaction to his brother's ambiguous stance, or perhaps to Moréas's scribbled note, or to both at once, just as he knew that his intransigence actually weakened his arguments, which were in principle correct—yet while his words sounded even to his ears like dry polemic, he refused to budge a centimeter, insisting on his extreme position.

"The last thing the battered Greek state needed was the beautiful masquerade of the Olympic Games," he concluded.

Silence fell once more. A cart passed by on the street below, its wheels letting out a prolonged, torturous groan. The echo seemed to reverberate for a long while in Moréas's sitting room.

Then Mardaras bowed his sheep-like head and said quietly, as if he were afraid of his words being heard:

"You speak as if you were not a Greek."

And John, in turn:

"It must have been the perch!"

What time must it be now? Better not to check. It would make his insomnia only worse. It was nearly dawn. He needed to sleep. He closed his eyes and saw a white landscape, vast and still, as if seen from above the clouds. He himself was outside of it, in some far-off place. A stormy wind within his body pushed him forward and in the distance he could see a tiny, faint speck growing ever bigger. He approached. It looked like a crutch floating in midair. The wind within him raged, swirling faster and faster, and as he went closer he saw that it was the chair with his clothes on it, hovering in the midst of the universe. A strange omen. In his mind he knew he was lying comfortably in his bed, wrapped in the blanket. This vast landscape, the crutch, the chair, were images from the beginning of a dream, or memories from an older dream whose flavor still lingered.

He found he was able to experience the dream while reflecting on it at the same time. He was certain that the chair was not in fact there before him, since he himself had tucked it between the door and the dresser. Even if he were to lift his head, he wouldn't be able to see it from where he lay. He wondered if the clothes still hung stiffly, encasing that nonexistent body. If the collar still stuck straight up, if the sleeves were still inflated. As when a man has died and is lying on the deathbed, and everyone else has left, gone to get ready for the funeral, and the room is otherwise deserted. On the coat stand in the corner hang whatever clothes the dead man had been wearing. The window is ajar, a south wind blowing. The curtain rustles, the clothes flap without a care. The indifference of those clothes beside the deathbed.

The scene struck a chord. It recalled the death of Prince Andrei Bolkonsky from Tolstoy's *War and Peace*, which he had recently read. That scene in particular had made a great impression on him. The prince, alone in his room, deeply ill, not only realizes he's going to die but knows he's already half-dead. Eyes closed, he experiences a sense of estrangement from all living things. Then, soon after, when he falls asleep ... that dream. The writer's skill at that point was superb. Such a devastating description of the struggle against death. And when the moment arrives, how the prince pushes for dear life against the door, and while he doesn't manage to close it, he struggles at least to keep it where it is. He summons all his strength as something terrible presses on the door from outside. The unknown. The unspeakable. The door closes, then opens again. That terrible thing thrusts its way in, and the prince dies.

Would he ever be able to write with that kind of force, to achieve the loftiness of Tolstoy's prose? What he desired above all was to shake his poetry free of lyricism and ornamentation, to uproot the unnecessary, to cut as close to the bone as possible. Would he be able? So often, reading a volume by another poet, he felt a kind of physical irritation at all the adjectives, the flights of fancy, telling himself with disdain that the poet simply made the language undigestible—but could he identify the same flaws in his own poems?

And what a masterly description Tolstoy gave of that languor, that absolute peace before death. How in that instant all the things of this world detach themselves from you. A strange clarity washes over you. The agony, the distress, the delirium are all over. The terror has passed. And if Prince Andrei had been frozen with fear those other times when he thought he was dying and leaving those he loved behind, now, when he knows for sure that he's dying, he is entirely unperturbed, almost hostile to his loved ones, feeling a lightness, like a butterfly fluttering by. That terrible thing that will push open the door and enter is irreversible.

Defeated by that terrible thing.

That incomprehensible thing you've always known exists, though you go on living as if it didn't. The unspeakable. The chair was hidden. The chair again ... He wondered if he was awake or still sleeping. He would have to try to stand if he wanted to find out, but his limbs felt numb, in no mood to move. Images passed before him. The clothes hanging from the coat stand fluttered so lightheartedly. Nothing impeded their swaying at a slight angle from the perspective of the room. Impelled by an unhurried breath very like the one that made them billow gently, then suddenly fall flat again when one windy day the living body that wore them was out for a stroll, attracting admiring glances. And if someone had once embraced those clothes, if he had bent his head to the shirt and inhaled the biting smell of starch and traces of sweat, if trembling with desire he had loosened the belt, the clothes had forgotten all that. Other images arose from the imperturbable existence of clothing. The hands that washed them in a wooden basin with boiling water, the thick suds, the bleach, and above all the fury with which those hands scrubbed out the stains, as one by one the spots vanished, the guilty traces, the kisses. In his dream he found himself once again in the room of the first dead person, who wasn't Prince Andrei. Everyone was leaving, going to dress for the funeral, those who loved the dead man and those who'd simply put up with him. It's springtime. The window is ajar, perhaps one can hear the chirping of birds. A humid north wind is blowing, heavy with scents. The clothes absorb the damp, and for a moment they seem to be growing heavier, but no, look, they're already dry, waving in the breeze. That motion is their way of taking part in the general festivity of spring. If they had a voice they would chirp like those birds. And the shoes! The dead man's empty shoes on the doormat, the heels worn. Pollen blows in through the window, dusting them. The left shoe is somewhat tattered, the leather shiny and drooping on one side, the side where the callus once was. But where were his shoes? He had to find them right away. The idea lodged itself in his head that something terrible might happen if he couldn't catch a glimpse of his shoes.

No. This had to stop. He was being ridiculous. Enough, he told himself. Stop. He needed to think about something else, to let himself fall back asleep. It was no use. He jumped out of bed, dragging the sheet behind him, to try to see where he had left his shoes.

When he returned to the bed his mood had shifted. There was no sense in trying to sleep, the effort only upset him more. Better simply to lie there awake under the covers until it was time for breakfast. There were so many things he needed to think through. Tolstoy's descriptions had awakened in him an appetite for writing. Prince Andrei's pale face, feverish, stripped of all human desires, seemed to stand before him. And that scene where he leaped out of bed and ran to the door. How had he found the strength, worn out as he was from sickness, weak and faint. Even greater was the writer's mastery a bit farther on, when it's all over, the terrible thing has won, and Prince Andrei collapses in defeat after his struggle with death, only to wake just then from his dream, lying in bed, and realize that he must die again, this time for real.

He could write a poem about that scene. He considered how profoundly art was inspired by art, perhaps even more than by life itself. Yet art and life were interconnected. It was true of all great artists. How could someone with a small, miserable life, hemmed in by prohibitions and fears, unable to let his senses run free, ever hope to fill his writing with such great emotions? How could he ever approach, even from a distance, Tolstoy's "terrible thing"?

And yet, and yet. It was no good getting swept up in comparisons. He shouldn't worry whether he would ever measure up to Tolstoy. Such thoughts merely moved him further from his goal, even if his goal was precisely that. He had time. What he needed to do was write. But first to reconsider his existing poems coolly, with composure. Line by line, with a surgeon's scalpel. The poem he'd been thinking about that afternoon was a good place to start. The streets had been swamped when he rose from his seat at Café de la Paix and as he wandered aimlessly, following the flow of the crowds, the throngs of people had caused in him a kind of intoxication. In that swarm of people, watching as strange faces approached and passed, he'd understood that his poem could acquire a more general force, could be made to refer to all these people who blackened the boulevard like flies, the tired old men and ambitious young ones whose gold monocles shone with an uncertain triumph, these people who had no idea they were already half dead, and others who would later come to wander these streets condemned from the start. The central idea surpassed any individual circumstances. "Again in the Same City." He hadn't included it in the envelope for Moréas. An oversight. Perhaps he hadn't chosen well, which poems to send. Perhaps that was it. He tried to put Moréas out of his mind. Moréas was the reason he couldn't sleep. Moréas and Mardaras. And John, in his way. No, John was merely the weak link, easily influenced. But if Moréas was right? That same thorn still pricked his side.

Weak expression Poor artistry.

A condemnation in four words.

He stared at the ceiling. In the weak light, vague shapes paused for a moment and then vanished, absorbed by the plaster moldings. His poems were still immature, he had to admit it. But something good might come of that awful note. He could read over his poems, decide which to throw out, which to keep and revise. "Again in the Same City." That was the place to start. He needed to forget Moréas and Mardaras. Something good would come of that note, he told himself, though he didn't really believe it, as even just the name Moréas upset him.

He pulled the blanket over his body. Day was breaking. The shapes on the ceiling slowly acquired mass, plump blossoms that timidly unfolded revealing trembling pistils. He remembered what Prince Andrei had said: "Love? What is love? Love thwarts death. Love is life." His lips grazed the sheet. His hands stroked his ribs. How soft my skin is, he thought. What a pity. This skin will age, become rough, wrinkled. What a pity it doesn't enjoy caresses now. For a while he lost himself in daydreams. The summers in Alexandria, after they returned from Constantinople. That first summer. Past the Corniche, up the narrow tongue of land where the Arab districts swarmed behind Ras el Tin Palace, was a long, isolated stretch of shoreline where families tended not to go, and where working-class boys went to wash off their sweat. Did they ask their bosses, or just sneak off? The beach was deserted. There were places in the dunes where one could hide. Each boy arrived alone, undressed hurriedly, ran into the water. Soon another would come, and he, too, would dive hurriedly into the water. For a while he would lose sight of them. Every so often an arm would appear, or two firm buttocks breaking the smooth skin of the sea. Then he would lose them again. No, there they were, emerging from the water. They shook the droplets from their bodies with quick motions like horses tossing their manes. A game of chase on the shore, boys tumbling in the hot sand. Laughter, shouting. In the end they wrestled. They always wrestled in the end. Strong, wiry bodies, dark under the blazing sun. From his hiding spot he watched and watched and could never get enough. How irrepressible his desires had been. How he had roamed in search of pleasure, though still emotionally naïve. Back then he believed everyone would bow before his talent, that the best journals would publish him, even in Athens. As if they were all simply waiting for him to appear from Constantinople and show them the way.

He opened his lips, closed them again, took a deep breath, and pulled the blanket all the way over his head. For the second time today, that same image: the figure of the young ironworker in

Yeniköy. Bent over his anvil, half naked, sparks landing on his glistening chest. Deep in his memory, long, long ago. His daydream about the boy that afternoon had been so vivid, before he went to meet John at Café de la Paix. And the image of the apprentice was accompanied in his imagination by another, of the boy near Galeries Lafayette sitting on the ground beside the cage of pigeons. The boy with the stick in his hand. Those sad, exquisite eyes. The wounded legs. Someone must have beaten him cruelly. There had been a deep wound on his neck, a trail of dried blood. He pushed the branch through the bars of the cage with such incredible care, lest he disturb the birds, controlling the movement so that the dry branch became an extension of his hand sliding gently over gray-green wings, following the line of a tail in a long caress, touching a whitish belly as the birds gurgled happily.

That day in Yeniköy. So many years had passed since then. He himself had been little more than a boy. He had emerged from the blacksmith's shop in a daze, it had been dark inside, and for a moment as he stood in the darkness he saw the apprentice crowned with ivy and laurel, saw him gliding between the colonnades of an ancient agora, nothing but a short tunic covering his noble body. The hallucination lasted only a few moments before he returned to his senses, in that same filthy shack with the wheels, hammers, and insistent pounding that drills through your skull, the apprentice still bent over the anvil hammering at the red-hot iron, and he hadn't noticed him, nor had the stout blacksmith leaning by the furnace with his mouth on the bellows, he was sure of it, yet his fantasy made him feel a strange agitation that he couldn't control, his knees shook, he had to get outside, quickly.

There was a pigeon coop beside the blacksmith's shop and as he stumbled outside he bumped against the wire and the pigeons flew off the ground, making a racket. Days later someone told him that the apprentice spent hours in there, amid the feathers and droppings. Stock-still for hours, staring intently, eyelids heavy with suppressed tears. Perhaps he was thinking of his mother, or the childhood friends he'd left behind in his city, Kütahya. It was a tall cage that looked more or less like a chicken coop, with a wire door and rows of shelves, covered by an awning of leaves to shade it from the sun. The pigeons cooed in pairs on the shelves, glancing around with their tiny, restless eyes. Disgusting glass eyes. There was a nest in the corner with two eggs in it. He'd seen the apprentice again, too, he'd just forgotten until now. One evening he'd hung around the blacksmith's shop, waiting for the apprentice to leave for the day, then followed at a distance. The young man didn't seem to be in a rush, walking slowly, wearing a cap and a short jacket over his work clothes. In an empty lot he stopped, picked up a stone, and threw it as far as he could, not aiming at anything in particular. Or at least he couldn't see anything from where he was standing. Suddenly the boy started walking more quickly. He had to run to keep up. He saw him duck into a small church in a deserted neighborhood full of wooden warehouses. There must have been vinegar manufacturers nearby, the acidity in the air stung his nose.

He waited a few minutes before pushing the door open to go inside. He moved silently in the gloom. There were two round chandeliers facing each other and the long tongues of candlelight licked the icons of saints on the old, blackened iconostasis.

Flushed, he had crossed himself and kneeled behind the praying boy. A hazy glow spread between them, smoothing the distance. Silver votive offerings glittered on the iconostasis and the smell of incense made him dizzy, and delicate shapes seemed to move over the floor, shapes as fragile as glass, hovering, then vanishing. They were alone in the church. The silence was unbearable. The flames on the candles writhed. Before them the pulpit was pitch-black, like the mouth of a whale. It was cool in there but he was bathed in sweat, burning up, as the faint portraits of saints on the icons seemed to lean toward him with expressions that grew ever more austere and angry.

He was thinking of getting up and leaving as quietly as possible when he heard a muffled, hollow noise. The boy was crying. He stayed frozen in place listening to the low sobs broken by little gasps. Women's tears disgusted him, but for some reason it excited him when men cried, those male tears that rarely flowed, that emerged only with effort and shame. One by one the tears slid over the boy's face, carving rivulets, falling hotly onto his worn jacket, onto a shirt already filthy with bird droppings and pigeon feathers, onto a chest strengthened by physical labor, onto breeches that clothed firm thighs. Kneeling a half meter behind the boy, he had been gripped by an irrepressable turmoil as if he were in the middle of a whirlwind, images from the apprentice's life moving more quickly and densely within him, his worries and dreams, his nostalgia for Kütahya, the poverty, the hard labor at the forge, the blacksmith's slaps, the stiftling afternoons in the pigeon coop, the horseplay and stolen moments in the sand with other working-class boys, the beloved figure of his mother becoming ever fainter as his body collapsed onto his straw mattress each night. In the silence of the church his sobs grew louder. The tears must have dried up by now, because what he heard was a kind of gasping, a harsh sound like the slap of waves or a knot of sea breeze whistling between the rocks on the shore. Around them the saints' figures had grown dark. He was lying in bed in the Saint-Pétersbourg Hotel, the bedspread pulled over his body and the apprentice just a few steps away. Trying to prolong the moment as much as possible, he followed the line of the boy's body in his mind, from the powerful neck to his sloping shoulders to the hairless chest and below, a bit farther down, a bit more. His lips wandered over the dark skin and the tang of sweat made him ravenous.

And then, as always, the easy solution. Panting, sheets in a ball, limbs sore from repeated spasms. A flash, a shudder like a burning wick, then nothing. He had fallen face-down and groggy on the pillows. He had succumbed again. Slipping from the bed, he dragged himself to the basin to wash, hands sticky with that disgusting resin. He felt like vomiting. His pulse had quickened. This habit was his downfall, and all his oaths were in vain. He leaned against the wooden dressing table, feeling as if he might collapse. He looked at himself in the mirror and saw a deathly pale face with sunken eyes. A repellant expression, tousled hair, those protruding ears with their enormous lobes. His careworn mustache drooped. His entire face seemed to droop.

He wiped his glasses, put them back on, and sat on the edge of the bed. The room appeared smaller to him, and cramped, the furniture mismatched. The candle in the candlestick had melted. He remembered the chair. Better to put it back in its place, so the maid wouldn't find it behind the dresser when she came in. He didn't want to give the help any cause for comment. He picked up the chair and set it back in front of the dressing table. Then he began to get ready.

"It's guarded on all sides. There are rumors of marksmen who keep watch in the forest," John said.

He tried to understand what John was referring to. On the silver tray the teaspoon formed an isosceles triangle with the butter knife and the burned edge of the toast. Three drops of milk had spread quickly over the linen napkin and been absorbed as if by magic. The light played hide-and-seek in the translucent curtains. The weather would be lovely today. And his mood would be fine, too, as long as he didn't hear people talking, as long as no one spoke, as long as the silverware didn't jingle in his ear.

Silence, he told himself.

"Would you like another croissant?" John asked. He spread a thick layer of butter on his toast, dabbed on a spoonful of strawberry jam, careful that it not slide off, and took a large bite. "The more I think about it," he murmured, his mouth still full, "the more convinced I am that the Ark doesn't exist."

"No coffee today, I'd prefer tea," he told the waiter and glanced at his brother. He had swallowed the bite, and his cheeks were no longer full.

"What do you think?" John asked. Not waiting for an answer, he began to expand on his own thoughts, continuing to eat with gusto. The idea that the Ark might actually exist was, to his mind, insane, all the secrecy, the carefully selected coachmen who had to swear a blood oath before they were hired, the marksmen who guarded the place ready to shoot at any moment, and above all the very idea that marquises would ever fraternize with coachmen, it was impossible, it seemed entirely implausible that a city like Paris would be home to such a place. Mardaras must have some sort of relation with a lower-class woman, he'd likely planned on meeting her and the Ark was his pretext, his attempt to escape detection. Or perhaps the Ark was just an ordinary brothel, albeit a high-class one. "Do you remember the house of Aline in Marseille? It's probably something of that sort."

He had kept Aline's card, with the calligraphic warning: *Don't trust coachmen who take you to second-rate houses for their own gain, look for "Aline" over the lamp, the only private house …*

Another memento from their trip to bring back to Alexandria.

For now, his pocket held a letter from their mother.

"We have a letter from the Fat One," he said.

"Have you read it?"

"I just picked it up from the concierge."

John smiled.

"No, I haven't read it," he said, pulling the letter from his pocket. Why doesn't he believe me? he wondered.

John opened the envelope. He began to read.

"My dear, my precious little children …"

He didn't hear the rest. He was having trouble concentrating. An insect crawling over a half-eaten piece of toast had attracted his attention, a little round bug whose six legs worked energetically, piercing the bread's flesh. He looked at the large pane of glass beyond the tables and at the other customers' backs. It was going to be a hot summer day, a day when crowds would swarm over the sidewalks. The sun outside would surely make him dizzy.

He still hadn't spoken to John about Moréas's note. The more time he let pass, the more difficult it became, not precisely difficult but as if specific conditions were required in order for him to raise the topic, as if Moréas's note demanded a particular atmosphere that would display the full range of its distressing consequences. Again he thought how the sun outside would make him dizzy.

"Your brother Pavlos doesn't take me anywhere," John read, laughing. "As if he were ashamed. I can't wait for you to return, my dear boys, you two aren't ashamed of your mother. Tell me about your meals, are you eating well? Costakis has such a delicate stomach, though he is rather a glutton."

The Fat One's chicken scratch. He always had difficulty reading her letters. He thought of the dining room in their house at night, the table, him sitting there, indecisive, weak-willed, burning with the desire to get up and walk out. The Fat One had already retired, but would call him from her room, wanting something sweet. Biscuits sandwiched with a layer of marmalade. That's what she liked. The most fattening snacks and yet she complained that she starved herself and grew fat on air alone. He would bring the dessert to her in bed and kiss her cold, clammy cheek. Noises wafted in from outside, the night beckoning him. How stifling that dining room was, he thought.

"I send you kisses, my dear boys, and eagerly await your return."

John folded the letter and put it in his pocket.

The waiters filed in through the service door, loudly pushing metal carts on which to gather up the place settings. The insect on the slice of bread had managed to dig a long hole like a tunnel, and was now approaching the crust.

"I wanted to tell you," John began, and for a moment his gaze, too, fell on the bug that now seemed to be sinking on its back into the bread, its six legs moving all at once. "I'm thinking that when we get home, not immediately, I might want to live alone," he said, and looked at him.

"You can't do that," he said shortly, still not certain of what he had heard.

"I've been wanting to speak to you about this since our trip began. I need for you to understand. I'm drowning in that house. I tried to tell you on the boat, on our way to Marseille. When we were sitting in the dining room of the *Congo*, remember? Sooner or later, all of us will leave."

"You can't," he said again.

He felt the annoyance swell within him, though at the same time he doubted his sincerity. It was a decision he himself should take, yet didn't dare. A move he needed to make that his brother would make instead.

"I thought you'd understand."

"You can't leave mother, we can't leave her," he said quickly and poured the rest of the tea into his cup. "Even from what little she writes to us, you can see the obstacles," he continued, though he had been only half listening to the letter. "How much she suffers when we're not there. Pavlos is entirely useless, all he knows how to do is make trouble. And her heart, you know, can fail at any moment … No, you can't do this. We can't do it," he said, raising his voice, bothered by the very words he was speaking, because he no longer had any doubt about his complete insincerity, though he wouldn't admit it openly.

Was it his fear of being left alone at the Fat One's mercy? Particularly at night, her presence crushed him. Her continual need for reassurance, how she sought his love all the time, at any moment. Every half hour, every five minutes. Night fell and they lit the lamps. The maid went off to bed. The two of them were left alone. She was constantly asking for something, wanting something. She interrupted his reading. And that flaccid, clammy cheek. If Pavlos would at least help. Pavlos was useless. Forever absent. But that wasn't the reason. He couldn't make up his mind to leave and had to admit that his mother's health wasn't the only thing stopping him. Was he simply a coward? Had he gotten too comfortable?

"Let's change the topic," John suggested.

Good idea, he thought with relief.

She also has that awful way of worrying about us all, he thought again. Even the slightest change in the daily routine was a source of distress, expressed in countless sighs. A cart might run over Pavlos as he was returning home at night, killing him on the spot, or he himself might catch a deadly contagion, or John might get dizzy while swimming and be sucked under by the waves. She fed on worry. It was one of her ways of keeping them close—and it was particularly obvious with regard to him. She was forever inventing new dangers. Of course she knew she couldn't convince him. She was unable to make him share her misgivings, couldn't make him fear illness or a badly cooked meal, something he might eat when she wasn't there to protect him, a sweet someone might serve him into which rat poison might have dropped, the swiftest passport to a terrible death in flailing pain—though on this point he had to admit she had affected him to some extent, he often picked at his food or turned it over to check the other side, in case a dead fly was hiding there, or a hair, which was worse, because you would find it only once it was already in your mouth, and be flooded with disgust. At any rate, the older she got, the more her worry for her children matured into a true art. The smallest outing, the briefest encounter outside the house, whatever happened *far from her* harbored grim possibilities, risks. For instance, that episode on the eve of their departure for Marseille. He was about to go out, had arranged to meet some friends to say goodbye, and she had begun her lament even earlier than usual, saying that she'd heard the weather was going to turn, the khamasin was coming, winds off the desert, he should really stay indoors rather than risk suffering some infection in the nose or rash in the ears when he was about to travel. He had borne as much as he could, and the idea of a rash in his ears pushed him over the edge. Tell me, he said, what if I were to get up from the table right now, trip against the sideboard, fall down, and as I fell swallow the wrong way and asphyxiate in a matter of minutes? If I were lying there blue from lack of oxygen, breathing my last before your very eyes, right here beside you, what would you do? She had looked at him without speaking, with that look in her eyes, but when he'd gone out into the street he felt guilty, and came back in to kiss her goodnight.

The breakfast room had almost emptied. A waiter approached pushing a cart. He asked with a frigid smile whether they wanted any more coffee or tea, obviously in a hurry to finish his shift.

As he stacked their dishes noisily, the half-eaten slice of bread bearing the little insect slipped into the bucket of scraps.

They rose, and John made a comment about their schedule for the day, which he had forgotten. According to the plan, they were supposed to go to Passage Jouffroy, they still had shopping to do and this was their only day. Most of the shops there would be open, and they could get their errands over with quickly. Then they could go to the Bois de Boulogne and have an ice cream at the Pavillon d'Armenonville; it was the perfect day for a country walk and the place was famous for its ice cream, which they hadn't had a chance to try during their last stay in Paris. Later, if they had time, they could go and see some final performance. As for dinner, there were several options.

Suddenly there was a rustling sound of people approaching. Almost immediately a group of men and women in gaudy hats and short white boots burst through the side entrance and headed for the reception desk, chattering all the while. The concierge with the gold epaulettes slowly took his position behind the desk and looked impassively at the swarm.

"The Russian Ballet of St. Petersburg," John said, "they always stay here when they're performing in Paris."

"What a rabble."

"Not at all, you're mistaken. It's a very famous ballet company." Then, reconsidering, he turned toward him. "What's wrong? Did you not sleep well?"

"I must have woken up too abruptly." He tried to smile. "I have a bit of a headache." It was as if the taste of that long, sleepless night still lingered in his mouth. An earthy flavor. Seeing his brother's concerned look, he quickly changed the subject.

"Look at that concierge, standing there as pompous as a cardinal," he said.

"As a hundred cardinals."

"With a little marquis thrown in."

"And a bit of general, too."

They laughed and went outside. The sun was already hot. Eighty-six degrees, he figured. The temperature was sure to rise as the day went on. It might even get up to 100. He had to fight this bad mood, not let himself get sullen. They had only two more days, and his pessimistic attitude affected not only John but himself as well. It drained him, made him unpleasant company, even his appearance became off-putting. He needed to apply his rules more strictly, he had gotten too lax with himself during this trip. The thought of his rules made him recall once more his languorous morning in bed. The messy sheets, his racing pulse, his face distorted in the mirror. Yes, it had happened, but it wouldn't happen again, he told himself. And something else was bothering him, too. The conversation with his brother, John's desire to leave home, to go and live on his own. He seemed decided, and it wouldn't be easy to convince him to stay.

"What are you thinking?" John asked.

The sidewalks were packed with people, just as he had predicted. Hats, umbrellas, lacy bodices and frock coats glided down the boulevard, cutting through the bright mesh of the diffuse sun which, already high, shone here on a satin bow like a rose in full bloom, there on the playful trim of a darkly colored ribbon around a narrow waist, further down on the fine line of a pair of pants that closely followed on a man's thigh. Frills, ascots, and white shirts paraded pleasantly—clothes that at night would wait sleeplessly in wardrobes, or draped over chairs.

"I was thinking about what you told me earlier, about the Ark," he said. It was the first thing that came to mind. He stood at the edge of the road and raised his hand to hail a cab.

"We're only going to Passage Jouffroy, have you forgotten?" John asked. "It's not too far to walk."

As they turned onto Boulevard des Italiens a beggar began to follow them, crying out, pleading. They began to walk a bit faster.

"There's something else I didn't tell you about the Ark," John said. "Last night I asked Mardaras if we could go together, if he could take us. He didn't object, but he did offer various excuses. It was obvious he preferred to go alone. I believe that confirms my idea that the Ark doesn't actually exist, but is just camouflage for other affairs, which for obvious reasons Mardaras prefers not to reveal."

The cafés were all packed. In front of a flower stall a smartly dressed middle-aged man stopped and touched his hat as if he recognized them. They stopped, as well, and the stranger threw them a confused look, turned, and continued on his way.

"La Maison Dorée," John sighed, stopping to stare raptly at the imposing building with the gold trim on the corner of Rue Laffitte. He looked at Café Riche to his right as if he wanted to burn into his memory each detail of a scene he wouldn't see again, an ethereal, elusive life, where elegance was the rule and luxury an innate virtue.

Most of the tables on the boulevard were already taken. Standing in the doorway with a monocle and one raised brow, the maître d'hôtel surveyed the waiters in black who wove discretely through the tables on the sidewalk, hastening to take orders with precise, refined gestures.

What gall, he thought, bothered for some reason. The waiters here seemed more aristocratic than the customers.

"Constantine," John called as if he were far away, not right beside him, "wouldn't it be lovely if we were to come here tomorrow? What do you say? We were so frugal on this trip, I believe we deserve a special treat on our last evening."

"I'd dine here very gladly if it were possible, you know that. But we can't. Don't make me remind you of how much our trip has cost so far."

"Let's leave off the accounting just for today."

"I'm coming up on eighty pounds. You?"

"I'd rather not know."

He left it at that. He didn't want to be harsh, and he had to admit he sometimes overdid it with his keeping of accounts, as if it brought him a perverse pleasure.

"Domus Aurea," he said, looking at the gilded façade.

"What?" John asked, his mournful gaze still trained on the tables of Café Riche.

"It was the name of Nero's palace in ancient Rome. It had three hundred rooms."

John didn't seem impressed.

"Domus Aurea sounds better than Maison Dorée, don't you think? *Maison* ... a maison can be anything, a tailor's shop, a brothel. *Domus* is more impressive. Though I can't imagine these people took any inspiration from the Romans."

Three hundred rooms and not a single bed for sleeping, everything designed for revelry and pleasure. After Nero's death the palace was plundered, then sank into the soil. The earth swallowed it up, frescoes, marble, gold, diamonds. He looked at John, who was entirely absorbed as if watching a theatrical performance. Like a little boy, he thought. He didn't want to spoil his brother's enjoyment, but also didn't want to stand there any longer in front of the café gawking at the French bourgeoisie.

"Shouldn't we be moving on?" he proposed. "We look like beggars."

"Did you know there are two entrances to Café Riche? One for mortals, and a side door off Rue Laffitte for the chosen few. Politicians, princes, even kings dine in special chambers, private *cabinets*. All the famous writers are regulars here," John said, watching him out the corner of his eye and waiting for some kind of reaction.

But his mind ran elsewhere, to Rome, to the pillaging of the palace with the three hundred rooms as soon as Nero died. The irony of fate. The wealth Nero had plundered being plundered once more.

"Balzac and Dumas used to eat here," John continued, still resolved on tempting him. "And Guy de Maupassant. I'm fairly certain Baudelaire had his own table. It's been the setting for many a novel. In fact, there's an entire mythology about cabinet six."

Who knows whether an environment like that might inspire me, he wondered, and for a moment abandoned himself to temptation. If he had the opportunity to dine in one of those private rooms, to wander soundlessly through the restaurant's corridors, trying to get a glance of what was happening in the other rooms. On velvet couches behind heavy curtains that muffled all noise, every compromising conversation. He might catch a scene reflected in a mirror: half-eaten delicacies on the table, champagne overflowing the glasses and spilling onto the costly rug, the quiver of a silk veil, shadows in the dim light, shadows that lengthened as bodies twined together and time stopped. Undoubtedly an environment like that, luxurious, uninhibited, where power made allowances for all sorts of pleasures and illicit passions, aroused his curiosity. Perhaps if he were to spend a few hours in such an establishment, collecting details as a natural-ist might, Maison Dorée would recall that other place, Domus Aurea, its opulence, its orgies, its entombment under the earth. That was the setting that truly interested him—he had no desire to write about French nobility. But the temptation lasted only a moment before his reverie was interrupted by the thought of how much such a dinner would cost.

"Let's go," he said, "we can't stand here any longer. It's ridiculous."

"If things had been otherwise we'd be able to dine here every evening," John said.

He was taken aback. It had been years since any mention was made of the family's bankruptcy. If things had been otherwise ... For the first time he realized that John, two years his senior, had been old enough during the period of that calamity to have understood far more. Which meant he suffered more, too. And during those years when the family was in Constantinople, John had remained behind in Alexandria, working like a dog to send them what money he could. He wondered if perhaps he should give in to his brother's desire to dine at Maison Dorée the next evening, he probably owed it to him—and as he was debating the issue his brother seemed to catch a whiff of his hesitation in the air, to think he had almost persuaded him, because a slight smile broke out on his face.

"Let's go," he heard himself say, instead of the declaration he had been preparing. He tapped his cane lightly on the sidewalk. There was still time before tomorrow evening for him to change his mind and give in to his brother's desire.

"Just a minute," John said.

Someone was headed toward them, waving his head in their direction.

"I'm so glad I caught you!" he called.

Mardaras?

Mardaras.

Smiling, he discovered that the encounter didn't spoil his mood, on the contrary it came at precisely the right moment to extricate him from this difficult position with John.

This afternoon was the *Promenade de la vache enragée* at Montmartre, Mardaras announced. As soon as he heard, he canceled all of his appointments and hurried to their hotel. There would be a decorated cow followed by floats and masqueraders.

"Like the great carnival parade in Alexandria," John said. "Flower fights, sugared almonds, flirting across balconies. Let's go!"

In the meantime, according to form, Mardaras excused himself and popped into Café Riche to greet an acquaintance. When he returned, he began to pontificate about the rules and whims of the café, which was frequented in the morning by bankers from the nearby Bourse, then journalists at lunchtime, while in the evening artists claimed their spots from early on, you were lucky to find a table, and you saw plenty of courtesans, too, including some regulars who came here for their dose of absinthe.

"Will le Tout-Paris be at the Promenade?" he interrupted.

"Of course," Mardaras replied, seeming not to notice the irony. "Though mostly artists take part, painters, poets, they're the inspiration behind the, what shall I call it, the event. You'll enjoy it. You'll see, it's quite a show—music, masqueraders."

"Like the carnival parade in Alexandria," John repeated.

"Oh, what memories you awake," Mardaras sighed.

Mention was made once more of the carnival parade he had attended several years ago in Alexandria—most likely the same year he and John had met in Cairo—and while he seemed to have strong memories, he also didn't seem eager to recount them. All he said was that he had watched the flower fight from a balcony on Rue Cherif Pasha, or Rue Constantinople, he wasn't sure, at any rate the balcony belonged to a very prominent family, he said pointedly.

And so the plan to go to Passage Jouffroy was abandoned and they set off, waving their walking sticks. The movement on the streets had grown even thicker, and as they moved forward side by side, he tried to imagine what impression they made on someone approaching from the other direction: three young men without a care in the world whose lives stretched before them.

The city rushed toward him and he would have liked to be pure and open, so as to meet it properly, to catch even its subtlest hints. Pure? Why pure? Where had that come from? Naïve would have been a better word. How else could he abandon himself to something entirely? Devote himself to writing without calculating the losses and gains? He needed to start from an unsuspecting, almost primitive state, primitive as concerned his desire to write as well as the goal of that desire, a tabula rasa that left no room for all the things he would miss out on, all the things his devotion to Art would deny him. And yet he was naïve. Behind the glasses, the mustache, and the expertly sour expression he had noticed on his face more than once as he'd passed a mirror, lay plenty of naiveté. He had to compose himself, to find his center. How much of his day was consumed by poetry, how much by dalliances, how much by the pleasures of life? The older he got, the larger the third share grew. Alexandria is killing me, he thought. Life squeezed from an eyedropper. If he lived in Paris things would be different. He needed to set a schedule. Perhaps the night before something had ripened and matured in him, perhaps he had grown a kind of shell. With these thoughts he quickened his pace and left the others behind.

He had almost reached Boulevard Haussmann and was wondering when they would hail a cab for Montmartre, but when he turned around he didn't see the others. Absorbed in his thoughts, he must have walked so quickly that he got ahead of them. He looked back again, down the street, where people came on in waves, their silhouettes melding into a blur. He stopped near the entrance to a building to wait for them. It was hot. The atmosphere seemed hazy. Men in top hats hurried into the building, others came out with a pensive air, and the doorman, wearing an ash-colored cap with gold braid, greeted each with a slight bow. It was probably an office building, a newspaper or insurance agency. He looked back again. Nothing. No sign of John and Mardaras. Only umbrellas, buggies, carriages, commotion, horses, manes.

Boulevard des Italiens forked at precisely this spot. Some carriages continued on, veering slightly to one direction, while others turned onto a narrower street, crossing the flow of those approaching from the opposite direction and blocking their path. Traffic suddenly came to a halt and the tumult increased, vehicles and animals standing in nervous immobility until a coachman urged his horse on to break the standstill, whistling and cracking his whip, and a young man with blond sideburns who had been trying for a long while to cross the road leaped, waving his arms as if he were swimming, and vanished between the carriages that were beginning to move, only to emerge a few meters farther on, bright red and startled. He watched him stop on the sidewalk, looking embarrassed, shaking the dust off his clothes and trying to recover his air of propriety. Then he left, striking his walking stick on the sidewalk. You had to be an acrobat to cross the boulevard just there, wiser to wait for a better opportunity, he thought as his eye fell on a sign reading Rue de Turbigo.

Rue de Turbigo? The name meant nothing to him. Nor did he remember having turned. He'd been walking the entire time on Boulevard des Italiens, always on the same side of the street. How many blocks had he gone? Three or four? He couldn't be sure, though he did remember small details about things he had passed, fleeting images he had caught out the corner of his eye: a shop selling canaries, dozens of birds chirping in their cages, a green parrot on a chain, then a very pale man who walked straight toward him with a wild look in his eye, swerving at the very last moment, he'd taken him for a beggar but he must have been mad, and then an old man mending woven mats under an awning, his feet in a bucket of water. A narrow ray of light fell into the water, marking the dark, swollen veins on the old man's feet. His toes were surely distorted, too, the nails sunken into the flesh, he'd thought. But was it something he'd thought then, as he passed by the pile of mats, or something he was thinking now? He had been walking quickly, not paying attention to what was happening around him. These images had been impressed upon him without any effort on his part, without his taking any active interest. Now no matter how he tried, he couldn't remember anything else from that walk. At any rate, it was impossible that he had crossed the boulevard or turned onto some side street and forgotten it.

They had been walking down the right side of Boulevard des Italiens, he was sure of it, all three of them together. At some point he had gotten ahead. If he'd turned, it must have been onto a street to his right, since he was absolutely certain he hadn't crossed the road. John and Mardaras had been following him. They would have seen him turn and called to him. They were talking, of course, about the Ark, about Dreyfus, the unfortunate war ... About poetic movements ... Under normal circumstances John would have had his wits about him, but drawn up into conversation, he may not have been paying attention. What a simpleton John could be sometimes. Charmed by an empty tin. Blah, blah, blah ... but dear John, I assure you this new movement will be a true turning point, yes, dear Nikos, but romanticism, too, was a turning point, and not only for Art, I agree, dear John, but the other day at Madame de Trianon's salon they had shovels at the ready to bury them all, romantics, symbolists, Parnassians ... my dear Nikos, just think of the role the romantic poets played in the Revolution of 1821, it was thanks to them that the spark of philhellenism spread through Europe, but dear John, we mustn't overlook this and that ...

It was unbearably hot. Not a leaf stirred. Rue de Turbigo. He went to the corner to see what the name of the cross street was. Rue au Maire. It didn't ring any bells. There was a tobacco shop on the corner, beside a dairy shop, and a bit farther down a few maids were gathered in front of a doorway. He went back to the building he'd stopped at before. He could ask the doorman for directions, find out where on earth he was and how to get back to Boulevard des Italiens, but for some reason this move presupposed an admission of defeat he was disinclined to make.

He retraced his steps once more in his mind. Something wasn't right. The shop with the canaries, the old man mending mats. There were no stores selling mats of that sort in the better areas of Paris. And the road he was on seemed to jog a memory. It was wide but neglected, lined with little shops with wooden windowsills, carafes and dishes stacked behind dirty windows. He must have wandered into some more working-class district. But how could that be? Could he have gone so far that he was now back in the center of town? It made no sense at all.

Church bells rang in the distance, then others that were closer, with an abrupt, metallic sound. It was already two, he thought, realizing that he was hungry.

"Can I help you, sir?"

It was the doorman with the gray cap.

He made a vague gesture.

The doorman waited.

"No," he said shortly. He looked up. Not a cloud in the sky. A hazy, gelatinous film, and behind it the sun, which continued to burn.

"Then I'd ask you to keep moving. For reasons of security."

He walked away and turned onto the street where the tobacco shop was. Rue au Maire. He looked into the distance, as far as his eyes could reach. A depressing Parisian street that seemed never to end. Haze sat on the rooftops like an upturned plate. Now he was very hungry. If he didn't eat something he would start to feel ill. He went into the dairy shop next door, bought two buns, avoiding the gaze of the disheveled shopkeeper who seemed determined to strike up a conversation, and devoured them as soon as he got outside. They didn't satisfy his hunger, on

the contrary it only intensified, but he couldn't go back in, monsieur, monsieur and those thick lips that moved as she counted
the coins. The temperature had risen even higher and a colorless
haze had spread over the area, sticking to your skin. How strange
that he was still able to stand on his feet. What with the heat and
his lack of sleep, it was only a matter of time before he collapsed.

Why did I just walk off, tail between my legs? he wondered
five minutes later. I should have put that doorman in his place.
He was right to say that the servants in France had taken on airs.
Such behavior would have been impossible to imagine back in
Alexandria. He would go straight back to Rue de Turbigo and
give the doorman a piece of his mind. Nonsense. He had to focus
and decide which way to go. There was no point in trying to find
Boulevard des Italiens again. Better to keep going and meet the
others at Montmartre, without any further delay. He would take
a buggy, or an omnibus, which he hadn't ridden a single time
since they'd arrived in Paris. They looked quite entertaining. But
an omnibus in this heat? Crushed in among the crowd? I'll walk
on just a bit farther and then take a buggy, he decided.

Then again, perhaps Montmartre was close at hand, just a
few blocks away. The coachman might refuse to take him such a
short distance, or even if he did, he might make some comment,
most likely an insult in slang he wouldn't understand, which
would ruin his mood. Even more humiliating would be to climb
into the buggy and tell the coachman his destination, and have
the coachman set out, sitting upright and tugging at the reins,
and the horses would trot for the slightest distance, practically
moving in place, before the coachman turned toward him and
said, here we are, sir, Montmartre. His collar clung to his neck.

It must be 104 degrees, he calculated. I've gotten lost, like a country bumpkin in Paris. Like a man arriving from the provinces with his bundle, wearing his best suit. I've lost my way and I'm not even drunk. And while the simplest, most logical thing would have been to stop the first passerby and ask for directions, again that same resistance within him kept him from taking such a step, as if he had made some bet. But what kind of bet? So he continued walking, drenched in sweat along a depressing road spotted with pigeon droppings and little mounds of dung, which he had just noticed, and which added to his great fatigue, the anxiety of watching where he stepped.

And if he went to Montmartre and couldn't find the others? It wouldn't be easy to locate them in the bustle of the Promenade, and besides, just the thought of being dragged along by a current of masqueraders made him feel queasy. Then again, how could he be sure that they had in fact gone to Montmartre? John might have gotten worried when they lost sight of him and returned to the hotel to wait for him there. John's worry. He would be even more annoyed if that had happened. And the letter that morning from the Fat One with the hint about his stomach, a transparent reminder for John to watch out for him. As if it suited them to keep him under their protection. The family pet. Weak-willed. Still a tadpole.

He was lost, that much was clear. The sights of Paris, the Trocadero, the Louvre, even the Eiffel Tower or the charred remains of the Bazar might be very close for all he knew. Perhaps Montmartre was a short walk farther on, as soon as he turned the corner he would see the Moulin Rouge, and the float pulled by a rabid cow trailing a mob of drunken artists. But what did it matter? At that precise moment he was lost. An old man with a beard dragging a sack overtook him, then turned to look back. Those eyes. They bore into him as if trying to stare straight into his soul. The man took a few steps forward, then turned to face him once more. His clothes were ragged but clean, he didn't look like a beggar. Who knew why he was staring like that. The man's expression had something sad about it, but derisive, too. He quickly crossed the street to the opposite sidewalk. The old man still stood in the same spot—and despite the distance his gaze was so piercing that it made him stop in his tracks. That gaze reminded him of something. A short story he had written. About an encounter with a ghost. A fantastic tale in which the main character is visited in his room by a strange man in the middle of the night, and of course he thinks it's a dream and pays no heed, but later he sees that same man outside in the light of day—that was the moment of reversal. A fantastic tale, but also entirely realistic. He was satisfied with how it had turned out. It left you uncertain as to whether or not the events had actually happened. That was precisely the sort of gaze he'd had in mind when he wrote that story, and now here it was in real life. It seemed to him that the old man on the opposite sidewalk made a gesture, somewhat vague, as if inviting him to come close. He turned at the first corner and put distance between them. As he walked he felt those eyes following him, clinging to him. He stopped to look back. The old man was on the corner. He had set his bundle on the ground, and again he made that same vague gesture. He started to walk more quickly. At the next corner he turned to look back without slowing his gait. He thought he could make out the old man with the bundle coming toward him. He wasn't sure. Parisian delusions. Exhausted hallucinations. He kept going. He turned at the first corner and again at the next. He walked on, stopped once more. He found himself at the entrance of an arcade and went in. It was an awful place. Hundreds of lamps burned all at once under the glass dome and the smell of gas was unbearable.

He stopped and pretended to study the array of lace in a shop window, keeping an eye on the entrance to the arcade. From behind the dusty glass a woman with a pointy chin and crimped hair was watching him, drinking from a blue glass. She nodded for him to come inside. In the neighboring window was a display of hats, top hats and bowlers, straw hats, fedoras, all sitting on wooden heads. Their faces all had precisely the same features, almond-shaped eyes, finely drawn eyebrows, full pink lips. They were all tilted slightly to the side, staring at the same spot with an expression of joyful anticipation.

"Come in, come in for a refreshment." The woman with the pointy chin had stepped outside and was calling to him.

Farther on a yellow dog lifted its leg and urinated against a shop window with a display of shirts. When it was finished, it lowered its leg and looked around impassively. People were coming and going. Weighed down with purchases, they jostled one another, leaned over to examine some bolt of fabric, walked on a few steps, turned back, began to bargain. A young man in a white apron walked by him. Short with strong, thick calves. A village boy. He unlocked a little door, glanced behind him and vanished inside. His face was handsome. The old man with the bundle was nowhere to be seen. He pulled his handkerchief from his pocket and held it over his nose. The stench was indescribable. Gas fumes, urine, here and there a strong whiff of something rotting that overwhelmed all the other smells and took your breath away. He kept the handkerchief over his nose all the way to the end of the arcade and went outside.

What did that old man want from me? he wondered a few minutes later, almost disappointed not to have seen him inside the arcade. Why had he been staring at him so intently? He would never know. If he had dared take that step earlier, had gone over to speak to him, he might have found out. His eyes seemed so otherworldly, as if they were trying to convey a message. Who knew what the man was thinking. It had been a strange encounter. The man must have been mad, of course. One of the dozens of madmen wandering through Paris. But how odd. How powerful description was. An image born of his imagination when he wrote that story—the peculiar gaze of the man who visits the main character at night, the person who can't be a person but must be a ghost, a supernatural presence—how strange to encounter that very same image later, in real life. As if imagination dictated reality. And just as the character in his story hadn't kept his appointment with the ghost despite his great curiosity, he, too, had preferred to ignore the call of that gaze and had instead merely continued on his way. Any contact with the supernatural or even just the foreign, the new, always carried a certain threat. Both he and his character had chosen to remain whole, untouched, safe at the borders of the known world. Something about this last thought rubbed him the wrong way. Something opaque and very small that he needed to unravel, though he wasn't sure he'd be able to follow this train of thought to the end. He knew he was still fairly malleable, but also closed, limited. He didn't embrace new experiences easily. An encounter with a ghost. The more he thought about it, the more he realized that the old man wasn't the ghost. The old man was merely the vehicle, the channel that allowed an uncanny presence to reveal itself. Now he told himself, try to step into his shoes on the sidewalk, to pick up his bundle. See that man with the mustache and little round glasses across the way? Still fairly young, though he's lost any youthful quality. Always trying to escape, tormented by fears, imagining someone's following him. When he looks ahead he sees insurmountable barriers, walls he himself has diligently built. He was the ghost. The old man had seen right through him, had tried to exorcise that ghost with his piercing gaze.

The idea pleased him, the reversal of roles. The ghost as his alter ego. It might work well in a poem that would flow freely from one image to the next, without rhyme or restrictions. Yet that free flow required effort, it wasn't easy to achieve. Often he had the suspicion that, despite their constraining nature, rhyme and meter in fact made the poet's job easier, as if they reduced the demands of the poem. It was always easier to be given limits. A free flow … Suddenly the lines from the poem he had been thinking about yesterday afternoon leaped within him.

The city will follow you. You'll grow old in the same gray streets. And through the same neighborhoods you will stray

The lines seemed lonely, unfinished. Orphaned words in a hostile universe. The poem felt abandoned to an endless loneliness. He realized he had begun thinking about it in order to avoid some previous thought that he had now forgotten, and at the same moment he saw his desk in Alexandria, his papers in the drawer, the half-finished poems, the volume of Gibbon with his notes in the margins, and back behind that, very far back, his childhood desk in Liverpool, the notebook with the blue and red lines, the fountain pen, his fingers stained with ink, night falling quickly over the smoky roofs, a severe voice scolding him. He mentally recited the entire poem again and as he ended with the lines, *Once you've ruined your life here in this small corner, you've ruined it in all the world*, Place de la Concorde appeared in the distance, it had to be Place de la Concorde with the obelisk from Luxor rising imperiously on the horizon—a good thing they had brought the obelisk here, the thought flashed in his mind, otherwise it would have been buried in the sands like Nero's palace—and he felt a sudden excitement, was flooded with a sweeping joy, not only because his hotel was close, but because the appearance of this grand square at the precise moment he was reciting his lines seemed like an excellent omen for the poem. The obelisk, which some called Cleopatra's Needle, was a granite colossus that had been brought to Paris from Egypt. It was the source of the square's grandeur. From Alexandria to Paris: a promise for the poem. Faces flitted by like flies circling the same streets, unable to escape. Scowling shapes, or unsuspecting ones. Prisoners. Always in the same city. Unlike the wooden figures in the window, for these imprisoned people there was no joyful anticipation.

He stepped lightly toward the Place de la Concorde, feeling newly invigorated. One thought led to another in a free flow—there it is again, he thought, that free flow, from the images of passersby to his lines, from Paris to Alexandria, and even farther, all the way to Luxor, whence the obelisk had come— deep in the desert where the mouth of the Nile bubbled, and from there to the quarries of Aswan near the Sudanese border, where granite had been extracted only to be carried, centuries later and hundreds of kilometers, all the way to this square where Marie Antoinette's guillotine had once been erected on the very spot where the obelisk now stood—and again to his poem, as if the poem were capable of crystalizing that circular flow, or rather of abolishing it, destroying all distance in a few short lines, allowing an unknown poet just setting out to capture this suspended world, to lay it bare, because History with a capital *H* was comprised not of events but of stories—and a wealth of new ideas crawled like ants in his head, searching for words, for the beginning of a line, behind which lay his ambition, an unquenchable thirst, he couldn't deny it, so many ideas and words, and ideas that hadn't yet found their words— it seems I'll have to write another poem, he thought, and the free flow was broken as he looked ahead. There was no obelisk. This wasn't Place de la Concorde. He was in some other square, vast with rectangular flower beds. In the middle protruded an ungainly statuette, mounted on a marble fountain whose water had run dry.

Some while later, dragging his feet, having crossed what felt like all of Paris for a second time, he saw in the distance a gilded building whose wrought iron trim glittered in the afternoon light. Maison Dorée. He felt as if he were returning from another life. Though he was still quite far away, he crossed to the opposite side of the street, worried that he might run into someone he knew, who would see him in this awful state. But who could he possibly run into? It was the journalists' hour, according to what Mardaras had said. Or perhaps the artists' hour. John and I will come here tomorrow, he decided. We'll come to dine here. It was as if he were taking a small revenge that made his heart leap at the sight of that carefree crowd enjoying an aperitif on the boulevard, elegant and aloof. Le Tout-Paris was a wasps' nest of fools, there was no doubt about that, just as in Alexandria, arrogant fools—and how vain, how grotesque to believe you're at the center of the world, when just a few steps down the street a banana peel is waiting for you, a beautiful, thick, fleshy banana peel that will bring you crashing down, how grotesque, how utterly grotesque, he repeated as exhaustion suddenly struck like an axe at the nape of his neck. The strong blow of an axe to the neck. His vision blurred and a faintness came over his body all at once. Across from him the carefree crowd trembled, figures swayed slightly, drinks in hand, before righting themselves again. Then his rickety legs continued on their way.

"What happened to you? You're drenched in sweat," John cried, jumping to his feet.

"No, it started raining. How long have you been here?" he said.

Mardaras ran to bring him a glass of water.

"Just for a few minutes, then it cleared up again," he added.

Inside he was smiling at the thought that he hadn't stopped for directions, that he hadn't asked for anyone's help.

20 June 1897

Dear Pericles,

I received both of your letters and apologize for
not replying sooner. I meant to do so at the first
opportunity—at some moment when I would be
relatively calm and not rushing around, but such a
moment never presented itself. I'm writing to you
now from my room at the Saint-Pétersbourg Hotel
in Paris, where I'm resting a bit before our evening
outing. Our journey thus far has been very interesting, though also quite tiring. It always seems it's
time to leave a place before we've even unpacked.

We're now in Paris for the second time. The
day after tomorrow we'll begin our return journey. I feel as if we've been away for months. So
many different events have impressed themselves
on me during this time, so many images, one after
another in an endless stream, sometimes entirely
unconnected, such that it would be difficult for me
to give a full account of the trip. We went to the
Louvre two days in a row, for instance, like diligent
schoolboys. That was during our first stay, before
we left for London. But how much did I retain of

what we saw? The Winged Victory of Samothrace, of course, to whom we paid our respects—they've set her in a very impressive alcove at the head of the Daru staircase—and when you see her from below you're overwhelmed with admiration, and then two or three small Chaldean statuettes that I liked very much. The Venus de Milo was exquisite, but didn't impress me. Likewise, Leonardo da Vinci's *Mona Lisa* is an excellent painting—and yet to tell the truth, it was as if I'd seen it before. A hint of déjà vu. But perhaps it's simply that we've all heard such praise for the painting's mysterious smile? Velletri's reclining hermaphrodite is expressive, with an ambiguity that makes you feel a bit troubled and leaves a rather melancholy aftertaste. I spent quite awhile searching through that labyrinth for a bas-relief that depicts Cleopatra presenting an offering to Isis—I read somewhere that there were later interventions, corrective engravings of the stone that interested me, since they show that this stele was probably originally intended for a different Ptolemy—but I never found it. However, I did see a statue of the dying Cleopatra by some Frenchman, which was quite sensual, her head thrown back as if in erotic ecstasy. I retained nothing else from the museum except for fragments, scattered impressions. And it's the largest museum in the world. What I mean to say is, the human eye retains things selectively, it can't absorb everything.

Certainly there are masterpieces that don't survive this process of selection. There was one painting, I believe in the Flemish room, a dark work whose shapes seemed snuffed out by a yellowish light, and something about it was transfixing, though the subject wasn't religious. I wanted to look at it more closely, but John was tired and in a hurry. I wonder if it might have been a Goya. In which case it must have been the Spanish room.

Of course I suspect this business of selectivity is true more of the representational arts, painting, sculpture. You know better about that than I. As for music, I'm not in a position to offer an opinion; I must think it over further. But the written word is different. With a novel, or even a poem, you have to give yourself over, devote time to it, even just the time it takes you to read, as opposed to a work of art, which you see all at once as you enter a room, displayed among others. Thus the novel or poem will make a deeper impression in the end, will leave its stamp on you and even after you've forgotten the plot, you'll still retain its "flavor," yes, its flavor ... I don't know precisely how to put it, but the poem seems to demand a kind of tête-a-tête from the reader. Exhibition halls are like a bridal bazaar, where paintings show themselves off, saying, look at me, I'm prettier than her (which reminds me, we also went to the famed Salon, which I found exhausting, as bad a bazaar as you can imagine, and that painting was there, the one by our own Theodoros Rallis that everyone's been talking about, though I find his *point de vue* a bit too Oriental, too affected for my taste)—but how is one to find time for a tête-a-tête in such an environment.

He stopped, feeling that he was rambling. He had no idea where this paragraph was headed, and apart from the wordiness, something had been off from the beginning, as if the entire stream of words was based on a misunderstanding. There wasn't time to begin again, so he crossed out the last sentence and continued hurriedly:

My dear Pericles, I shouldn't tire you with my theories. From what you write, I take it you're well and that your summer has begun pleasantly with excursions and swimming in the sea at Ramleh. It's an easy journey by train. You describe the evening of cards you enjoyed—excellent food and plenty of gin—and how you were losing at first but eventually broke even and left feeling pleased. You don't mention who else was there, or comment on the conversation, or the gossip the following day, which is always the most entertaining part, as if you're leaving me room to imagine it all. You ask if I miss Alexandria. I believe I do ... but I'm not sure. At times I feel nostalgia, which is different. Nostalgia without the sense that anything is missing. I miss my close friends, you first among them, and I dream of our delightful conversations. But I don't miss the city. I think I could easily settle in Paris or London. I'd have no difficulty adjusting. In fact London might suit me better, as a result of my upbringing. Such a move would be excellent for my poetry. Plans written in sand, you'll say. Soon I'll be back and the memories of this casual traveler will quickly fade.

It's true that one's perspective changes in Europe. In Alexandria everything seems so distant, as if everything is unfolding in some other reality, even our own alarming affairs, which we witness at a strange distance. Events, wars, conflicts of ideas all take place somewhere else. We watch as if through a foggy lens and don't experience their intensity. Like the prisoners in Plato's cave, we see only shadows. Is it because we're émigrés, almost stateless people? I don't know.

I'm rambling again, he thought. Besides, the letter had become rather disagreeable, with what one might call a note of complaint or self-pity.

Your first letter, which mentioned your family friends in Marseille, I received on the night before we left that city for Paris. There was no time to visit them, though I dearly wished I could, especially as it would have allowed me to see their lovely villa with the cacti and the rose beds you described. I'm afraid we won't manage to see them on our return trip, either, as we have only a few hours between the arrival of the train and the departure of the *Congo*.

I don't remember which of your letters told me about the new volume by Ruskin that you bought. Have you started it? What impression did it make? The book interests me greatly, I'd like to borrow it and promise to return it promptly. After you've finished it yourself, of course. I know I still have your copy of that novel by Anatole France, I kept it far too long, I wanted to read it one last time before leaving for Paris and I truly did find it very useful. I'll bring it to you as soon as I return.

You wrote that T. may publish one of my poems in his journal. It would please me greatly. I wasn't sure from what you wrote whether he's already decided or is still considering the issue. Either way, the poems I gave him will need some revision. Please do me the favor of trying to meet with him, and if you think he has indeed made up his mind, ask him to wait until my return, at which point I can give him the final version. Don't forget, my dear Pericles. I thank you in advance.

We visited several good bookstores in London. I saw a lovely edition of Shelley's *The Revolt of Islam*, leather-bound on matte paper that was like woven fabric. It was quite expensive, I didn't buy it. Apart from that, London lives and breathes the Jubilee celebrations. Throngs of people everywhere. We saw relatives and old friends. We ate at the Star and Garter in Richmond, the service and fare were both excellent, the quality and presentation quite fine, but as for the flavor, *laissait à desirer*. You could serve the English a plate of oxtail and they'd gulp it down without chewing.

Here in Paris there's quite a buzz about the Dreyfus Affair—you must have heard of it, the Jewish officer who was convicted of treason three years ago. Since then he has been held in terrible conditions on Devil's Island, and many claim, and indeed seem to have legitimate cause to suspect, that he is innocent, that his trial was merely staged. The issue has assumed the proportions of a national schism. All of France is divided into two camps; the artistic community is likewise split on the issue. Siblings refuse to say good morning, spouses pass notes at home rather than speak.

He paused. Those spouses passing notes rang a bell. He'd heard it somewhere. They were Mardaras's words. It was inconceivable, that such a ridiculous character would chase him even into the letter he was writing. He crossed out the last sentence and sat there thinking. Outside the daylight was fading. John would be expecting them to take tea together. He would finish the letter quickly and go down to meet him.

There's something I wanted to ask you about, too. Didn't you watch the carnival parade at the Benakis home one year? I remember you describing the baskets of petals you tossed from the balcony, and how the middle daughter, Penelope, behaved a bit oddly, and seemed to have a rather particular temperament. When we discussed it later, you hypothesized that she might have been unlucky in love, and we later learned who was involved. Do you remember whether there was another guest that day by the name of Mardaras? Does that name mean anything to you, Nikos Mardaras? Short with a head like a sheep's. He's stuck to us like a burr in Paris.

He crossed out the last sentence.

He seems frivolous and narrow-minded to me, despite his large head.

Again, he crossed out the sentence.

We met him yesterday and I'd like to hear your opinion, if you have indeed come across him. John seems to like him but I find him a bit *superficiel*. He's Moréas's secretary, unpaid, of course, and takes care of his correspondence. Yesterday he took us to Moréas's house—Moréas himself is in Greece at present. His library is enormous. I thought it

somewhat limited in range, but then I didn't have
time to study it systematically. Moréas, as you
know, has made quite a name for himself in Paris,
and every so often he baptizes a new poetic movement. I must say, I'm skeptical. The last book of
his that I read, *Le Pèlerin passionné*, didn't leave me
feeling at all *passionné*.

He crossed out the entire passage about Moréas and looked at
the sheet of paper. It would be best for him to copy the letter
out from the beginning. He certainly couldn't send it as it was. It
gave the impression of a man who changed his mind constantly
or who got carried away with his thoughts and wrote things he
then wanted to hide, and decided to smudge them out. But
there wasn't time. He sat there absentmindedly for a moment,
pen in hand. The matter of Moréas required delicate treatment.
He bent over the page and began to write.

I learned that Moréas has praised my poetry. His
library is impressive, it's quite well-known in Paris
and he seems to keep abreast of the latest pub-
lications. Speaking of Moréas, I realize I haven't
yet returned your copy of his *Le Pèlerin passionné*
—I'm afraid I have no excuse to offer. I'll bring
it to you as soon as I return, along with Anatole
France's novel. As for Mardaras, see if you can
remember anything. Yesterday we spoke of the war
and found we were not at all in agreement. You
know my opinions on the matter, and must realize

I am unconvinced by those who believe lamenta-
tion to be a sign of patriotism.

Be that as it may. I forgot to thank you for
visiting our mother. You brought her great joy.
You wrote that you found her alone with the
maid, and she complained of not having been out
in quite a while. I fear Pavlos spends too much
time out at coffeehouses, and seems not to realize
his obligations.

He crossed out the last sentence and continued.

Pavlos does what he can, but I fear our absence has
put quite a lot of responsibility on him. And of
course he has obligations of his own. He can't very
well ignore the invitations he receives.

One last thing that will please you. I've heard
reports of an enigmatic "house" known as the Ark.
It's not clear precisely what transpires there—it's
rumored to be a den of pleasure frequented by
aristocrats and commoners alike. It's in a remote
location out near the fortifications and is under
constant guard. John and I will try to go, and I'll
share our impressions with you.

On rereading those sentences, they seemed exaggerated to him,
and he added:

Of course it may all be mere *fantaisie*. Our informant is Mardaras, after all, so I have my reasons for doubting the accuracy of what we've heard.

I must say, I am rather fatigued. I spent the entire day wandering over all of Paris. Today was the *Promenade de la vache enragée* at Montmartre, a carnival organized by artists, with music and masqueraders. Something like our carnival parade. It was quite a madhouse.

That's all of my news, and of course we'll speak soon in person. I'll be home in a week. I wrote to you that it feels as if I've been away for months. Perhaps when I see Alexandria at a distance, from the bridge of the boat as it enters the port, it will seem as if I never left.

I thank you, again, for your letters.

Yours,
Const. Cavafy

P.S. Looking over my letter, it seems very careless, with so many sentences crossed out, and the thoughts haphazardly expressed. I would copy it out more cleanly but I'm too exhausted—I know you'll forgive me. John sends his best.

He put the letter in his pocket without reading it over. That last bit about Alexandria rings false, he thought. And I let him believe I went to the Promenade. It doesn't matter.

I t's the light falling over the Punta della Dogana that creates the reflection. If you're in Piazza San Marco the water level seems higher. Waves slap at your feet on the pier, making little whirlpools as they recede. You watch as the foam rises. How much cognac had you drunk? Believe me, the canal is utterly tranquil, the surface as still as oil all the way to the Rialto. Of course the water hasn't risen, the level is precisely the same. It's just an optical illusion. At that time of day the light is stronger. The sun falls on the Punta della Dogana and seems to shatter. I've noticed that, too. It made an impression. So much light and yet the waters below so dark and threatening. Around the time of day when we're headed to rehearsal. It's a strange sight. I'd say it's the cognac the lot of you drank at the hotel. Cognac? More like barley vinegar, it goes straight to your head.

The last one to speak broke into a deep, exuberant laugh, and some of the others joined in.

"The dressing rooms at the Fenice are awful," said a male voice he was hearing for the first time. The French was hesitant, thickly accented.

One woman tossed out a comment in Russian and another added in French:

"And that old cleaning lady followed you around with an outstretched hand."

"And the rats. I've never seen rats as big as the ones in Venice," pronounced the same male voice. The man must have been quite young, and his voice had a melancholy ring.

He tried to get a good look at the young man, but he was sitting at the edge of the group with his back turned that way. Again the conversation returned to the Punta della Dogana. The man who was now speaking seemed to be almost in ecstasy, he'd felt as if the heavens were opening, he said, with all that light flooding the scene, huge boulders of light, and the water rising—he expressed himself in French with greater ease than his companions, some of whom mixed in a fair bit of Russian. Every so often someone seemed to be translating, so there must have been someone French among them as well.

"Venice has the most beautiful clouds," said the same young man. The tone of his voice wasn't sad, as he had at first believed, but empty, flat. It was the voice of someone who has not yet lived.

He stood up to get a newspaper from the next table, hoping to get a better view of the group. The young man's head leaned gently toward one shoulder. Seen from the back, he appeared to be of medium height with wavy chestnut hair. His body rested loosely against the back of the armchair and his right hand dangled, tracing vague circles in the air. There were another five or six in the group, all Russian, probably ballet dancers, and the Frenchman with them was older, most likely their impresario. The troupe was presumably touring Europe, and Venice was one of the stops. John was very late, he must have fallen asleep. He needn't have hurried to finish his letter after all. With the newspaper in his hand he crossed the room and sat at a table across the way that offered a better view. A misguided move. Now he was too far away to hear their conversation, and the young man, though turned three-quarters toward him, was screened by two women who kept fanning themselves energetically. He folded the newspaper and rose once more to his feet. There was a small table off on its own that he hadn't noticed earlier, lodged between the group and the wall. He went over to it and sat down, then shifted the table back to make room for his legs. It would of course seem strange that he had chosen this uncomfortable position. The arm of his chair touched the back of the one in which the young man was sitting.

John appeared in the entranceway and waved to him.

"I'm sorry, so sorry ... The Promenade wore me out," he said, coming closer.

A man with graying hair and a rather dry expression wearing a wing-collar came up behind him, escorting a portly woman cinched into her corset who kept emitting little cries.

"A drink, a sherbet, quickly," she gurgled, turning to scan the room around her.

"Good evening, Comte," a waiter called, hurrying over to greet them. "Madame la Comtesse," he said, lowering his voice, and bowed. The maître d'hôtel appeared at a run. When he arrived he bowed, too. Then the two began to back away, bowing all the while, waiting for the couple to decide where they preferred to sit.

"There, over there," the comtesse pointed. A valet in white gloves appeared out of nowhere carrying a small poodle. As soon as he set it down at the countess's feet, the poodle made a sound like a crow and the valet kneeled and gathered it once more into his arms.

The young man had turned around and was watching. His eyes were gray, shaded by heavy eyelashes. His skin was pale, almost translucent, and in profile his nose seemed quite small, slightly upturned, with delicate nostrils. They were light gray, his eyes. The color of the sea on a rainy day.

"Madame la Comtesse," John said, smiling. "I apologize for being so late, I simply couldn't rouse myself from my lethargy. But why have you squeezed yourself in here?"

"Unacceptable. I'm quite annoyed. There's been no sign of a waiter all this time. At least not until the comte arrived.".

At the other end of the room, the comte was peering soberly through his monocle, the comtesse was fanning herself, and the valet was standing at attention with the poodle in his arms.

"Well-fed rats," said the young man. The entire group of Russians laughed loudly.

Was it a jab at the comte and comtesse? The boy must have a sense of humor, he thought.

"Did you hear the news? Due to inclement weather there will be no crossings on the English Channel for two days. It's a good thing we got across when we did," John said. "What shall we have to drink, tea or chocolate?" He glanced around for the waiter. And then, "Are you sad to be leaving?"

He didn't answer. A curl of the young dancer's hair had fallen over the back of the armchair, close enough to touch if he reached out his hand. Soft, freshly-washed hair gleaming with lighter streaks. And something like a scent, divine, wafted his way now and then. Something fresh, something he couldn't quite place.

"Just a minute, I'm finishing a thought," he said. He closed his eyes and inhaled deeply. A scent of milk and fresh wheat. Then he turned to his brother. "So, what were you saying?"

"Will you at last solve the mystery for me? Did you come to the Promenade? You were so exhausted when you got back to the hotel that I didn't dare ask."

"Of course I came." He turned slightly toward the wall and let his shoulder rest on the young man's armchair, rubbing his sleeve gently against the brocade upholstery.

"I still can't understand how we got separated. Mardaras and I waited for you on the boulevard for quite a while. You must have turned off it somewhere, there's no other explanation. To be honest, it crossed my mind that you might have done it on purpose to be rid of us."

"No, it wasn't that. I must have just let my mind wander," he murmured.

"We looked for you at Montmartre, too. Where were you standing, near the Moulin Rouge?"

The slow rubbing had aroused him.

"We stopped at Place Blanche and watched the parade from there. I left Mardaras for a bit and pushed my way through the crowd to look for you on the other side. Such an enormous crowd, a truly impressive sight. Not to mention that Mademoiselle Stumpp, the Muse of Montmartre."

"A bizarre choice for a muse if you ask me."

"You think so? I found her charming, and more demure than I expected. Mardaras showered her with confetti."

Now the Russians were laughing loudly at some joke.

He shifted his weight onto the arm of his chair so he could recline more comfortably. He stretched his legs. His palm touched the fabric of the young man's armchair and stroked it gently.

"What float did you like the best?"

There was something rough about the texture that excited him. The fabric felt like silk but was shot through here and there with coarse threads like nerves.

"What did you think of the float depicting Imagination? The starving artist with the magic baguette in his atelier was thunderously applauded when it went past. I thought the Chimera quite a success, too." John was looking past him, recalling images from the Promenade.

The Russians were laughing again. The young man's chair seemed to move. Just a tremor, practically nothing at all. His hand palpated the fabric in circles. He sought out the coarse threads, rubbing them with his thumb.

"*Vivez d'amour et d'eau fraîche,*" John was saying.

Across from them the comte, comtesse, and valet seemed to be frozen in a tableau vivant, eyes empty, mouths sealed. The young man's chair shifted again and the lock of his hair slid a bit farther down. He continued to stroke the fabric gently, pressing it lightly with the tips of his fingers. Smaller circles, then larger.

"The French certainly know their way around satire, it's in their blood. Wasn't it a blast? *Vivez d'amour et d'eau fraîche,*" John repeated.

He once again inhaled the scent that drove him mad. Quickly, slowly, quickly, he thought. The lock of the young man's hair was very close. Slower, even slower. His palm grew still, continuing its gentle pressure. He felt the stitches of the brocade rise against his skin. Something harsh stood out, a gold thread, thick, as if starched. He reached out a single finger—under the stitches the surface was smooth, uniform, the thread no longer there. He groped for it, felt it, lost it, found it again. It was a vein that wound through the weave, vanishing at times. He traced it with two fingers, fumbling for it blindly. Some sort of ornament tightly sewn to the fabric tickled his touch. His arousal increased and his thumb rubbed ardently against the fabric.

"Of course I prefer the carnival parade in Alexandria. Perhaps because it holds so many memories. We've been going since we were children. And of course all the friends you run into there."

"Our parade is more of a family affair," he said, just to say something. His voice sounded husky, as if it were rising from some unknown depth.

"My thoughts exactly."

The young man's elbow jutted out over the arm of the chair. Curved, in a black baize sleeve that seemed a bit worn. "*Ochi chornyye, ochi strastnyye*," one of the group sang, and someone else broke in, soliciting the singer's opinion on something. The young man's elbow withdrew. Immediately the lock of hair danced in the air as if it were toying with him. His hand opened and closed. For a while he stroked the tips of his fingers with his thumb. The motion ceased, the fingers froze, contorted in a spasm. Enough. He had to calm down. His mouth was dry, his lips clung together. Enough, this has to stop, he told himself. And then the same divine scent wafted toward him again, reeling him back in, and he inhaled deeply, eyes nearly closed, wanting to hold it all in, to savor it with his mouth, which now felt moist, full of saliva, wanting to trap it all inside, to inhale again and again, to drink it all in, the milk, the fresh wheat, the crisp, newly-cut stems, the south wind whipping fiercely over the thirsty earth, the first raindrops falling onto dry, sun-scorched soil, which drinks them in greedily, still unsatiated, the young shoots that spring up, gentle necks swaying. The fresh smell of this white skin had intoxicated him. He breathed more deeply and tried to hold that breath inside. His fingers groped the brocade, located the embroidery, the coarse, golden threads, and chafed against them. He dragged his index finger along the back of the chair, stopping at what he figured to be the middle of the young man's back, guessing where those gentle dimples must be, the dips above the kidneys. He sank his nail into the fabric until it hurt.

"Whatever can that blessed waiter be about? At this rate we'll be taking our tea at dinnertime," John complained.

Go on, go on, he thought.

He was in ecstasy.

"What's wrong with you? Do you have some itch?" John asked.

"Yes, no ..." he said, his voice emerging as if out of a well full of stones.

The waiter came to take their order and left.

"Wasn't I right to speak to him? The service today is unacceptable," John said.

His face was on fire. Tiny specks danced before his eyes as his hand continued to stroke the back of the armchair a little lower, outside his brother's line of vision, close to those dips in the lower back.

"Though perhaps I should have complained to the maître d'hôtel, taken him to task, don't you think? Or better yet, the hotel management."

He needed to find some relief. He could barely contain himself.

"I," he started to say but was unable to continue.

He would go to the toilet. No, to his room. He would find some excuse. He would say that ... Go on, go on, he told himself as he pierced the fabric with his nail.

"Let's change tables," John said, seeing the waiter approaching with his tray.

Impossible for him to stand right then. Just a bit more, he thought. A bit more. His finger slipped into the slit in the fabric, opening it wider, then slid all the way in, entering something dense but soft, a network of threads both fine and coarse. He twisted his hand, inserted a second finger. Deeper in, the material became something he couldn't identify, spongy and warm. It was as if the heat of the young man's body had reached all the way there, his sweet heat, and that divine smell that surrounded him. His ears hummed. He felt something harder and continued to dig, holding his breath. He slipped a third finger in, grabbed hold of something metal, or a tangle of threads. Lord, just a minute more. The waiter bent over their table. Another metal bit, more tangled threads, and finally a wire pricked his finger and he almost cried out.

The waiter was setting the tea things on the table.

"What on earth is he doing? There isn't room at this table. Tell him to gather it up again," he said and rose to his feet.

S omething was happening at the far end of the room. The comtesse was scolding the valet, waving her handkerchief. The comte jumped to his feet, pushing the armchair back, a pained spasm on his ashen face.

"Georges," the comtesse cried.

Three waiters ran over.

A black turd adorned the marble floor. The poodle sniffed it, tongue hanging out, trying to decide whether to lick it.

"Georges, Georges," the comtesse repeated. The comte stared into space with the same pained expression. The waiters stood in a circle around them, awaiting instructions, while the valet had dropped to his knees and was trying to pull the dog back, who lunged forward to bite him and let out that awful sound like a crow. Face flushed a deep red, the valet scooped up the dog and rose to his feet.

Meanwhile, the group of Russians seemed absorbed in some disagreement. They had raised their voices, the impresario was gesturing as if annoyed, but the young man didn't seem to be taking part, he had turned his head and was following the scene with the dog.

A servant came into the room carrying towels and a mop. Another followed with a bucket of water. Then the old concierge appeared in the doorway, glanced in and then disappeared again.

"Poor Georges, I bet he'll be the one to take the blame," John said.

"Georges is the poodle, not the valet."

"Nonsense. Why would you think that?"

"Shall we bet?"

How strange that he now felt almost rested. And in a fine mood, too. The head of chestnut-colored curls that was now across the room had certainly played its part. He had an almost direct view of the young man from the more comfortable table to which they had moved, and despite the distance that divided them, he could observe a number of small details, or rather not details but the features that render a whole unique, how the muscles of his thighs flexed in his pants, how he crossed his legs, then uncrossed them right away as if he were about to rise, yet sat there sinking even deeper into the armchair. There was something dreamy in his movements, too, in how he cocked his head or combed a hand absentmindedly through his hair or let a finger rest for a moment at the corner of his mouth. Those lips are made for kisses, he thought, and the memory of the madness that had gripped him a short while before, that paroxysm in the armchair, brought a faint smile to his lips.

"Look, Georges bit the valet."

"So you insist?"

"About Georges?"

John laughed. The two of them were in fine form. Mardaras would be coming by to pick them up later that evening, accompanied by a lady, Madame de something, he had forgotten her name, but she was nobility of some sort. Continuing to observe the young man out the corner of his eye, he thought the time might be ripe to tell his brother about Moréas's note. It was the only way of bleaching a stain that wouldn't easily be rubbed out.

Each time he remembered that note he felt as if it were digging a poisonous burrow, and he knew it would torment him for a long time, perhaps years, erupting in his memory at the most unlikely moments, piercing him time and again until it crushed him entirely. But perhaps he and John could discuss it calmly, examining all possible explanations—as if there could be many for those four terrible words! As if they didn't signify his literary condemnation, he thought, seeing them again in his mind's eye, written in red pencil on the envelope on Moréas's desk. *Weak expression Poor artistry*. But at least John would placate him. He couldn't bear another sleepless night. They had discussed similar issues in the past, and John had a way of dealing with them, entirely logical, free of prejudice, as when a journal once rejected one of his poems and they spent the entire evening poring over the letter, which was only a few lines long, not even, and his brother's words had helped him to view that rejection unsentimentally, to remove the husk of failure from around it, and above all to conceive of himself as a poet whose path included hardships and obstacles, ones that his talent could surely overcome—a course through the stormy seas that seemed, in the end, quite exciting, coming to life before him during that long, terribly hot evening, until the cicadas had grown quiet, the candle had gone out, and his brother's shadow flickered in the dark room as his calm voice reassured him, exuding confidence, yet without falling too much into flattery, which would have been the easy way out.

He was about to speak when he noticed a movement in the group of Russians. The impresario had risen and was approaching the young man. He pulled a chair over to sit beside him, the young man scooted to one side to make room, and the entire back of the armchair with the hole presented itself for all to see.

"I have a plan, as long as I can convince Mardaras," John was saying.

"Just a minute."

"I'd like your opinion. Where are you going?"

"I forgot my newspaper."

"Listen, if the Ark exists ... I mean, in the truly unlikely circumstance that the Ark exists, we really must go before we leave Paris."

"Let's go to Maison Dorée tomorrow," he said, then hastily walked away before his brother could react.

He passed the trio with the dog, who had once again assumed their tableau vivant positions, and progressed deeper into the room. The newspaper was still there, folded on the table. He stood behind the young man's armchair and bent over, pretending to read. He could see the hole, as big as a walnut, a worm-eaten walnut. Threads, gold threads and something brownish and wooly sprung from within. How did I manage to do all that, he thought, and felt like laughing. He pushed the table over to hide the hole. He bent once more over the newspaper, dragging his finger slowly across a line of small black letters. *Their Royal Highnesses the Prince and Princess of Naples departed yesterday morning from Paris on a private train ...* He stretched his foot out to touch the young man's armchair.

Now he'll turn to look at me, he thought.

Le Figaro, Sunday 20 June 1897

He waited. Across the room he could see that John had turned to look at him.

Bombes et cyclones was the title of the main article.

Investigations continue regarding the man with the bomb, or rather bombs: three have now been found that seem to have been constructed in the same manner. They were transported to the Municipal Laboratory with the greatest of care …

He skipped down a bit on the page. *We have learned that the bombs contained gunpowder, nails …* Perhaps the doorman who shooed me off this morning had taken me for a bomber? he wondered. For a moment he closed his eyes and inhaled. The scent was no longer there. But he'll turn to look at me, he repeated to himself. He was sure of it. He felt an illogical certainty that the young man would turn toward him, he just needed to stay there, just had to want it strongly enough, his desire simply needed to maintain its intensity. As if this were some spiritualist encounter in which the spirit's appearance depended on his faith and commitment.

Across the room, John gestured impatiently.

He continued to read. *In his fiction Dickens has described the mental state of the common criminal, the murderer for whom the police are searching but are unable to find. In those days, however, the press was not what it is today, there was no reporting to speak of, and* faits divers *did not assume that role in people's lives …* The Russians were speaking loudly, another disagreement about something. He heard none of it. With the back of his calf he gently grazed the brocade fabric. I'll wait here until you look at me, he thought. Look at me. I know you'll look at me. *The bomber surely belongs to this type, and so we must suppose that he is one of the Parisians currently most entertained by the affair—or, if we assume him to be more educated, then we might say that he has a very pleasant understanding of art.* The armchair knocked against him with a jolt, jarring him in the ribs. The Russians were getting up to leave. The young man turned and looked at him.

Gray eyes streaked with damp. Their eyes met silently. A full, ripe mouth, out of place in the boyish face. A perversity about that mouth. A constriction of the lips, something pained in the creases. Kisses, kisses, then nervous sobs, he thought.

They were already leaving, shoving one another like a common crowd. Just a minute, he gestured to John, who was waiting for him fretfully. He bent over the newspaper. *The storm seems to have passed, the barometric pressure ... Yet bad weather continues over the English Channel. The temperature has dropped. In Paris the temperature was 15 degrees yesterday at eight in the morning, 17.5 degrees at noon, and 19 at two.*

Was he merely imagining that the young man's eyes had lingered on his, not insistently, but as if they wanted to speak to him? That gray with its hidden currents, the mouth that could easily become carried away. The full lips, a bit heavy, something like a twitch at the corners. You could bite those lips, you could suck on them and they would respond with passion, and afterward as you pulled back to look, you would glimpse something slightly dissolute being suppressed at the edges, the nearly invisible traces of something like perversion. As he crossed the room, he tried to picture himself through that young man's eyes. Was I charming, at least? he wondered.

"I've been working something over in my mind for quite a while now," John said. "I want you to tell me whether you agree."

"About the Ark?"

"Yes, yes. Though your suggestion about Maison Dorée left me speechless, and now I'm a bit confused. You're remarkable, dear brother. You constantly surprise me, as if I'm just meeting you for the first time. Let me think … Perhaps there's a way for us to combine the two? What do you think?"

John's plan was for them to pretend that some other acquaintance had mentioned the Ark to them, as well. Someone who'd stopped by the hotel to take tea with them that afternoon, or, better, someone Constantine had run into at Montmartre. That would sound more convincing, since the length of the Promenade had allowed plenty of time for confidences. So, this acquaintance—they could invent a name and profession later— had invited them to go with him to the Ark, had in fact insisted. But they preferred to go with Mardaras, because of the strong bond of friendship that had swiftly grown up between them in the course of a single day. In John's view, this would be the tricky part. Mardaras hadn't invited them to accompany him, and in fact had always spoken of the Ark as if it were a masonic lodge, off-limits to outsiders. Which meant that they would also have to pretend there had been a sort of invitation on Mardaras's part, or at least that they had understood his references to the place to constitute an invitation. A double pretense, the pretense of pretense. The second was of course the more difficult, they would have to behave in such a way as to make Mardaras believe that at some point, at some indefinite point, perhaps the previous night, he had suggested or let it be understood that he was suggesting that they visit the Ark together. It was like bluffing at cards. Of course the plan concerned the following evening, their last. Tonight the presence of Madame de would be prohibitive regarding the Ark, unless she took her leave at a reasonable time, and the three of them were free to continue their evening together.

"I want to tell you something about Moréas," he broke in.

Moréas's note needed some introduction, so he began to speak of the previous night, when he hadn't slept well, in fact hadn't slept at all, woke with a headache, and so on, but as he spoke he realized that the introduction was pointless, it was enough to pronounce those four words without prologues or prefaces, four simple words and his brother would immediately understand, and yet for some reason he couldn't, so he continued this monologue instead, staring into the depths of the room, focusing on the spot where the young dancer had been sitting, and mentioned the carriage that had taken them to Moréas's house, the horses' dirty manes, the still waters under the Pont Neuf and something about Dreyfus. What on earth did Dreyfus have to do with anything? All he needed to say were those four words. He slipped once again into his description of the carriage ride along the streets of the Quartier Latin, lit by those depressing streetlights, of the steps at Moréas's house, the sleeping servant, then suddenly jumped to poetic movements, and how meaningless these conversations were, how they tried to fit Art into various molds, all those *isms*, romanticism, symbolism, and so on, molds they fitted on by force, as if Art needed an excuse, as if it had to account for itself before those idiots, he concluded, realizing that he had raised his voice.

"And yet there has to be some form of necessity shaping Art," John said. "We can't just leave everything to chance. We can't be sure that the apple will always fall beneath the apple tree."

"Necessity?" he heard himself ask. Art was pleasure. An exacting pleasure few were capable of appreciating. As necessary as the game that frees a child's mind from the dry teaching of the schoolhouse, necessary because it enables expression to overcome the constraints of conventional thinking—and if John would admit that, he would agree with him about necessity, but if he insisted that Art had some social role, some domesticating mission, then he was diametrically opposed, and at any rate all those *isms* didn't make for better poems, they were like enormous, floppy hats that always failed to flatter. What am I saying? he wondered. If they were to speak of Moréas's note he had to put an end to this garrulity, otherwise they'd run out of time. *Weak expression Poor artistry.* Weak expression. What time was it now? The conversation tired him. The armchair with the slit was diagonally across from him. How he would have liked to see that wavy hair tumbling down its back, slipping over the brocade fabric, to see those eyes, those lips again. But he really needed to get to the point, so he spoke of Moréas's library, which while large had seemed to him rather lacking in depth, and about the book by that young writer, Marcel Proust, Anatole France's protégé, which he'd sought in vain, and hearing his voice sound more and more shallow and macabre, he stepped like a sleepwalker into Moréas's office and approached the gallows of the desk, in the alcove illuminated by a single gas lamp, whose sloped ceiling made it look like a lair. Or perhaps a refuge, though the light was raw and cold ... He went closer, then closer still. The lamplight fell on a table that was almost bare, exaggeratedly neat. It didn't look like a poet's desk at all. More like that of a high-ranking civil servant. There was a double candelabra and a stack of blank paper. "Inkstand, letter opener, blotting paper, all perfectly aligned," he said, and stopped.

He could see the envelope containing his poems. He saw his own handwriting, *Monsieur Jean Moréas, rue ... Paris, France,* and then the note in red pencil.

It was impossible for him to continue.

"You describe it so well. A poet's private apartments are fascinating, they reveal so much," John said.

Apart from the trio with the dog, the room was nearly empty. At the other end of the room, in the corridor leading to the kitchen, the shadows of waiters passed by. Huge, headless shadows.

"I've heard that Hugo's house in Guernsey is truly extravagant. Where he lived in exile. Like a mausoleum, but all in black. But don't let me interrupt, go on, we've arrived at the most interesting spot, Moréas's desk."

"These meteorologists are entirely ignorant. They said it would be cool in Paris, fifteen degrees Celsius—that's about sixty degrees Fahrenheit, whereas it has to be over 85."

John looked at him, taken aback.

"What does that have to do with anything?" he asked.

"Nothing."

His brother's expression continued to show surprise, so he added:

"I read it in the newspaper, it just came to mind."

Already his thoughts were running elsewhere, to something small, the most minor of details. When he'd mentally entered Moréas's office just a minute earlier as he tried to tell his brother about the note and instead wandered ever further from

the point, unable to spit out those momentous words, had he
noticed something on the floor, something shiny on Moréas's
parquet? Made nervous by the note, it had escaped him at first,
he had walked right by as with steely steps he approached his literary condemnation, headed straight for the gallows, pressured
by the need to talk so that he might break free. Now he took
a slight step backward. He turned around, leaving the envelope on the desk. He bent down to get a better look. There was
nothing on the floor. Yet it had been there just a moment ago.
Something small and shiny, perhaps a scrap of rubbish, a slip of
gold foil, useless, a bit of rubbish he noticed out the corner of
his eye, shining in a peculiar way, tremulous but discrete—no,
it couldn't be rubbish, it was probably some charred piece of
paper, words snuffed out before he had a chance to read them.
Or perhaps it wasn't something he'd seen but rather something
he'd heard. A name skated past his ear like a white whisper as
he moved toward Moréas's desk. A word. A single word on the
floor. I'm becoming ridiculous, he thought. And yet the word
was there and he needed to bend down and pick it up. He tried
to concentrate, turning his back slightly so as to isolate himself
from his brother. A little nothing. It's nothing, he told himself.
A little nothing, already snuffed out, erased. Yet he didn't give in
to despair. He struggled to concentrate harder, and in fact there
was a word, which had been lost because he couldn't remember
it or perhaps had overlooked it, or not heard it well, and yet
he would have recognized it from among thousands of words,
a solitary word that had something to do with Nero's Domus
Aurea. How those rooms had been buried beneath the earth. The
statues, the damask curtains that swayed as night fell, the gold

couches where adolescent bodies had tasted pleasure for the first time and older men had felt an ecstasy that verged on death, it had all become debris, piles of rubble, thick dust. The dust of time. Marble columns buried beneath the earth, which ground them down until they, too, became earth, and the mirrors, with diamonds embedded in the artful carvings of their frames. Those fateful mirrors whose reflections hid so much. But why fateful? Mirrors, mirrors ... He was close to the word, he felt he was getting close, though he was still only circling it. He looked in the mirror, which wasn't one mirror but many, and tried to see his way through a series of reflections that returned the same images, only fragmented. Harmonic limbs, thighs whose skin is as pale as alabaster, blond fuzz on a chest, on others hair that is dark and curly. Vigorous buttocks. Gray eyes, the color of the sea after rain, flitting through every shade from ashen to lilac. Full lips. A mouth as red as a cherry, as if it's been bitten. Those bloody lips.

"How can they write that the temperature is falling when we're dying of heat?" John asked.

"Tell me a word that begins with *m*," he replied.

He had been hungry at school. How very hungry he'd been. Around eleven a cold gust of wind would blow through his chest and he could think of nothing else. Sweet rolls, raisins, chocolate. There was nothing to eat. He would have to wait for lunch.

"Myself, misery, myzithra," John said and laughed. "What kind of word are you looking for? A noun? Something that lends itself to metaphor?"

Setback, shortage, starvation, he thought. What if the word began with *s*?

"And why starting with *m*?" John asked.

Hunger, hankering. Hunger means being alive, he thought. How the desire to eat overcomes you, to chew, to swallow, nothing else matters in that moment, the need rises, your stomach cracks, your vision blurs and you know you're alive because of this hunger. Liverpool, listlessness, lynx. Without intending to he had left Domus Aurea and was now in his old school in England, on a winter day or perhaps autumn, drizzle falling, the cold cutting bitterly through his short pants, and it was eleven o'clock, eleven on the dot, when the bell for playtime rang. It was a time when all the children were hungry, and their hunger pushed them to wild acts, to sadistic hazing, as green snot slid from nostrils. Green snot. The word was gone.

The word was gone.

"I've forgotten what I was talking about. And why I wanted

to remember that word. It sounds like a fine plan, about the Ark," he told John.

Hunger, Liverpool, alive. They weren't allowed to stay in the schoolroom during playtime. No matter what the weather, even if sleet fell in gusts from a foul sky, they had to run outside into the school yard. A flight of stairs sprouting weeds led to the servants' quarters and at the top there was another, smaller yard before a wooden door with a padlock, a yard guarded by thick walls, whose narrow, pointed windows protruded like battlements. There no one could see him. The servants' quarters were closed. He climbed the staircase and waited with his back to the wall until playtime was over. He would rather stand there freezing than fall victim to the other children, become the laughingstock of all their games. He shook with cold, his teeth chattering. His hunger was so tyrannical, so absolute, that he barely felt the cold. There was a large brown flowerpot in the yard packed with black dirt from which a bare, crooked branch sprung, and a tin watering can abandoned by the door. How had it happened with that boy ... He must have followed him, or perhaps one day they went up together. That winter, they met at the top of the stairs almost every day. First one would urinate into the watering can, then the other. They didn't speak, he couldn't remember them ever saying anything at all. The urine issued steaming from their childish little specks, aiming for the aluminum base of the can. As one urinated the other watched, greedily taking it in. He had seen his brothers' members but this one seemed whiter, larger, thicker. Slightly flattened at the tip. And it produced so much urine, which sprang from that tiny hole and drew a lovely, bold arc in the air, ending in the watering can. A jet of golden droplets that sprang up triumphantly, their proud trajectory aimed at the gloomy world and then suddenly drying up. Golden droplets in the miserable fog.

Golden rain. Domus Aurea.

"What was the name of that school in Liverpool?" he asked.

He didn't hear the answer. Through the plate glass he caught sight of the young dancer waiting alone at the reception desk. He wondered if it was a good time to approach him. Perhaps he could engage him in conversation. He could ask about the company's performances. He murmured a vague excuse, picked up his hat, and stood.

The central chandelier was lit. Against one wall were two display windows where porcelain figurines stood alongside some transparent boxes containing Lilliputian figures, like insect sarcophagi, which he hadn't noticed before. He stopped to look at them. The young man was standing beside the reception desk, one elbow on the counter. The concierge was occupied, head bent over the large guest book.

He spun on his heel and headed toward the concierge.

"I'd like to make a reservation at Domus Aurea," he began.

The concierge gestured for him to wait.

Idiot, he thought, and at the same moment realized his mistake. Domus Aurea.

"Maison Dorée," he corrected.

He turned to the young man.

"Reservations in Paris can be such a nuisance," he said, and smiled.

The young man didn't seem to realize he was being addressed. Those gray eyes, that same dreamy expression.

I'm smiling like a dragon hiding its teeth, he thought.

"If you don't make a reservation in time," he tried again, "you're liable to go hungry in Paris."

Finally the other understood.

"In Paris?" he asked hesitantly.

He touched his hat with his hand and bowed slightly.

"Constantine Cavafy," he said.

The young man didn't offer his name, only a *bon après-midi*, and then seemed to rethink it and added *bonne soirée* in the same hesitant tone. But he fixed his eyes on him and continued to stare, not examining him, exactly, yet with a kind of insistence. Might he be recalling the moment their eyes had met, when the armchair bumped his ribs?

"I suspect you're a dancer," he began, then stopped.

Mardaras was entering the hotel, accompanied by a tall, haughty woman.

"Excuse me," he said and touched his hat again, thinking how ludicrous the scene was, how ludicrous he himself was. "We'll speak again."

The young man was still observing him with a serious air. He thought he saw the full lips move slightly. The voluptuous lines parted, or rather relaxed into an expression suggesting a smile. And then he noticed an element that had been there all along but to which he hadn't paid attention, of which he now slowly took note as it appeared before him, as if revealing itself only to him, especially for him, an insolence about that mouth, a trace of brazenness in that hint of a smile, which aroused him greatly.

"At your service, Monsieur Cavafy," said the concierge.

He gestured vaguely that he would return and went over to greet the newcomers.

Madame de. Mardaras's introductions were full of trimmings and frills. The entire time she held her long neck, weighed down with jewelry, tilted to one side, and examined him intently. As if he stood before her as the very last specimen of the human species. It was very unpleasant.

He heard laughter at his back, and caught a motion like a comet's tail out the corner of his eye. The valet held the glass door open for two dancers to pass through. The impresario appeared in tails and a shiny top hat. Three more Russians arrived, making a ruckus, perhaps already drunk. They all went outside and waited on the sidewalk for the rest of the group. More laughter. Finely stitched, girlish laughter, and the young man's voice, too, sounding slightly dull or perhaps insincere. The light had faded, night was coming on quickly. The young man was the last to leave. And before he went outside, he turned to look at him.

"John is expecting you. I'll be right back," he said.

He took two aimless steps, then went toward the door. The group of Russians had disappeared down a side street. A dark-skinned man with an accordion stood in front of the building across the way, his back to the wall, gaze fixed on the entrance to the hotel. The movement on the street had thinned. He saw the comte, the comtesse, and the valet with the poodle approaching in formation and stepped aside to let them pass. When he looked again, the man with the accordion had vanished. He needed to go up to his room. At least for a while.

No.

What foolishness.

He must go up to his room.

But who am I fooling? Who am I fooling? This was his last

thought as he hurriedly climbed the staircase with its polished banister and the ochre glow from the plaster candelabra fell across his face as he took the steps two at a time, approaching his floor, running down the hall to his door, which he unlocked with trembling hands, then pushed it closed behind him, panting. That mouth, that mouth, he thought, all his senses reverberating. Something tangible and alive at the tips of his fingers.

It seemed that mouth couldn't get enough of his kisses. And as he feverishly unbuttoned his clothes, he already knew that his desire was far greater than the satisfaction would be, that the satisfaction would betray the desire, that the body of the young man was an abyss that went down and down without end, that his own body was an abyss that went down and down without end, that this immediate relief would only disappoint him.

He saw his pants fall to the floor. He saw the hair on his legs. His shoes.

Those lips. Those lips, he thought.

The smooth body that had only just left childhood behind.

How it gives itself over to caresses, that body.

To kisses.

Kisses, kisses, then nervous sobs. Knots in the chest. The craggy sigh of pleasure. Sobs without tears, sobs that don't necessarily indicate sadness.

He was sitting in the chair with his legs spread. His suspenders were loose. His tongue stuck to the top of his mouth. He was still on fire but felt a shiver pass through him. He had succumbed again, for the second time that day. The bed at his back a battle zone. Sheets, pillows, blanket: the empty companions of his embrace, the very sight of which made him feel nauseous.

And that awful whitish darkness that slipped in through the half-open window.

A chameleon. I'm a chameleon, he thought.

He got up and stood before the mirror.

He turned his head to the right, then the left. He had his mother's cheeks. What if he kissed the way she did, too? Those lips that press into you like cotton, repeatedly. That sound. How could he describe that sound? Not a sucking sound, something else.

He raised his hand, pulled up his sleeve and kissed his arm.

His lips left a neutral, pharmaceutical impression.

He was entirely lucid, that was what saved him. He was able to examine his symptoms.

He tried to see himself through the dancer's eyes. The image of his mother passed before him again, more irritating than ever. Eyebrows, drooping mouth, flabby cheeks. So what if he resembled his mother. The dancer didn't know her, would never meet her. In her youth, they said, she had been a beautiful woman. They said. Of all her children, he bore her the closest resemblance. He inspected himself carefully in the mirror, trying to identify similarities. He looked nothing like her, and this realization offered a temporary relief.

He quickly freshened up, splashed a bit of water on his face. He opened the door and went down the stairs. The reception area was empty. The concierge still stood in the same spot behind the counter, glasses low on his nose. From a distance he saw John framed by their visitors, Madame de with her long neck and Mardaras with his curly locks. A sheep and a giraffe, he thought. Instead of laughing, he felt a sense of despondency wash over him.

"And the poor valet has become a servant *à tout faire*. He even has to play the comtesse's lady's maid. She'll be calling him any minute now to undress her." Mardaras broke into a shrill laugh. That was his reaction to Madame's gossip, that the comte had fallen on hard times, lost everything, a famous courtesan had taken him for all he was worth, plucked each and every feather one by one, estates, vineyards, castles, even a little lake, all in just six months.

"Record time," the Madame stressed, calmly sipping her tea.

"So that's why his face is as long as a grave digger's," John said.

Madame was of Greek descent, or rather of mixed heritage. Whenever she used a Greek word, she gave it a particular emphasis, then seemed surprised at herself for having uttered something so exotic.

The conversation turned to the Grand Prix, at the hippodrome. Had they been this year? Yes? No? The weather was divine, so warm and sunny after a fussy spring full of thunderstorms and mud. That sudden summer weather seemed heaven-sent to reward them, wasn't it so? A recompense to those who loved that noble sport, who would have traveled all the way to the Bois de Boulogne even in a downpour. Everyone was there. So many smart dresses, such wonderful hats, each a work of art in its own right, all those pearl pins, ivory opera glasses, all that caviar and crackers with foie gras.

"Though I wouldn't want to be in the duck's position," Madame commented.

The hippodrome had never seen anything like it. Champagne flowed in the grandstands and carriages, until at last they started emptying bottles into the grass just to enjoy the sight of the foam. And how they had celebrated the winning horse, Doge, hero of the day. An exquisite brown colt. A whip-smart creature. He had hung back so as to conserve his energy, then on the final round he sped up and passed Roxelane, jutting his strong chest forward so as to ensure his medal. The crowd, which had been holding its breath, dissolved into cheers and shouts. There had been many Americans, too. An unforgettable day. According to Mardaras the Longchamp races were the social event of the year. You simply had to be there, and under no circumstances would he himself miss the event, for any reason.

There's that le Tout-Paris again, he thought. He glanced at the reception desk though the plate glass window. Who knew when the young man might return. Where he might be at that precise moment, in what neighborhood he might be wandering, on what street. Who knew whether he would ever see him again.

"You were right about Georges," John said, winking at him.

"Who?"

"The poodle, that was Georges."

Now they were talking about the Promenade. Madame hadn't gone, she couldn't bear those kinds of crowds. She avoided places where too many people were likely to gather, once she even fainted at a reception. It had been very unpleasant for her, and for the hosts, as well. It must have been around the end of the Second Empire because she was still a girl then, had just made her debut in society, and not only were her parents at the reception, but so was her governess, who stood waiting in the vestibule with violet water to freshen her up between dances or pin fresh flowers to her dress. Madame loved that governess like a mother, a real mother, she'd died the year before in a poorhouse in Provence, or perhaps not Provence but a small city in Jura, in the mountains, no, it was Provence, she decided. Whenever Madame spoke, Mardaras responded like an automaton, cackling loudly or shaking his sheep-like head meaningfully, and upon hearing of the governess's death, he began to repeat the word Provence in a heavy tone, adding, "Remarkable, quite remarkable," but she had already moved on to another topic, much more pleasant, about how the juice of the birch tree was an aphrodisiac, and Mardaras was left hanging rather awkwardly.

Most of the time Madame simply ignored Mardaras. To all appearances she was a rather idiosyncratic woman who didn't easily admit defeat. Her age was uncertain, and she wore a creation like a theater box perched atop her head. And that expression as she inspected you, tilting her long neck, a habit she'd likely cultivated on purpose. In other company she might have been amusing, he thought. In company not quite so discordant as their own.

"There are no birches in Egypt," John was saying.

"But you must have beetles, no? The juice of beetles is an aphrodisial, too," Mardaras said.

"Aphrodisiac, not aphrodisial," Madame corrected.

The room was empty and the lighting seemed to have been dimmed, two shades lower. Trays of tea things had been forgotten on the tables. Where the group of dancers had been sitting the chairs still stood in a circle as if continuing the conversation. He felt hungry and dirty. His hands were clammy. He thought he caught a whiff of himself. But it was probably his imagination, all that accumulated exhaustion, so many emotions in a single day. And that flat beginning of the evening, which seemed to level everything that came before. Perhaps he should order a sandwich, it would calm his stomach until the others decided about dinner. He listened as they conversed without coming to any agreement; Mardaras kept trying to second Madame's suggestions but was mistaken each time in his interpretation of what she preferred, meat or oysters, a large restaurant or something more cozy, picturesque, and bohemian, and she kept correcting him, continuing to be entirely ambiguous about her preferences yet precise in that ambiguity—it was a true art, he thought, and then his brief meeting with the young dancer sprang to mind. "I suspect you're a dancer," he had said. How ridiculous. And the way he'd smiled the entire time, his lips frozen into a kind of grimace. An unnatural smile that attempted to perform social ease. The Fat One's smile.

The conversation continued about where to dine. A fine restaurant or a bohemian one? Pigalle or the Left Bank? Somewhere they'd been before, where they could be sure of the quality and service, or a new place where they'd risk disappointment? He paid no attention to what they said. The conversation seemed to fade into the distance, the words floating off one by one. Dirty cups, empty teapots, linen napkins waited stock-still on the tables. The lighting in the room had grown even dimmer. Outside it must now be truly night. He was alone at the edge of the world. At his desk in Alexandria bent over his papers.

Muffled sounds wafted through the window from outside. The last carriages lingered in the Quartier Grec as guests descended the stairs of a mansion and bid their hosts goodnight, laughing. The footsteps grew silent. Solitary figures in the velvet light. Farther off the neighborhood of Attarin was emerging from its lethargy. Again the cheap music, the drawn-out complaint. An elegy. A voice that bled at the refrain. Raki glasses clinked. One customer cursed, another muttered to himself. Behind smoky glass a young apprentice, deeply submerged in the sink, washed the remains of meals off the dishes. A few men were playing cards on the ground floor, they'd been playing since the night before, their eyes heavy and expressionless, though at times they gleamed strangely at good luck or bad, then grew dark again. Someone ran up the stairs, ascending quickly to escape detection. He pushed open the door. Before him, the unmade bed. Still untidy from those who had come before. The clefts in the sheets. The lingering, nauseating scent of a man's cheap cologne. Yet even that revulsion has an edge of sweetness, a foretaste of the pleasure to come. He needed to stay there, transfixed, needed to persevere. Bent over his desk in the lamplight, over those same writings he had corrected time and time again, he was alone at the edge of the world. If he raised his head in an imaginary line his gaze would fall on the spot where the Lighthouse of Alexandria once stood. Six hundred years before, it had still been there. Ptolemy I Soter, who ordered it built at the height of his glory, never lived to see it completed. The seventh wonder of the world. Shattered, destroyed, buried in the depths. Lost, just like the shipwrecked vessels, beside corals that slowly grew over the course of centuries, and corpses consumed by the waves, which continued their journey indifferently. A refreshing breeze blew off the sea. Every so often he felt that gentle breeze slip into the room. Like a caress come to fool this boring night at his desk. At this hour his mother would have gone to bed. He hoped she had fallen asleep and wouldn't call for him again and interrupt his work. He looked down at the mass of manuscripts. "The Horses of Achilles," one of the poems he'd sent to Moréas. He set it aside. "Again in the Same City" required more thought, it still needed something, a spark to light it up. He put it, too, aside. "The Funeral of Sarpedon" still plagued him, still wasn't finished. How spare his handwriting was. As if each letter, each alpha and delta wanted to announce its presence to an uncertain world. The obstinacy of his handwriting was disheartening. He looked at the scattered papers, the jotted alternates, the smudges and crossings-out. He could tear everything up, destroy it. Then the weight would lift. Or, even better, he could burn it all. That would make quite a scene. He could see flames licking the manuscripts, then imagined the very next moment, how he would plunge his hand in the ashes to save some line, the beginning of some stanza. He had to persist. Alone. Famished. Feeling an insatiable hunger. Those two poems, "The Funeral of Sarpedon" and "The Horses of Achilles," were related in some way. Strange that he hadn't noticed before, this barely perceptible commonality that went beyond *The Iliad*, their shared source. It was also their placement in time. That retrospective chronological perspective. Both deaths were described in Book 16, and both took place on the same day. First Patroclus kills Sarpedon. In his poem, "The Funeral of Sarpedon," that killing had already taken place, and a weakened Zeus—unable to prevent the death of his child, and now trying to keep his corpse from being dis-honored—ordered Apollo to attend to the remains, to bathe the body in myrrh. Later that same day, Hector will kill Patroclus. In "The Horses of Achilles," he already has. Both killings, or rather each one separately is already a thing of the past when we read the respective poems. In some sense, each of these two poems unfolds in the wake of the main event: the curtain is pulled back and the scene revealed after the dramatic event has already taken place—and this sideways lighting shifts our sense of the drama. The tragedy is what follows, not the event itself. Not the disaster in and of itself. But there was something else that connected the poems, too. Perhaps a philosophical stance? Something about human fate. Does a man become what he himself chooses? Is he free to choose?

"I believe I'd prefer to go home," Madame said.

"Oh, please don't go, don't abandon us," he heard John say.

A fitting response. The idea of being left alone with Mardaras was unbearable.

"In that case, let's go to Place Pigalle," Madame decided.

As they headed out the door she changed her mind. They would go to Le Procope. Le Procope, again? No matter. Thoughts thronged inside him and so he didn't object, not wanting to interrupt the flow. The two poems still needed work, that was certain. What troubled him was the form. One of the two was more advanced, more mature. "The Horses of Achilles." Though something still bothered him about the rhyme in the very first lines:

When they saw Patroclus dead,
once so strong, noble, and young,

> *the horses of Achilles flung*
> *their lovely manes and cried in dread;*

Dead, dread, young, flung. It didn't sound bad, on the contrary
it had a nice ring, and that was what worried him. It was too
easy, a gentle gliding that might tarnish the lines that followed.
He needed to reexamine that rhyme. And to rethink the placement in time. How the action began before the poem itself,
and how the shared perspective of the two poems evoked some
eye external to both, which pulled them into its field of vision,
whose limits they couldn't exceed. Yet constraint wasn't necessarily negative. On the contrary, it provided a backbone for lines
that might otherwise seem disjointed. For now, though, he was
concerned with something else: Was human fate, the human
condition, at the core of both poems?

Once they were in the carriage, John leaned toward him:

"Earlier today I got confused. I thought tomorrow was Pavlos's name day and that we'd forgotten to write."

"We'll be home by then."

"My best wishes, in advance," Mardaras interjected, having
overheard. He started to explain to Madame what a name day
was, that in Greece it was more important than a birthday, and so
on and so forth, facts of which she was apparently already aware,
since she cut him off and turned to ask something of John.

John said that it used to be a major celebration in their
house. Visitors came and went all day long. After all, it wasn't
only Pavlos's name day, but their father's, as well, and that of the
family's second son, Petros—both of whom were now dead.

"My condolences," said Mardaras.

From best wishes to condolences in an instant. Was that how poetry worked, too? Was a poem supposed to be a condensation of the circle of life? To reflect that circle? Seen each time from a different perspective, illuminating another shard of a shattered mirror. Did a poem have to express *that* to be successful?

In the end they had come to a different neighborhood altogether, somewhere near Place de Clichy, on a side street with low houses and sagging, moss-covered roofs.

A cow's head hung outside the entrance to the restaurant. Mardaras went in first to make sure a table was ready for them. He came back out displeased. The establishment was not suitable for ladies.

"I assure you, I am in no need of a chaperone," Madame said and stepped forward to enter, then turned around again, saying she knew of a much better place, rather odd, almost repellant, and not exactly a restaurant.

Up to that point Mardaras had displayed only his worldly, elegant side. Just then he seemed suddenly to remember his other identity, as *homme de lettres*, bohemian, or perfect *puriste*, depending on circumstances, and he tried to recover that side of his persona with a toss of his sheep-like head, exclaiming:

"Delightful! We'll follow you anywhere you like, to wherever this fascinating place may be hiding." He made an ostentatious gesture intended to embrace the entire district before continuing: "I'd be so pleased if you were to reveal a secret I don't know, some hidden corner. In my ten years living in Paris I've explored the most out-of-the-way places, even dubious settings of uncertain morals, and I dare to boast, if you'll allow me, that I know the city better than even born-and-bred Parisians."

No one listened to the rest of his speech. Madame gave her arm to John and they led the way. He followed behind with Mardaras.

The neighborhood was lively despite the late hour. Carriages stopped and smartly dressed couples emerged, perhaps illicit couples, since without pausing for an instant they hurried toward the lighted marquee of some cabaret or restaurant and slipped inside. Farther down, as they passed a *café-concert*, he caught sight of the continuation of one such scene. A couple had just entered the establishment and the shiny black door closed behind them. On the other side of windows framed with little red curtains and lit by the fluted glow of gas lamps, their figures appeared to hesitate, otherworldly, theatrical. They hadn't yet taken their seats. One of the waiters was preparing their table. They stood to one side, an ordinary looking couple, man and woman, yet something set them apart from the other customers. An erotic invitation, perhaps, some secret pulse? He noticed the woman's bare shoulders as the maître d' took her light coat, the man leaning slightly toward her, a sense of expectation saturating his body, as if something trapped inside of him was finally about to be set free. He saw the two silhouettes approach each other in the suggestive lighting—yet it occurred to him that perhaps they appeared to come closer only because he had witnessed the scene as he passed by, walking past the café on the sidewalk outside. They had clearly come closer, but without moving at all. The other tables around them were all occupied, the atmosphere thick with smoke, someone gestured to the waiter, an imposing woman was applying lipstick, the man beside her had fallen unconscious in his soup, the orchestra played with gusto, a massive singer shook her plump, gloved arms, pigs' heads appeared from beneath silver lids, the ambience in the café must have been noisy, chaotic, irksome. And yet the young woman heard nothing, noticed nothing, saw nothing but the man leaning toward her, he, too, held hostage in the same sphere of influence. Nothing could stop that attraction, the convergence of two bodies that hadn't actually converged. He tried to return to his poem, to the thoughts that had been preoccupying him most recently. He had come to a kind of conclusion a short while ago. Not a conclusion, exactly, but an aesthetic model of sorts, a concept that might relate to poetry more generally and which, were it to be applied with talent, might be the key to a poem's success. The circle of life. Life, death, the in-between. Each poem should present that circle in miniature. An attempt to condense. Could the rule hold true? It would be very appealing, an unexpected solution. A life in miniature. Something alive. A leaf, a tree, he thought. He looked up at the dense foliage in the small park he and his companions were crossing just then, the swaying branches that glistened with a slight silver tinge in the weak lamplight. It seemed so simple. The progression from the tender shoot trembling as it emerges to the sturdy trunk that falls with a single hollow thud, that crumbles and rots and turns to ash and slime in the bowels of the earth, until a tiny new shoot emerges once more from within … Life, death, the in-between. The perfect model for a poem.

Though of course other poems concerned themselves with only a single detail, he thought. They grabbed hold of a thread, a scrap from the weft of life, something so small as barely to register in the grand turmoil of passions and events. They grabbed hold of it and stripped it to the bone. Sometimes compositions that began with something so slight could end up becoming masterpieces. He was drawn to poems of that sort, poems that took an image, an episode, anything at all and dug down into it. Baudelaire's "The Albatross" was one such poem. It was a perfectly balanced composition, one he often brought to mind as an example of a gradual unfolding, a continual accumulation of poetic intensity from one stanza to the next, which you experienced as something almost tactile as you read. The poem's technique was impeccable. It was neither empty nor burdened with excess meaning. It was like a sonnet, only not a sonnet, but four stanzas of four lines each.

> *Often, to kill their empty time, sailors*
> *play with albatrosses they shrewdly catch,*

That was how it began, jolting the reader with a taste of things to come.

> *enormous birds that fly above the sea,*
> *idle companions, following the voyage.*

Again the lines drew you in, made you want to read on. The birds were still flying freely but you already knew, from the second line, that they would be taken captive. What came next? How did the second stanza go? He couldn't remember. And the third? That, too, he couldn't recall. He knew the fourth by heart, but had lost the intervening two. What had stayed with him was the sense of a bitter irony, and the sailors' scorn for those migratory birds. Far from the sky, netted on the deck of the boat, mocked by the sailors, who tickled their beaks and jeered at how they limped when they tried to walk, unable to spread their wings for balance. How craven and dejected they seemed, almost indifferent, these kings of the sky with their huge wings, not resisting but simply enduring this humiliation. That was what Baudelaire had written in his first three stanzas. Then suddenly, in the last, he likened those birds to the figure of the poet. That was the key to the entire poem. Like the albatross, the poet ignores what's happening around him, lives a life of exile on earth, dragging his weighty wings, which keep him from walking as others do. It was an exquisite poem. To be sure. And it focused on just a single detail from the circle of life: the poet's position in contemporary society. A small thing. Utterly insignificant if viewed in the context of the circle as a whole—if you compared it to the vast model of genesis and decay.

> Just like those princes of the air, the poet
> cares not for arrows nor for thundering skies;
> an exile on society's scornful earth
> whose giant wings impede his every lurch.

And yet. He wasn't sure. Was it only a detail? An insignificant scrap from the weft of the circle of life? Or perhaps in "The Albatross" there was that same expansion of meaning, when you reflected on the poem after reading it? What it made you consider far surpassed the words of its handful of lines; the poem's meaning exceeded its literal bounds. That was what made it so effective. And didn't Baudelaire's marvelous metaphor, his likening of the poet to an albatross, how both lumbered awkwardly on earth dragging their giant wings, also encompass the human condition without pointing explicitly to it? The albatross had a deeper meaning, Baudelaire hadn't chosen it only to shed light on the poet's condition. There was a duality there, a tension in human nature. Wasn't everyone, not just the poet, condemned to live here on the ground, yearn as they might for something higher? Didn't everyone long for the infinite and seek refuge in religion, comfort in alcohol, or gambling, or a lover's embrace? Humans were mortal yet longed for immortality, and at times, waving their enormous wings, they could fool themselves. Though only briefly. The feeling never lasted long. The desire proved vain, the wings useless, a merciless, daily reminder of all that remained beyond reach. Their very existence, the fact that he was equipped with wings, mocked a man's fate. Cruel wings. Wasn't that what a human being was? Life, an extended attempt to banish death—and at times, amid the bustle and confusion of the day, you might manage to forget. But the terror always returned. And so you would throw yourself once again into that unequal struggle, that awful attempt to distance the object of terror, Tolstoy's terrible thing, and through all the numbered years of your life, from childhood to old age, you advanced like an earthbound albatross dragging your enormous wings over the ground, lurching and stumbling. He needed to give it more thought. The circle of life. Awkward, feeble steps.

He walked beside Mardaras, a strangely silent Mardaras. Madame and John were just ahead, arm in arm, and from their lazy gait you could tell they were chatting pleasantly, enjoying each other's company, Madame's full skirts sweeping the sidewalk, John's cane tracing brushstrokes in the air. It was a mild summer night. The stifling atmosphere, the heavy heat that had been so oppressive throughout the seemingly endless day had finally broken with nightfall and a light breeze now blew in invisible gusts, the leaves on the tall chestnut trees rustled faintly as he raised his eyes trying to distinguish some sign in their dark mass, some omen to guide his thoughts. His own poems were not like "The Albatross." Not nearly as good. It wasn't only a matter of craft, he knew. They were rudimentary attempts, downright juvenile beside Baudelaire's. He wasn't capable of achieving that gradual condensation of a poem's dramatic essence. He wasn't yet capable. How dearly he would like to clear his mind of such thoughts, to stop thinking altogether. To abandon himself to this walk, observe the movement in the streets, experience this moment. Carefree, without the worry that gnawed at him. He watched people blithely coming and going on the sidewalk and felt a stab of envy. As passersby approached him, their faces opened in unhurried smiles. There was a light in their eyes, an impatience to see how the evening would unfold. Laughter echoed on street corners. Groups of friends crossed paths in the dim light of streetlamps and made arrangements to meet again later on. Perhaps the young dancer was also enjoying the coolness of the hour. Who would want to return to his hotel on such a pleasant night? And the Russian dancers were probably night owls. Perhaps the young man was out meandering through the streets of Paris with the others, or perhaps he was alone, had stopped at a café for an ice cream or one last drink. Who knew, he might be wandering that very same neighborhood. Perhaps their footsteps were even now bringing them closer. What a lovely night. Poetry could wait.

A t Le Rat Mort two young men rose from their table to greet Madame with overwrought compliments. "The Duke de Losange and his cousin Edmond," Mardaras whispered behind their backs.

"And why the dead rat?" John asked.

"When they first opened the café, everyone said it smelled like carrion inside. As for Edmond, he's an illegitimate son, all of Paris knows, but he keeps challenging people to duels to clear himself of the stigma."

"You have no idea what you're talking about," Madame cut him off. She nodded slightly to the two young men, who were heading back to their table, then turned to John and began to speak of the Commune, those terrible seventy days when Montmartre had been a battle zone. "They set up barricades right here in Place Pigalle, Le Rat Mort was a watering hole for leaders of the sans-culottes, blacksmiths, bootblacks, mule drivers and tinkers, laundresses and milkmaids who had taken up arms, and now here we are as if none of it ever happened, because history has no logic, my dear John, history is written to be erased. A certain tailor who had his shop in my neighborhood," she continued, "a little hunchback with thick glasses who was always bent over his needle, used the Commune as an opportunity to put himself forward, people like him took on airs during those days," for instance her aunt, Baroness von Schröder, had a servant, not even a chambermaid, a girl who wasn't even allowed in the kitchens, and she'd been made captain and guarded the archbishop of Paris, she'd been the one to lead him to the execution squad at La Roquette prison, since they'd abolished the guillotine during the Commune. "Do you think their objections were aesthetic?" she tossed out, and laughed once with a laugh that wasn't a laugh because her expression remained the same. "Perhaps the guillotine wasn't sophisticated enough for the sans-culottes?" she added without a trace of irony, in the same neutral tone. Then, catching sight of a round table in the center of the café laid with a crisp tablecloth and lorded over by a hefty pheasant on a platter with yellow claws and shriveled skin, she craned her neck slightly, declaring dispassionately: "That's history, my dear John. A dead carcass. Du Rat Mort."

A remarkable woman. Capable of making the most extravagant pronouncements in an entirely neutral tone. He didn't particularly like her, but was drawn to something about her, these odd opinions and the strength of her convictions. He glanced at the two young men who had stood to greet her with all those bows and curtseys. Strange that Madame hadn't introduced them. One might have thought it rather rude if she hadn't been so idiosyncratic. One of them, probably Edmond, limped slightly as they returned to their table, he must have some infirmity. He had excellent posture and a handsome face, if rather cold, a coldness that detracted somewhat from his beauty. Beside him, the duke, his cousin, seemed to have been born an old man, already bald, a shrimp of a man with wispy black sideburns. There were three women at their table, all blonde, very thin. Young, with gaudy hats that shaded their weary faces. They were models, Mardaras explained, following his gaze. There was a models' bazaar each Monday morning at Le Rat Mort and outside by the fountain in the square, painters would come by to select their models, some were highly sought after but they all faded quickly, by eighteen they were spent, eaten away by absinthe—Edmond preferred them that way, in decline, the more bedraggled the better, strange tastes which Mardaras didn't share or understand, perhaps it was because Edmond was illegitimate, who knew what a psychiatrist might have to say about his case, at any rate he was illegitimate; to be sure, Mardaras said and suddenly fell silent, worried that Madame might overhear.

The maître d' and two waiters had been standing at attention before them this entire time, waiting to see whether they should prepare a table. Every so often the maître d' mechanically reached up to smooth his thick mustache, and while it was likely a gesture of impatience, Madame paid no attention, continuing her conversation with John, and since no one seemed prepared to take the initiative, they all remained standing before the large pheasant, which looked embalmed, its hooked claws at the ready, its glassy eyes about to burst from their sockets.

"Doesn't that pheasant resemble General Le Brun in his tomb? Bug-eyed fools, the both of them, even in death," Madame said and returned to her reminiscences of the Commune, when her neighborhood tailor had become a general of sorts, and a particularly bloodthirsty one at that, she wondered if he wore his thimble when he pulled the trigger, at least that, in her opinion, would have shown a bit of originality, and as she spoke she scanned the room with her eyes, the diners at the other tables, the stained glass windows that refracted the light, the posters of rats on the walls, rats living the good life, stretched

out on sofas, yet she didn't so much as glance at the maître d'
or the two waiters who stood waiting there like columns. She
was obviously undecided as to whether she should commit to
an evening here and therefore give the signal that they would
stay, or whether they should leave, an indecision that lengthened
even further her narrative about the little tailor, who had been
part of the mob that had rushed to set fire to the Tuileries and
the Imperial Library, established facts that she remembered with
great vividness even though she had been only a girl back then.

She'd always been only a girl, he thought. All the events the
Madame had spoken of, at least those accompanied by personal
memories, had taken place twenty or thirty years earlier. What
had become of her life in the interim? he wondered, watching her turn and head for the door trailing Mardaras, who had
remembered that Le Rat Mort was also where Rimbaud stabbed
Verlaine. The poet Charles Cros had been there, too. Show me
your hands, Rimbaud said, we're going to do an experiment, and
he pulled out a knife and cut Verlaine's hand deeply, but Cros
managed to jerk his away in time.

"And then Verlaine went to his little wife that night to bind
the wound," Madame said dryly, gesturing for John to follow her.

"Had Rimbaud already written 'The Drunken Boat' at that
point? I believe so, but I'm not certain," Mardaras said, struggling to keep control of the conversation.

"His defense of the Commune," Madame chortled.

What an era, what passions, he thought. How a life like that
could burn a man to ash in just a few years. He ended up useless, but not before he'd written his masterpieces. He himself was
incapable of such explosions. His passion was internal, subdued,

though no less tyrannical. Perhaps even more tyrannical precisely because it never erupted in that way. The question, he thought, is who can produce better poetry? The one with the quiet life, bent timidly over his desk, his mind fired by desires and the most wild imaginings, fantasies he knows will never become reality, or the other, who rushes at life with gusto, who taunts life like a foolhardy warrior, daring it, betting his very existence in a game of heads or tails? Which of these two will become a better poet? he wondered, realizing as he did that this "other" was Rimbaud and that he had placed himself and his handful of mediocre drafts on par with him, that he had dared even to conceive such a comparison. The one or the other, me or him? he thought again. It was such an unlikely, implausible question that it made him feel a kind of melancholic amusement.

"And what was it all, in the end? A historical farce. That's all the Commune was. The maidservant became a captain and then went back to being a maidservant," Madame was saying to John.

His fatigue had passed the bounds of physical exhaustion. Every so often he felt his knees trembling. He lit a cigarette, then fumbled for another, even as he held the first burning in his hand. Confused, he tossed them both. But when they stepped outside into the sweet night air with its gentle breeze, the tall trees and shapes of people passing by in the mild dusk, he felt better and again wondered whether the dancer might be wandering somewhere close by. Immediately afterward came the image of himself in his hotel room a few hours earlier, the unbuttoned shirt, his scrawny, hairy calves jutting out of his lowered pants, and behind him the bed, the sheets, the pillows, a scene of degradation.

Who cares, he thought. Who cares. Those eyes, those lips. The hint of insolence in that suggestion of a smile. He wished he were alone, so he could lean on the trunk of a tree, sit down on a bench in some dark corner and think about the young man at his leisure.

"There's Nouvelle Athènes, perhaps we should dine there?" John said.

The lights of the café across the street trembled with bluish sparks.

"My dear friends, follow me and you won't be disappointed," Madame said.

"Did you know Émile Zola lives near here?" Mardaras began. No one paid him any attention. In other circumstances John would have been impressed, but he'd been taken entirely under Madame's wing, as she stood in the center of the square and talked about the fountain in Place Pigalle, how it once flowed with well water and then became a dump, a truly formidable rubbish heap, with fish heads, worn-out shoes, the torn stockings of courtesans, quite a unique collection, until at some point they planted flower beds and surrounded it all with an iron fence.

"It's a pity, because you would have gotten a glimpse of the true Montmartre," she said, leaning toward John almost conspiratorially to explain her theory that rubbish revealed a neighborhood's true face; rubbish dumps were silent witnesses, entirely irrefutable, since the rubbish in Montmartre was different from that on the Grands Boulevards or in the sixth arrondissement, and before historians dared to dip their pens in ink, they should try sticking their noses in a pile of rubbish instead of running off to libraries and lectures.

This speech wasn't devoid of originality and had some basis in truth, he had to admit—and perhaps at some other moment, if he hadn't felt so exhausted and empty, he would have wanted to delve further into the topic. Now the lecture ended with Madame's inimitable *ha*, the laugh that wasn't a laugh. She offered John her arm and the two advanced toward the street, stopping only once, just for a moment, undecided. Then they set off again and continued at the same slow pace, making the rounds of the square.

He was hungry. His stomach felt as if it were splitting in two. The uncertainty of their destination was getting on his nerves. He counted one, two, three benches waiting empty in the dim light, their thick wooden slats forming wavy ridges, then five lampposts in a row, one where two lamps hung from the same post, both suspended from spirals of tiny tendrilling vines.

Mardaras walked beside him, spewing names.

Names. Names.

Who frequented Nouvelle Athènes and who Café Guerbois—but only on Sundays and Thursdays, he wanted to be entirely clear on that point. Who went to the Chat Noir. Who got drunk at Abbaye de Thélème, which they were passing just then and which was a restaurant, not an abbey, a unique place worth a special visit, particularly if you were new in town. The decor on all three floors was inspired by Rabelais's *Gargantua and Pantagruel*, the waiters dressed in monks' robes, and the restaurant embodied a kind of utopia, one might even call it a transubstantiation of utopia, though it left Mardaras himself entirely indifferent.

"When you've lived in Paris for a decade, you're not easily impressed," he said.

He kept hoping for a break in this constant stream of words, but every door, every façade, every stone in the road was a source of inspiration for Mardaras, who peppered his speech with little enthusiastic cries, hoping to garner Madame's attention. She, meanwhile, had tightened her wing, or her noose, around John, and spoke only to him. That leaves me as his quarry, he thought. He saw a large stained glass window depicting underwater scenes on the façade of a building hemmed in by a finely wrought fence and stopped, furrowing his brow, pretending to study it. But Mardaras, undaunted, launched once more into his monologue, explaining how he considered himself an initiate, that was the perfect word for it, he had been initiated into Paris, he had reached the highest stage of initiation into this city and knew everything, which spots the modernists frequented and which their enemies, where the impressionists exhibited their work, and so on and so forth.

As he listened with half an ear, the image of his workplace in Alexandria came to mind, the entrance to the Third Circle of Irrigation, the stairs he climbed every morning and would probably continue to climb for the rest of his life. He saw his feet on the stairs, his black shoes which, though freshly shined, were already dusty again, and then his face, rather anxious and slightly sweaty, since he was always running late in the mornings. His agitation at the idea of encountering his English supervisor on the way to his office. And his great relief when he slipped inside without meeting anyone at all.

"Tell me, how would you describe Montmartre, as an artists'

base, or as a haven, a retreat?" he made the mistake of asking. "Is it a springboard for those seeking fame and glory, or rather a place where people take refuge because they feel protected and unharrassed?" he added, believing that these two options might inspire some contemplation on the part of his interlocutor, and therefore a few minutes of silence. Right away the expectation proved false, as the other's torrent of words swelled, interspersed with new details about the peculiar behaviors of certain artists, their arguments and their passions, until finally he began again to stray in all directions at once, mentioning roads, addresses, particular episodes, where Camille Pissarro's studio was, where Paul Cézanne kept his mistress Hortense without his family finding out, who'd argued with whom and who owed whom money. Mardaras had met Pissarro once, he looked like Abraham with his long white beard, cut a very imposing figure. He'd met Cézanne, too, but Cézanne was a lunatic, dangerous; once in Café Guerbois he refused to shake Édouard Manet's hand, saying he hadn't washed his own in eight days, though everyone knew Cézanne copied Manet's work, admired him and hated him, too, and had painted his *Moderne Olympia* specifically hoping to surpass Manet's *Olympia*. Cézanne had gone mad, that much was clear, ever since he'd recognized himself in Émile Zola's novel *L'oeuvre*: the painter who commits suicide in front of the piece he's unable to finish was clearly based on him. Then again Zola was just as bad, in the last few months he'd lost all sense of reality, too, over the Dreyfus Affair ...

"Just a minute," he said.

His ears were ringing.

He took a few steps forward.

"I think I'll go back to the hotel," he said.

Madame and John turned toward him.

"I have to go back," he repeated.

Then Madame said something about a child who lived with pigeons, it seemed to be a continuation of her conversation with John, and he walked with them for a moment, intent on hailing the first free carriage that passed. The child had disappeared, that's what was worrying Madame. He was the son of a doorman or perhaps a seamstress and he had a way with pigeons, a very particular talent. Though it wasn't exactly a talent. More like a gift. With the smallest movements, or perhaps no movement at all, he could make birds follow him. The way the mice followed the piper in the story by the Brothers Grimm. The child trained them in a courtyard, he must have been given special permission. He lived with them, spoke to them. Though it wasn't speaking, exactly. Anyhow, each Thursday, at Madame de Filion's *séances de spiritisme* at her mansion, the pigeons would fly up to the second floor and wait on the balcony of the summer salon, settled among the azaleas, the hibiscus, the scheffleras. No one had called them, they just sat there in pairs, always peacefully, forming a tableau in which the purple and pink azaleas with their tight little buds were interspersed with pigeons, then bright green, wide-leaved scheffleras, then more pigeons, then yellow hibiscus, and again pigeons. These last were probably the oldest, the wise men of the brotherhood, and the birds did in fact operate as a brotherhood. Finally, at the very edge of the balcony, came the azaleas that were already in bloom, trumpet-shaped blossoms spread wide. When the séance was over, the pigeons departed without a sound.

Though they had never discussed it outright, they all felt that the amazing success of Madame de Filion's spiritualist meetings owed itself to that calm, inexplicable presence. Each Thursday the spirits simply appeared, they didn't make trouble or shy away as usual. They answered questions precisely, not resorting to riddles, as if a channel of direct communication had opened with the other world, a corridor through which the dead and the living could communicate unimpeded, or, more precisely, the living could obtain all the information they wanted. Thus it was that they found out about General Legrie's mistress and acted right away before she could get her clutches on his château in the Loire. Thus they learned, too, about the sapphires and gold coins that had belonged to a distant ancestor of Madame's close friend, which were hidden in a chest with some other articles of fine jewelry, buried in ash in a bricked-over alcove in the wall of the laundry at her crumbling manor house. The ancestor appeared at the séance and described in great detail the location where the chest was hidden. Of course they hadn't noticed the pigeons right away, since the curtains were always closed. One evening when the humidity from the Seine was stifling, when it clung to your skin, the Marquesse de Saint-Michel began to faint and they opened the middle balcony door to let in some air. Then they saw the pigeons. Motionless among the flowering plants, as if hypnotized. In a tableau of perfect harmony that took your breath away. Often before a séance began someone would walk over and peek between the curtains. Queitly, without comment. Of course Madame de Filion had tried several times to tip the child but he always refused. Even though he was as poor as can be. Now the child had disappeared, and the pigeons with him. The séances since then had been utter failures. Nothing but ridiculous antics, a Karagiozis puppet show, to put it in Greek terms. It was dreadfully absurd. Unthinkably absurd. Unthinkable.

"What's wrong?" John asked him.

"Your friend has worn me out ... But wait. The boy with the pigeons. Remember yesterday, by Galeries Lafayette?"

John didn't remember.

"There was a boy beside a cage of pigeons. He had bruises and a wound on his neck that looked to be from a knife. He was sitting on the ground. Beside the stall where we stopped so you could get that gift for Rozina."

The uncomfortable look on John's face seemed to spur him to continue.

"You bought Rozina a red kerchief, don't you remember?" he said again.

"Stop a moment, stop, this is where Victor Hugo lived," Mardaras called. "On his return from exile. At number forty-eight Avenue Frochot, and do you know who lived at number fifty, just next door? I'm sure our Alexandrian friends couldn't even guess. It was Madame Sabatier, Baudelaire's Apollonie! Just imagine him sitting at Nouvelle Athènes, it makes me shiver just to think of it—sitting there at a corner table, writing her those exquisite poems. Baudelaire, a young man at that point, with manicured nails and green hair."

"His hair had turned green from the absinthe," Madame explained.

The road snaked, climbing almost imperceptibly between elegant villas smothered in greenery and manor houses of various architectural styles. Avenue Frochot. Really too narrow to be called an avenue.

"*Je t'aime, ô ma très belle, ô ma charmante …*" Mardaras recited.

"A red kerchief, have you forgotten?" he insisted, looking at his brother.

John pretended not to have heard.

"*Que de fois … Tes débauches sans soif et tes aurores sans âme. Ton goût de l'infini …*"

"Will you be quiet, at last?" Madame said.

John's face was pale, drained of blood. He turned to the others and said, "Constantine has worked on Baudelaire."

That was unnecessary.

"He's translated his poetry."

It served me right, he would think later that night when recalling the evening's events. He put me in my place quite nicely. It hadn't been John's intent, but the result was the same.

Mardaras murmured, "Which poem, which poem?"

"'*Correspondances.*'"

"Splendid."

"Correspondences According to Baudelaire." He saw his own title before him, neatly copied out on a white sheet of paper, carefully and with a sure hand. The little tail on the *l*, the capital *B* slightly crimped. Sparse, insistent letters, pressed firmly onto the paper. As if obstinacy could make up for a lack of talent, he thought. What had he been thinking? What had he been trying to do? To appropriate the original? "*Correspondances.*" A masterpiece. Whereas what he had written was a pastiche, lines translated from Baudelaire sandwiched between lines of his own. It had seemed brilliant at the time. Now it sickened him.

Fortunately Madame was interested only in the pigeons. Ignoring Baudelaire, she brought the conversation back to that earlier topic.

Baudelaire, Rimbaud, Hugo, you demolish me. Your stature crushes me. "Your stature crushes me," he said, raising his voice. No one reacted. He'd only thought the words.

As when you start to tear open the canvas of a large painting and discover another painting behind it, then another and another, until in the end the fibers fray and unravel, he saw himself, the self he thought was his—but what self? Nothing but a tadpole—torn and falling in tatters. The echo of these names rattled in his head. Baudelaire, Rimbaud, Hugo. Rimbaud. Verlaine. Mallarmé. Baudelaire, and again, Baudelaire. The list was unrelenting. Enough, he said loudly. But again he had spoken only internally. He looked bitterly across the table.

The faces he saw all wore the same expression of weary joy. John sat directly across the table and behind his shoulders other, smaller faces swayed, displaying thin, wrinkled smiles. How had they ended up here? Another of Madame's inspirations.

Two rows of tables ran the entire length of the narrow room and a boy with a dirty apron dragged a worn-out broom around heavily, pushing rubbish from one corner to another. The space seemed more like a corridor or a closed passageway alongside train compartments. And from the far end of the place, in erratic waves, came a haze of feathers and wings, whitish bellies and tiny glass eyes—the hum of Madame's mythic pigeons, of which she was still speaking, sitting with a dispassionate expression as her gaze wandered to the blurry mirrors of Le Café Sans Nom.

Racing pigeons and rowing pigeons. Simulated pigeons. Chinese pigeons. Wind-up pigeons. Miniature pigeons. A pigeon exchange. Though the pigeons that attended the spiritualist meetings at the home of Madame de Filion had belonged to another breed. Not another breed, that was imprecise. They had an aura. And as Madame remembered it all, seeing again the image of incredible harmony on the balcony of that summer salon as the pigeons stood motionless among the flowering plants, she almost believed they had expressions, human expressions. A mysterious serenity. No, that was wrong. It wasn't a human quality that they exuded, but something strange, otherworldly. They gave off the grace of a higher power, something almost divine—a claim which in the past Madame would never have accepted and which to be entirely frank was painful for her to admit even now, since she had always considered herself an agnostic. And the strangest thing of all was that each year on October 15, when the séances moved from the summer salon to an almost circular room on the ground floor beside the large dining room, an odd chamber with a vaulted ceiling, painted a red that was somehow both subdued and passionate and seemed more suited to the boudoir of a refined courtesan, out of keeping with the rest of the decor, the pigeons followed them. There was no balcony here. The pigeons took up their positions, again in pairs, on the awning and above the lampposts, while others stood on one leg on the fence outside whose monstrous railings had been designed by a Belgian architect, scalelike with pointed spikes and linked coils depicting a serpent eating its own tail. They stayed there for hours, perched above the void, perfectly balanced. Of course they didn't present the same impression of sophisticated harmony as they had outside the summer salon. There weren't the proper conditions for something of that sort. And yet the birds lined up in formation—each knew its precise position—and even in those adverse circumstances created the tableau of a studied presence that hinted favorably for the spirits. They fulfilled their roles admirably throughout the winter, through those many damp, endless, misty months. *Bref.* These days the *habitués* of the séances had lost heart. The spirits no longer came. And on the rare occasion when one did, it was invariably a lesser spirit, almost entirely insignificant, who merely teased them before vanishing in the dim light with an awful little laugh. The child had disappeared thirty-three days ago.

"Christ's age when he died," Mardaras said.

John leaned toward him.

"That red kerchief," he began.

"For Rozina?"

His brother's hand grazed the lip of his glass, then froze.

"Rozina's gift?" he insisted. "It struck me as odd, how you suddenly got it into your head to buy a gift for the maid."

"It's not what you think."

He hadn't thought anything. The boy with the dirty apron was now sweeping at his feet. He would have liked to kick him. To give him a swift, hard kick on the shin. Of course he did nothing. He just drew in his feet to make room.

"I'll explain when we're back at the hotel," John said.

"Well?" Madame had tilted her long neck toward him. "You mentioned something earlier about a boy who kept pigeons."

Nothing escaped her.

He glanced at the waiter who was setting steaming plates down on their table, and said:

"He was about twelve or thirteen years old, I'd say, and had a cage of pigeons. He was playing with them, heedless of what was happening around him. He wasn't wearing shoes, and was wounded, too. Someone must have attacked him and beaten him badly, it's the only explanation. I don't think it would be too difficult to find him. He was sitting beside the stall of a gypsy woman selling cheap kerchiefs."

Why was he being so cruel? For some reason he had associated the purchase of the tacky gift with John's announcement that morning that he wanted to leave home and live on his own.

"We should go look," Mardaras offered.

"We could pass by again tomorrow morning," John said.

Madame looked thoughtful.

"Why not tonight? I'll interrogate the child myself. I have my ways."

But Madame again ignored Mardaras and changed the topic. She said something about the raspberries which were very late this year, then mentioned a certain Léo Taxil and asked if they knew anything about him.

On the plate before him a fat sausage with shiny red skin floated in a pool of sauce. Lentils with pork fat in the middle of summer.

"I like this sort of humble food," Madame announced. Seeing his expression, she added, "Oh, I ordered for you, too. They say the food of the lower classes is much tastier."

She frowned at the sausage and dug her fork into its spine.

Was it merely his hunger? It did seem delicious. Rich, thick, relieving. But not too rich, with just the right amount of salt. The Fat One's voice echoed weakly in his head: "My dear boys, please be careful what you eat in France, those sauces can cover up so much!" And he drowned out the voice with thick spoonfuls in which swam something indefinable but intriguingly crunchy.

"What's wrong?" cried Mardaras, who'd hurried to clear his plate, loudly praising the humble meal all the while.

Madame's plate was untouched.

She was feeling a bit ambivalent, she told them. She wasn't hungry, or perhaps just the sight of the food had satiated her, or perhaps it was the effect of some news she had received that afternoon. She couldn't be sure. Friends of hers in Greece had informed her that the situation was critical. The economy was balanced on a razor's edge and the state was crumbling. Practically speaking, that shouldn't upset her, her ties to the country were weak to nonexistent, and yet she still felt concern for that forgotten corner of the world. Everything was doomed. There had been one misstep after another. Along general lines she agreed with the opinion that the Greeks were reaping what they'd sowed, yet in her innermost heart she felt a kind of compassion. An inexplicable compassion. From bands of thieves and petty local lords, they'd become a state overnight. To say nothing of the priests with their goat beards and dirty black robes who always insisted on having the last word. And that abysmal prime minister, Diligiannis … Madame had met him in 1867 when he came with a delegation to Paris, and he hadn't made a very good impression.

"Have you heard Georgios Souris's brilliant line about Diligiannis? 'The prime minister art a dreamer and about many things art troubled …' " Mardaras said and began to laugh. He translated it into French for Madame. "But in Greek it's something else altogether. It's Diligiannis in a nutshell."

"I believe Souris composed that line earlier," John said, "about Prime Minister Koumoundouros."

"And yet it suits Diligiannis perfectly. The prime minister art a dreamer and about many things art troubled …"

"I don't know if he's dreaming or troubled, but that war was a debacle," Madame said. "Who is this Souris?" she asked.

"A little mouse of a poet. You see, *souris*, for mouse?" Mardaras broke into loud laughter.

Some of the patrons at nearby tables turned to look at them.

Those drawn-out shrieks. How his laughter turns my stomach, he thought. Like a peacock's cry.

John was laughing, too. His face, slightly flushed, still seemed undecided as to how much hilarity it was allowed to express. Beside him the sheep's head was thrown back, the hands crossed over a chest that shook as those washed-out blue eyes shed slow tears of hilarity. Around them, blurry faces swayed with tired smiles. Small faces, tired joy. Then the door of the café suddenly opened and remained open as if held by some invisible hand. They heard curses. Two young customers appeared in the entrance and the boy with the dirty apron carried a table over the heads of the seated patrons to make room for the newcomers. There was an alcove by the window, dimly lit by a lamp in a little bell that hung from the wall. At times the light grew suddenly stronger, throwing a harsh glare on the torn tablecloth, then quickly died down again. A woman dressed in green, a deep green laced with silver, sitting alone and somewhat cut off from her surroundings, drew his attention. She was well dressed, in clothing that appeared to be expensive, though the ensemble seemed haphazard, as if she had thrown on whatever was close at hand. Her hat was crooked and her silk frills dragged on the ground. Her head was bowed and he sensed a peculiar charge, a brief internal tremor passing through her body. Behind her, other faces appeared like figures cut from paper. Vague, perforated. He would have liked to think about his poem "Again in the Same City." Perhaps he should try to retain this image, jot it down to consider later. It might provide background for the scenes in the street, the kind of hazy, subdued background one finds in a painting, in contrast to the tyrannical intensity of the individual who wanders through the anonymous crowd, always in the same city, incapable of leaving. Or he might use that image in some other poem. But he felt exhausted. Empty. Weighted down by meaningless events. Small faces, tired joy, he thought. He must try to remember it later.

How many hours have I been awake? he wondered. And what was he doing there? He watched the boutonniere in Mardaras's lapel dance as he laughed, then suddenly settle down. The camellia had begun to wilt, its petals limp against the black fabric.

The chortling died out with a gurgle.

"I'm glad your mourning over the defeat in Crete hasn't prevented your enjoying yourself this evening," he said with half a smile.

The other man hadn't heard, and it was necessary for him to repeat himself. Why did he care? Why was he so determined to pick a fight with that fool?

Mardaras sat up in his chair.

"But …" he stuttered, looking at him, then turned uncertainly toward Madame.

"I'm referring to that fiasco you described as a heroic defeat," he insisted, raising his voice, and his desire for confrontation vanished.

"Our Alexandrian friend has trailblazing ideas."

"I would say, on the contrary, that he's a bit too much of a realist."

That was his brother, always eager to smooth any sharp edges.

"*Quelle folie de grandeur,* this involvement in Crete," Madame said.

"On the contrary! The spirit of the Revolution of 1821 is what inspired the intervention in Crete. The dream of an ethnos, a poetic vision. Unlike the strangling of the Greek spirit some at this table seem to support. Quite unlike that. It's a shame Moréas isn't here, he'd explain it all to you."

Moréas, the cherry on the cake.

"*Un drôle de bonhomme,*" Madame said. She saw him often, always in the same spot at the same café in Saint-Germain with his papers spread out on the table. A strategic position, she thought, because from where he sat he could keep an eye on all the comings and goings.

"He seems to have quite a following, particularly among young poets. One might say he directs the fate of cultural life," John began.

"You mean he plays traffic patrolman from his café table?"

"You'd be surprised. Several important movements had their

start with him. Just think, all these new poetic trends might never have found their expression if it weren't for Moréas, who provided the theoretical foundation for their existence."

"Exactly," said Mardaras, grateful for the support.

"You've deified him, my dear." What she saw was a funny little man who sat day and night in the same café, following the goings-on and scribbling in his notebook, with that thick mustache and heavy expression, like a greengrocer keeping track of customers' credit. But perhaps John was right, or perhaps Moréas at least sincerely believed he was controlling the circulation of ideas in Paris from his table. In that case, the prefect should provide him with a policeman's *bâton blanc*, so he could do his job more properly.

Jean Moréas, wielding a white stick.

He put his hands in the pockets of his waistcoat, pulled out a cigarette, and lit it.

A funny little man.

He threw a glance at Madame, sensing he had an ally.

"The heart of poetry beats in the sixth arrondissement," Mardaras was saying.

He didn't listen to what came next. The woman in green by the window seemed to be waiting for something. Again, that sense of an internal vibration moving through her body. The waiter approached with a tray and she appeared to draw back slightly from the table, as if trying to establish some distance, perhaps inhaling deeply to control that inner tremor. Still leaning back, she reached out a hand. On the table sat a jug with a strange spout, a tall glass with a bit of transparent green liquid, and beside it a small white bowl that probably contained sugar.

She brought the glass toward her and bowed her head even lower. She seemed to be purposefully taking her time. What was she waiting for? Then he noticed that she was holding a little spoon in her hand, resting it on the lip of the glass. With her other hand she picked up a sugar cube and set it in the spoon. She stooped even lower. Her movements were exaggeratedly slow, as if she were theatrically performing some ritual. She raised the jug and began to pour water over the sugar drop by drop. The liquid in the glass grew cloudy and changed color, first a rotten yellow, then white. She was sitting at a distance, however, so he couldn't be sure. The woman set the jug down. She scooted toward the table, almost bumped into it—and he saw her fingers cinching the glass like a noose.

"We had lunch at Le Procope yesterday," he heard John say.

"Voltaire used to keep a table there."

"And Verlaine was a regular, as well. It's where he wrote '*L'Art poétique*.'"

"*De la musique avant toute chose …*" John murmured.

Sans rien en lui qui pèse ou qui pose, he thought. It was the final line of the stanza and for many years had been his highest standard for poetic technique. He pushed his seat back and stood up. He walked toward the door of the café, winding his way between the crowded tables. He opened the door, glanced around. Then he turned and looked at the woman. The glass before her was empty. Her arms hung limply. That internal intensity was gone. Her body was propped up only by something accidental, hypothetical, an obstinacy that in better days she believed to be her own personal strength, and if she ever realized it was gone, she would collapse. Her head jutted unnaturally from beneath the brim of her hat as if sprouting from a dead trunk, her long, expressionless face was pasted on like a mask. She seemed to notice him and her mouth opened into a smile, giving him a glimpse of a gruesome shadow. Her front tooth was missing.

I rise I surge I leap, he thought. An image came to him, as when you peer down from the top of a staircase and see someone climbing, and the man climbing was him, headed with steely steps toward his office. In a week. In a week he would be climbing those stairs at the Third Circle of Irrigation. He knew the way by heart, the striped marble of the landings, the wooden banister, the walls, the cracks, which steps were worn in the middle into dips. He once again saw his feet hurriedly climbing the stairs, while at the bottom, three floors down, that mouth waited, frozen in the spasm of a smile, that gruesome shadow in the center.

When he returned to the table Madame appeared to be ready to leave. The name Léo Taxil was mentioned once more. John had heard something that piqued his interest and she admitted that for a while she'd been quite interested in the case. Of course she had her own opinion, she wanted to make that clear from the start, as to why the Taxil case had assumed exaggerated dimensions that it didn't deserve. He was a debonair fellow. A braggart of little learning. But dangerous, as it turned out—after all, a little learning truly was a dangerous thing. In hindsight she'd come to the conclusion that he must have been sorely mistreated by the Jesuits at the boarding school where his parents placed him. As a sworn anticleric, he published a few books that didn't meet with the reception he had expected. Then came his sudden about-face. He repented, publicly converted to Catholicism, repudiated all of his writings, and to top it all off was absolved by the Pope, who had excommunicated Taxil two years earlier for writing a pornographic piece about him. And finally the biggest *coup de scène*: he begins to release his reve-lations about the masons. The Freemasons are agents of Satan, what could be simpler? Taxil names people, exposes members of society. He becomes the bishops' pampered pet. The public hangs on his every word, as an anti-demonic madness sweeps over the whole of France.

I rise I surge I leap, he thought again. Why were those words stuck in his head? The woman in green was still sitting in the same place, the glass before her empty. Every so often the lamp in the little bell behind her abruptly brightened, and her figure assumed an almost granulated look, as if thick grains of sand were breaking loose in the sudden glare.

Madame was of the opinion that the Taxil affair was what finally brought an end to the Second Empire. Not the War of 1870 or the Paris Commune. The Second Empire, or at least its ghost, lingered in everyone's mind, waiting for the appro-priate moment, until the Taxil affair knocked it to the ground like a house of cards. They were all such dupes, she commented in the midst of her narration. Pope Leon gave Taxil an official audience, which made him unstoppable, gave him the clout to proceed with new revelations about the Palladists, a powerful sect devoted to Beelzebub. He published eyewitness accounts of rituals and orgies. He made quite a stir. And then the new *coup de scène* ... The high priestess of the Palladists arrives in Paris. April 19, two months ago. The room at the Société Géographique is packed to the gills with the crème de la crème of Catholic society. Taxil had promised that Diane Vaughan, the high priestess of Satanism, would be there. He appears alone, stands at the podium, and reveals that it was all a hoax.

"They say this Diane Vaughan was a typist from Ohio."

"What difference if she was a typist or shepherdess, seeing as she never existed?"

He enjoyed listening to Madame as he let his mind wander. That dry, dispassionate tone. Her exaggerated insistence on being precise, yet without relinquishing a sort of ambiguity. Perhaps this ambiguity was a matter of elegance, a form of courtesy to her interlocutors. His mind ran elsewhere, to something that had taken place when they still lived on Rue Cherif Pasha. He was hiding in the garden. He must have been crying because his eyes burned. As darkness fell the heavy leaves of the palm tree drooped over him. Whispers echoed, footfalls, wheezing, labored breathing. The sky had closed and the shadows disappeared on the grassy path. What had preceded this scene? He couldn't remember.

Mardaras was laughing again and Madame cut him off with a gesture of her hand. There was still more to tell of this saga, another installment of the *feuilleton*. The Taxil affair had become mixed up with another case, of Édouard Drumont, and the two men exchanged abominable accusations about each other. Drumont had rabidly attacked the Jews in his writing, he was now in Brussels issuing calumnies about Zionist conspiracies. Be that as it may, such incidents were fueled by society's age-old tendency to divide into factions. People's deep need—an antediluvian need, to be sure—to support this position or that. Or, rather, not to support but to oppose. In her opinion, this was the true substance of the Dreyfus Affair, too. But what substance was there, really? None at all. Her friends had split into two camps, half in support of Dreyfus, the other half against. People who had grown up together since the cradle, who belonged to the same circles, who dined at the same restaurants. They had all given in to this primordial urge to split into factions. Was there any logic in it? None at all. The masses thirsted for a spectacle, for violent jousts, even if those masses lived in châteaux and manor houses, knew how to ride and how to distinguish a béchamel from a béarnaise. For instance, when Charcot was still alive and running his clinic at the hospital in Salpêtrière, hadn't they all gone to see those miserable, disheveled women falling in ecstasies of hysteria? Even she had gone. Was it out of scientific interest? "I ask you that," she said, and stopped.

"Le Tout-Paris," slipped spontaneously out of his mouth.

"Precisely, my dear."

It was her world and she loved it. But that didn't mean she was blind to its faults. Which were, of course, her faults as well.

With those words she stood, signaling their departure.

Pigeons, shadowy dancers, passed in front of the window. A strong north wind, musical, accompanied by the echo of the sea. He lay there waiting for his cousin. There must be a storm on the Bosporus. Between the two shores the fishing boats would be buffeted by wild foam. The drone of the wind whipped through the house like a mournful song and he imagined fishermen lunging at the rigging, grabbing ropes, ties, anything, struggling to shimmy up the mast as the soles of their feet slipped, the small craft pitched dangerously to one side, and the hold flooded with water. Please, fishermen, don't cry. Fishermen with your unkempt beards and the salt tang on your strong chests. The windstorm raged in Therapia and an ominous haze covered Yeniköy. Over Hagia Sophia four minarets pierced the mist like skewers. The low ceiling hung over the empty room. He'd covered himself with an old overcoat but the cold was still piercing. His cousin was late. Perhaps he wouldn't come at all. It wouldn't be the first time. The pigeons passed in front of the window.

He must have dozed off with his eyes still open. He remembered Madame rising but now she was sitting again.

His brother kicked him under the table.

They were talking about Byzantium.

"Constantine's opinion is that … Well, tell us yourself," he urged.

His cousin always wore cologne, he remembered. In those

days in Constantinople, that cologne and the care he took with his dress were viewed suspiciously by most people. But he liked it, and admired his cousin greatly. Even though his cousin betrayed him in the end. That didn't change the initial attraction, the magnetism his cousin held for him. Or the fact that, thanks to his cousin's company, those unpleasant years of poverty had acquired a certain spark, an unanticipated color. They hadn't kept in touch. Wretched, dismal years.

Strange how the pigeons continued to pass back and forth, entirely unperturbed, untouched by the violence of the wind. They performed their shadowy routine at the window, the spinning, the backward pirouettes, the sudden falls. Two by two in a harmonic pas de deux and then a sudden vertical drop that took your breath away. And everywhere nature was at a fever pitch of agitation, the moaning wind, snapping branches, swollen waves, fishermen hanging from their masts. Flashes of light tore through the darkness. The house shook to its foundations. Far off, beyond the Sea of Marmara, Hagia Sophia seemed submerged in hoarfrost. A blind man ran to take cover, a shadow like a tiny dot in the marble atrium of the church. Stray dogs howled. A black cloud of dust whipped over the neighborhoods. By now the apprentice would have left the blacksmith's shop. He, too, would be lying with open eyes, listening to the storm. On his back on a straw mattress, uneasy, not understanding what was happening in his adolescent body, what this strange excitement was that made him fling himself about for no reason, then curl into a ball, that made him want to stroke his backside, or the insides of his thighs. The piercing cold and his fear of the next lightning strike mingled within him, stimulating his desire even further. He hadn't told his cousin about the apprentice. As if he wanted to keep him as something apart, somehow. He suspected that his cousin might make fun of him, or worse, would want the boy for himself. The wind howled. He pulled the coat tighter, seeking warmth. This exquisite stillness in the storm. The pigeons, shadowy dancers at the window.

His eyes were open, yet he was asleep.

The ecumenical synod in the year 754.

Iconophiles and iconoclasts.

They were burning the icons. Thick smoke rose from the atrium of Hagia Sophia, blackening the floating dome. A heavy cloud descended over the city. Illuminated manuscripts and holy books in the flames. A pile of cinders beside the fountain inscribed with its palindromic phrase: ΝΙΨΟΝ ΑΝΟΜΗΜΑΤΑ ΜΗ ΜΟΝΑΝ ΟΨΙΝ. Wash the sins, not only the face. How ambiguous Christ Pantocrator's expression looked beside Constantine IX Monomachos. Cautious. Distrustful. And the angry crowds. Humiliations, castigation. The expulsion of the monks, whom they dragged crippled by the necks like donkeys. Eyes put out with burning sticks.

Fire.

Flames.

Greek fire.

Gunpowder flames smoke. At the edge of his field of vision the pigeons continued their maneuvers. More quickly, pausing now and then. Spinning, pirouettes, and falls that he tried to catch in his peripheral vision as the movement dissolved into a haze.

"I didn't say that," he heard Madame object.

"When the emperor pronounced himself patriarch, too."

"That doesn't interest me. Or rather, it's yet another indication of the paranoia of the Byzantine Empire, its fanaticism. What's certain is that its greatest strength was fear."

"It's true that fear creates coherence," John said.

"Be that as it may, I find that period of Greek history repulsive, quite repulsive."

"I believe I would have taken the iconoclasts' side. For all their fanaticism, they did have a *pureté*. In fact, I find them fairly close to certain poetic movements."

Who had said that? Mardaras, of course, who else.

"Constantine believes the iconoclasts were led primarily by military interests. Just consider the pressing need for troops to resist the continual assaults of barbarians from the East. And since military recruits came mostly from the races of Asia Minor, where given their proximity the anti-iconic beliefs of the Arabs and Islam were widespread, the campaign against icons seemed necessary."

It bothered him greatly when others spoke on his behalf. But meeting John's gaze, which was straightforward and kind, he realized he was being unreasonable, that he was utterly consumed by exhaustion. His room at the hotel floated like an oasis before him. The bed, made up with fresh sheets, the soft pillow, his nightshirt folded neatly on top of it, and in the background the outline of the water jug in the gentle, dim light.

"Westerners consider iconoclasm a period of barbarianism and darkness. Constantine has kept notes from his study of Gibbon. But others see in it an early attempt at social reform. Didn't Paparrigopoulos make an argument to that effect in his *History of the Greek Nation*?"

John looked at him expectantly. If you think I'm going to chase this snake out of its hole on my own, you're quite mistaken, his expression said.

"He described it as an attempt to limit the role of the Church and the monks. And the system of serfdom, too. Remember our discussions on the topic? If I'm not mistaken, your views weren't too far from those of Paparrigopoulos. Putting aside the acts of violence, you said, which can only be characterized as primitive, iconoclasm could be seen as a modernizing movement. A challenge to the old world, the old order of things. Though on a personal level I'd say you're more of an iconophile than an iconoclast."

"If I venerate the cross and the lance and the rod and the sponge," he said.

They were the words of Saint John of Damascus.

"The Europeans have got Byzantium all wrong," he averred.

Cross, lance, rod, and sponge. If I venerate those tools with which the Jews killed my Lord, as the cause of my redemption, how can I not also venerate icons created with purity by those who believe, for His glory and in His memory?

There were so many ways he could respond. He could contradict Madame and her stale, prejudicial distaste for Byzantium, but also John, who was looking at the issue far too logically. At the why and the wherefore.

There was no why, no wherefore.

Spring, season of eros. Good Friday in Alexandria. Banners depicting seraphim behind the raised cross. *Oh my sweet springtide, my sweetest child.* Christ's funeral bier strewn with flowers, parishioners standing with lit candles, silver everywhere, and a reverence so strong it bordered on pleasure. There were so many things Westerners didn't understand, things they knew only as abstractions, theoretical constructs. Whereas the Orthodox faith was full of pagan elements. And perhaps it went deeper than paganism. The circle of life. Death, birth, and that poignant stretch between the two that one should rightly dedicate to preparing for the end. Which was not an end at all but a new beginning.

He felt a sudden wave of nostalgia for Alexandria. As if he had been imprisoned in this place for years. Captive in Café Sans Nom. New customers continued to arrive, despite the late hour. The woman in green was gone. The empty glass still sat on the table, and beside it the jug with the strange spout that resembled the snout of a fox.

"What I'd be more interested in studying is the end of iconoclasm," he began, but left it there.

There was a line in one of his older poems. A young man in white is carrying the cross at the head of a procession. In one neighborhood after the next the Christians come out of their homes and bow down to it. The beautiful young man moves forward holding the cross aloft. It was an imposing image. Nothing else he had written about Byzantium satisfied him. As if he were forcing historical context into a poem, and the lines rebelled.

John said something. Then Madame asked him a question, but he wasn't listening.

"I'm sorry," he said, explaining that he was so exhausted that even the most bloodthirsty iconoclasts seemed to him like deities of sleep.

Madame found the comment quite inspired.

As they arrived at the Saint-Pétersbourg, John stopped for a moment at the entrance. He watched the carriage as it pulled away.

"What an evening," he sighed.

The hotel was dark. Only a dim light shone from inside, probably the lamp of the young valet on night duty.

"Madame's last point was superb, how she likened the Dreyfus Affair to the clash over the use of icons. Were you listening? Mutatis mutandis, in her view, the scene is the same and Zola and Anatole France the iconophiles of the present day!"

John laughed, his gaze still fixed in the direction the carriage had gone.

"How did she come up with it? The single difference, she stressed, was that the iconophiles in the Dreyfus Affair don't stroke their icon until the paint rubs off, as the Byzantines did. And that story about the pigeons, what did you make of it?"

He paused and searched in his pocket.

"The pigeons who enchant the spirits. An unlikely story. I wanted to ask, too … Why didn't you back me up during that conversation about Byzantium? You're the specialist, after all. You'll owe me next time."

Again, that same nervous laugh.

He started to head into the hotel but John stood in the entrance, blocking his way.

"Oh, and there's another bit of news about the Ark that you

didn't hear, since you had walked on ahead. When Mardaras offered to go looking for that boy with the pigeons in the middle of the night, Madame seemed reluctant, there was obviously something on her mind. Suddenly she said she had a suspicion where she might find them. Guess where? At the Ark! Out of the blue. She thinks they've been secreted away there. She's heard that guests at the Ark—where her son-in-law is often to be found, along with any number of feebleminded folks—bet great sums on the pigeons. Mardaras's color changed ten times—"

"What's going on?" he interrupted.

His brother didn't turn toward him.

The red kerchief.

He should have guessed.

The red kerchief was a gift for a lady friend of John's. A very special friend for whom he harbored the most exquisite feelings, he repeated twice, avoiding his brother's gaze.

An English governess in Mansoura! Who no doubt kept her savings hidden at the bottom of her trunk. Pale, with freckles. A governess. Who probably assumed not only the care of the children but a few household chores as well. Perhaps she washed dishes, swept, or even scrubbed dirty clothes in the basin on the maid's day off.

They climbed the staircase toward their rooms. It was a good thing he was so exhausted; otherwise he might have let slip certain expressions and characterizations that he would later regret. At the top of the stairs John stopped and asked him not to speak on the subject to anyone. To keep it a secret. No one else knew. He was the only one to whom he had revealed his feelings.

His feelings.

The valet walked before them, lighting the way with his lamp.

This will kill the Fat One, he thought. And I'll be the one to suffer the consequences in that stifling dining room, the sobs and moans, the teary eyes hidden behind handkerchiefs.

"Did you think at all of our mother?" he asked.

Without waiting for a reply, he gestured to the valet that he no longer needed him, and walked on in the dark.

He made his way forward blindly, tracing the wall with his hand, unsure whether he would, in fact, be able to locate his room.

The news had crushed him.

He heard voices behind a door. A man's voice and a woman's, arguing. He stood there for a moment. The woman's voice climbed two notches higher, repeating the same unintelligible word as if it were a question that for her was an answer. It sounded to him like Russian. He pressed his ear to the door. The man started to say something, toneless, apologetic, but the woman talked over him, drowning out his voice in a torrent of consonants. He heard glass breaking. The woman laughed hysterically. Then a thump, probably from some other floor. Footsteps approached, then hurried off.

His room was at the end of the corridor. He went in and pushed the door closed behind him. He fell onto the bed like a slab of wood. The sheets were smooth, starched. The pillow sank beneath his head. This is my bier, he thought. No flowers, no procession. The angry woman's voice echoed in his head like the clatter of stones tumbling down a hole. Tumbling and tumbling until they silenced the feeble male voice. He wondered whether the man behind the closed door might have been the young dancer. Imprisoned in that room. Prey to a crude, hysterical woman. What dreadful laughter, full of spite. How contemptible when compared to Madame's noble laugh. That dry, dispassionate *ha*. The thought of Madame enveloped him in a kind of unease. He wasn't sure whether he had made a good impression. He had spoken very little over the course of the evening, letting all the opportunities pass when he might have elaborated on his opinions. In two cases in particular, during the conversation about Byzantium and then about the war in Crete, he had listened irresolutely as the others spoke, like some sort of fool. Tossing out an irrelevant phrase now and again, always at the wrong moment. While he easily could have challenged their positions. He could have proven to them that, though he came from Alexandria, he was much more than Madame's aristocratic friends. Much more what? More educated? More refined? He was not at ease in society, of that he was painfully aware. This knowledge had tormented him on not a few occasions. At the Benakis residence, or the Salvagos residence, or any of the great houses to which they were invited, he often felt that they went as poor relations, in a way. And now this coup de grâce: John's feelings. The ambiguity of their social position in Alexandria would cease to be ambiguous—the respectably fallen family that for years had managed to conceal its plight. A governess. In Mansoura. Petticoats dragging in the mud. Raised on oats, a pastor's daughter for all he knew. He hid his head under the pillow. He felt like crying, and perhaps he did, and then dozed off in that position.

Five minutes later he was lying on his back with his eyes wide open. The steady progression of their downfall. The family's slow decline, ever since their father died. And not all that slow, really. He could vaguely remember a scene. He must have been sixteen, perhaps seventeen years old. They had returned from England. Bit by bit the Fat One had resumed all her old habits. The visiting, the teas, the occasional evening drive to Ramleh in the carriage. It was interesting for him to realize how others viewed their fall, rather than how they themselves experienced it from within—within the four walls of a house filled with innuendos, sudden shouts, sobs. Sobs that inevitably led to midnight snacks of spoon sweets. One of the brothers would suddenly rise in the middle of a meal, slamming the door behind him as he left, and the others silently took their leave in turn, only one remaining behind to console their mother. That one had always been him, even when he was a little boy. But outside the house? Outside things were different. The façade changed. The Fat One continued to show the same interest as before in diamonds and jewelry, to ask around for a good cook, to rattle on in irritation about some mistake the French had made in the digging of the Suez Canal. As if nothing had happened. Of course everyone saw right through this bit of theater. He remembered one moment in particular, at the Benakis residence. He and his mother had gone for a visit, it must have been January, the name day of Saint Antonios, and the young son of the house was celebrating. Though perhaps it had been some other holiday. They had just climbed the stairs. A servant waiting in the vestibule took their coats. Madame Benakis appeared through another door. And he registered something. A remark. No, nothing had been said, it was expressed only as an awful, wordless gesture. The servant, weighed down with their coats, asked Madame Benakis something. She made a curt gesture with her hand, no, no, as if the very idea filled her with revulsion, and pointed to the coat rack in the hallway behind her.

Now of course, he understood the implications of that awful gesture. At the time, he had merely been impressed by the intensity of the expression on her face. The maid must have asked Madame Benakis whether he and his mother would be staying to dine, so she would know where to hang their coats. Poor relations' coats in the hall, those of the guests invited to dinner in the wardrobe in the office. Later he had felt strange when one by one the other visitors began to rise with affectation and pleasantries to head into the next room, where a large table had been laid. The same servant stood in the door to lead them in, wearing an embroidered white apron and a ridiculous cap. He listened to the voices, the laughter, the clink of silverware. Silver trays passed by in the background. A divine smell of roast meat. At last the two of them were left alone in the salon, apart from an old woman whose wits were not all about her, and who spoke of the virtues of a German education, and above all of the Germans' fondness for cold baths. But something had registered. He had surely felt the humiliation. Because, on the way out, he considered going back and stealing that book.

That day at the Benakis residence he had flipped through it absentmindedly and chosen a poem at random to read. It had shocked him. His French must not have been very good at the time, but he had lingered on certain lines, reading them over and over, looking around to make sure no one was coming. *"Femmes damnées."* That was the poem's title. He had never heard of Baudelaire. The book was *Les Fleurs du mal.* It must have been the first, uncensored edition. He was sure of that because when, much later, he bought a copy of his own, he looked for the poem and didn't find it. The French censors had removed it. But where had he come across that book in the Benakis house? Certainly not in the salon, where he sat with his mother listening to the ladies' boring conversation.

He remembered another edition with the poet's portrait as a frontispiece. The poet was no longer so young, and seemed to be looking right back at him. Even if you turned the book upside-down, the poet still stared at you. You can't escape me, reader, he seemed to be saying. At any rate, that day at the Benakis residence, he hadn't held on to the poet's name. What he remembered was the title: *Flowers of Evil*. In hindsight it seemed entirely unlikely that any of the Benakis family had ever bought such a book. Some guest must have forgotten it there. He'd found it on a low table, perhaps over by the piano, behind some other books, he no longer remembered. At some point when he had gotten up and walked aimlessly around, not daring to go into any of the other rooms, waiting for time to pass, for the visit to end, so they could rise and take their leave. The mere thought of stealing the book had been his revenge. His response to humiliation. To Madame Benakis's terrible gesture. *"Femmes damnées."* Lying on scented cushions, behind heavy, dark curtains, given over to a sweet lethargy that disturbed them rather than putting them to sleep. Their eyes burning embers in the darkness. Their kisses, which dug into flesh. Marks from a beast's teeth in white flesh. He couldn't understand what that beast meant, how the poet intended it, but he felt that it was something terrible, unavoidable, just. As he flipped through the pages, he kept stopping at that same poem. He remembered the feeling of the book as he held it, the coarse corners somewhat green from use, an embossed pattern on the cover, tiny lilies that stroked the tips of his fingers. An entirely erotic feeling, how had he not realized earlier? He remembered sniffing the book, that he remembered with great vividness. The book's odor, indefinable but distinct, from the various hands that had flipped through it, hands that had stopped at this page or that, prickling with sweat at some daring description, as the erotic arousal intensified. And that other book, what had it been? In Constantinople, at his cousin's house. His aunt was out. In the next room his cousin was getting ready to go out, too, ironing his mustache, putting on cologne. Tobacco, jasmine, and some other note, faintly sweet, vulgar. He'd been invited somewhere—and announced with a self-satisfied smile that he wouldn't be taking him along. The cover of the book was yellowed, the corners worn, a shape like a fishhook beneath the title. It must have been a bad day—something must have upset him, there was a terrible pressure on his chest, tightening like a vise. It wasn't his cousin's behavior, he was used to that, something else must have happened. He held the book open before him, paying no attention, not even registering what he was reading, eyes trained always on the same page as he felt the stitches on the cover like tiny gashes in the leather, the fishhook tickling his finger, and the words on the page swayed and blurred. Then they assumed their proper places again, all in a line, vividly printed, urgent. As if forming a protective shield. It had seemed to him that all his desires, all his sadness, his rage and fear could fit into those lines. He couldn't remember what the words said, and it didn't matter. What counted was their therapeutic quality. Their power to bring order to the chaos of the world and to the chaos inside of him. And then there was that other book, when he was very small. He always had to skip a page because he was afraid of the wolf. It may have been his very first book. The page showing the wolf dressed as a sheep. He liked all the pictures on the early pages, of little lambs frolicking peacefully in the field, and even the one of the wolf licking his lips as he watches them from his hiding spot, that picture in particular brought him enormous pleasure. So why was he so afraid of the disguised wolf? There were other illustrations that were much more frightening, but he could look at them for hours on end. The wolf had covered himself in a sheepskin and the shepherd, unaware of the trick, shut him up that night in the sheepfold with the other sheep. The image on that page was very dark. All you could see was the wolf's mouth with a bright red, huge, glowing tongue. That was the image he couldn't bear. At night the shepherd went into the sheepfold and grabbed a lamb to slaughter. That lamb was the wolf. He slaughtered it at dawn, as the sun rose in the distance. There was a pile of logs burning and the shepherd sliced off the wolf's head with a large knife, a scene that reminded him now of the sacrifice of Abraham. In the final image the little lambs were once again frolicking joyfully in a green, grassy clearing. The evil had been redeemed. Little lambs on green grass. What a dull picture. Far more dramatic was the one of the disguised wolf, the four hairy legs sticking out from beneath the white sheepskin, the long tail dragging on the soil, and that gluttonous snout that gave away the wolf's identity. The snout of a greedy old man, so unlike the sheep's silly benevolence. But was it really benevolence? More like ignorance. Not even. Indifference, the infinite bliss of their breed. An apathy that can kill—that will, in fact, kill the wolf, will kill the old man who lusts after something impossible, something unattainable. Fat, fluffy, delectable little lambs. Like the member of that boy at his school in Liverpool. The arc of golden urine. Why had that image come to him now? Golden rain. Domus Aurea. He needed to remember the word. The word. The word that had been lost on Moréas's floor.

He rose from the bed. He went to the window and looked down. The road was a metallic strip between silent buildings. This night needed something else to bring it to a close. Some spark, some promise. He opened the door and let it close gently behind him. Third room to the left down the hall. He approached with a spring in his step.

A lamp must have been burning somewhere because he could see his shadow. A bent, crooked, threatening shadow that skimmed over the wall like a taut cord. A hunter stalking his prey, he thought. He follows the trail of its scent. For the first time during this endless failure of a night, which snaked its way over the failure of the day before, he felt an excitement, a wild surge of joy.

He could hear nothing through the door. The quarrel had ended. Holding his breath, he made out a hoarse, indistinct sound. Someone was crying beneath the sheets. Then a small shout, a sigh, and another sigh that had nothing to do with tears. He glued his ear to the door and waited.

Hazy copper liquid snakelike crimson. Crimson glimmers in the water of a bog near Mansoura. The surface swells, ripples. For a moment it's dyed with blood, then turns gray. Reflections in a dirty glass. If you put your eye to the glass you can see exquisite colors. The remains falter, a few sink to the bottom, others pass them as they rise, the saliva leaving behind a little trace of light—each bit of grease, each gracefully floating crumb an incredible explosion of blithely undulating microscopic details. The dentures curled in the water. Three sharp teeth. Sometimes it seems to move, to rotate slightly, allowing a better view. That imperceptible movement liberates new remains, a tiny scrap of apple skin, then something fibrous, stringy, perhaps a morsel of beef. The dentures motionless, lying in wait. Waiting all night on the bedside table.

The water in the glass was cloudy. He couldn't see anything. Just a blur. No glimmers at all. Hazy copper liquid snakelike crimson. Nothing.

He opened his eyes. There was no glass.

A church bell rang in the distance. Four times. Four in the morning. All this time he'd been squeezing his eyes shut so as to hear better. His ear on the keyhole. Crimson glimmers slipped past under his eyelids.

His limbs were numb. He needed to get up and leave. He tried one more time to imagine them in bed. The young dancer with the woman. The image came and went. Enough, he told himself. How humiliating. Kneeling outside a stranger's door, sleepless, sweating, terrified that the valet might pass by, or some insomniac hotel guest, or that a fire might break out, or an earthquake hit, and everyone would rush from their rooms and catch him in the act, the honorable Mr. Cavafy. Just a bit longer. Two more minutes. The room would be dark, the candle burned down in the candlestick. The atmosphere heavy. The bed unmade. The horrid, hysterical woman had fallen into a lethargy—she would be young, though, and perhaps beautiful, since she was a dancer. The young man lay beside her. On his back, thighs parted. A golden fuzz on his limbs. His lips. Those lips. Full, slightly plump. A perverse twist at the corners. Those voluptuous creases that deepened into grooves as the night progressed, stretched out, overflowed, dawn still hours away. Now he himself was lying beside the young man. He hadn't touched him, was holding back. He shivered at the sight of that body, driven wild by the thought of what was to come, and so he kept delaying, putting up barriers between them, though he could have swallowed him whole, his desire now paroxysmic. He held back. With great effort, he held back. He slowly trailed a hand over the sheets and stopped just shy of that firm, hairless chest. The young man turned toward him. A brazen glimmer flashed on those wet lips. What's taking you so long? said the eyes. A half a centimeter more. And as his fingers crept over the sheets, another bed appeared, another image, disagreeable, repulsive. A bed with heavy curtains that hung from gilded rings, with worn lace and thick bronze posts that glinted dully. A smell of damp in the covers, a plump hand beckoning him, and the rancid taste in his mouth as his mother's head appeared, magnified by the pillows, weighted down with rollers and pins. On the bedside table the dentures sat in a glass of water. Her new dentures. She had called him in to say goodnight. And she would call to him later to bring her something sweet to eat.

He closed his eyes, pressed on them with his fingers, saw tiny flies.

Only a week until he was back in Alexandria. That depressing house. That dining room, like a stage set in a theater. The setting for a drama that kept repeating itself over and over until it felt like a farce. "Do you know when I want to die, Costakis?" she asked him one day. The two of them were alone in the dining room, shortly before he and John left on their trip. He looked at her, surprised. "Never!" she cried, laughing triumphantly. He laughed, too, while at the same time saying to himself, I believe she disgusts me. But he would never let Pavlos or John know, never let them even suspect that he, too, couldn't stand her.

No one touches her anymore, he thought. No one caresses her. So why, now that she was growing old and needed him more, did he avoid her? A year ago when she would embrace him and launch into her coquetry and sweet words, he responded without annoyance. Sometimes she lisped, pretending to be a baby. He would laugh, and answer her in pig Latin to entertain her. Ethay abybay. Ethay abybay antsway iceyay eamcray. But in recent months whenever she squeezed his arm as they walked together on the street, he would pull back. He loved her very much. But she disgusted him, too.

And what if she died while he was gone? What if that was his final image of her? Begging for a bit of tenderness in the night. The baby wants ice cream. Ethay abybay.

There was a sound. He pricked up his ears. He caught a low sound, a gurgle. Then nothing, silence.

A half-erased scene came to him. An old man at a window, watching the traffic in the road with a certain intensity in his gaze. Daydreaming. Or not old but rather middle-aged, his opportunities for pleasure not entirely extinguished. Perhaps it was a line from a poem he had read. He looked nothing like the old man with the bundle who had followed him that afternoon on Rue au Maire. The look in his eyes was different. The old man with the bundle had fixated on him, pinning him with his gaze. As if he wanted to turn him inside out, uproot all his certainties. The old man in the window, on the contrary, gazed at an internal landscape. He watched the traffic, the young people passing by, and longed to be with them as memories besieged his mind, of hot afternoons spent in some bed, in some anonymous embrace, and a procession of naked bodies passed before him, coarse caresses that had marked him like hot sealing wax, and his senses awoke, blood coursed impatiently through his veins once more, yet this desire, while fervent, entered another framework, too, a somewhat philosophical framework. The things he observed so ravenously prescribed an attitude toward life, a way of being. He had written about an old man. His poem about a café where an old man sat hunched over a table, pining for the years that have passed, all the missed opportunities. The poem now seemed so weak.

Again he heard a gurgle.

Someone in the room was washing. He closed his eyes, pinned his ear once more to the keyhole, then curled his hands into a cone. Nothing. His mind was inventing these noises on its own.

WHAT'S LEFT OF THE NIGHT

It was strange. He was drawn to old age. No, that couldn't be it, since old men disgusted him—their sagging skin, the blank look in their watery eyes. It was something else. He was still young and yet as nostalgic for his youth as if he were an old man. Was the problem that he was timid, a shrinking violet? A coward despite his desire to experience strong passions? He felt imprisoned in a body that would quickly age, was already declining day by day, his back growing more hunched, while those lips, his own lips, still rosy, seemed not to belong to him at all. How he longed to kiss a young mouth—a mouth like his! As if it were forbidden him, as if he were missing teeth, or his gums had withered, or his breath stank with the stench of old age.

He yearned to yearn, was nostalgic for nostalgia itself. He wanted such things—which he could in fact be enjoying now, a beautiful male body, eros as he understood it, things that could be his were he not such a coward—to become inaccessible, unattainable, so he could experience them with the power of memory and of Art. Or was he just afraid? And all the rest was sophistry?

Weak expression
Poor artistry

Again that sad refrain. He thought he'd forgotten, but every so often it returned. It was the imprint that would remain from this trip to Paris. If only he could have spoken to John, confided in him, they would have sorted it out. But after John's revelation that night on the stairs, it seemed unlikely. He would have to make concessions in return.

And yet ... just a minute ...

He pricked up his ears again. That was certainly the sound of water.

Someone in the room was washing. Water ran from a jug, falling into the porcelain basin.

Two hands were rubbing that strong neck, splashing water on that face.

A faint light spilled in through the window. He lay in bed awaiting the young dancer. Whatever had transpired between them earlier was just the beginning, a tiny bite before the meal. He now saw those naked buttocks outlined in light, as in a painting, the sturdy shoulder blades, the golden indentations just below the hips. The young man turned toward him. A small, exquisite bite. He closed his eyes. The water still fell from the jug, rushing in a torrent into the porcelain basin. A scent washed over him. Fresh, elusive. With just a hint of sweat pricking his nostrils. He reached out his hand to stroke a chestnut-brown lock of hair—the very same hair that had tormented him the previous day in the armchair, falling down over the brocade and continually escaping his grasp. The bed creaked as the young man lay down beside him. How warm and smooth his body was, how finely defined the muscles. Tensed, at the ready ... How much violence that tender abdomen contained. Bites. Deep, wild kisses. Hands tightly gripped, pinned behind the back. Slaps. Light blows. Mouths that struggled to come together, blocked by limbs that had entwined like octopi. Be still, he said. The young man's breathing was labored. Still, he said again. His heart was about to burst. He grabbed the other by the wrists, twisted them, trying to still the young man, who slipped from his grasp. They struggled. The other gave in. He kissed him, caressed him insatiably. And then he noticed a detail that made him shiver. Something small, at the edges of the imaginary. His hand was curved so that his fingertips groped the head of the young man's penis while the testicles rested on his palm, rubbing gently against it, and there was a tiny hair … A hair that grazed his palm, a single hair that was stiffer or perhaps longer than the rest—all the others were soft, like a baby's—and at times scratched his skin, making him feel almost dizzy. Just a single hair. The rapid ascent of pleasure. Art is not what you say but how you say it, came to mind as with a sudden thrust the young man's body came to ride him, pinning him down.

His whole body felt numb, his muscles cramped. He couldn't bear it any longer. He needed to go back to his room, to lock the door, to find some relief—for the third time in twenty-four hours! He stroked the door frame. A tiny hair. And feeling the weight of the young dancer pinning him down, unable to move, he tried to concentrate on that hair so he wouldn't lose it, to hold it in his hand until he reached his room, to let it scratch him and set him ablaze for ten, fifteen steps until he could open the door, close it behind him and lower his pants, and his brain burned, his eyes ached, how could the hair not escape, how could he keep from losing it on the way, how could he leave that exquisite feeling behind, where would he find the strength to abandon it, *abandon*, he repeated to himself, *abandon*, a word from Plutarch, how do you find the strength to abandon what you hold most dear, and at what cost? His eyes stung, burning in their sockets, and he wondered if he could possibly say no, deny it thrice and erase this pleasure he worshipped.

He clutched at the wall, leaned his weight against the frame and stood. Then he lurched forward. Back in his room, he opened the wardrobe and fumbled around, looking for his loofah glove. He hadn't used it since he left Alexandria. He stood in front of the mirror and stripped off his shirt. He plunged the glove into the basin and rubbed himself vigorously.

He splashed water on his ears. He rinsed out his mouth several times.

Three deep toe-touches.

Breaths.

Toe-touches until he grew dizzy.

Inhale, exhale.

Toe-touches.

Now he was fine.

He hadn't given in. Not this time. His rules had helped. He felt almost relaxed. Just now he would like to read a good poem, or to write. He went to the window and glanced outside. Yes, he was in a mood to write. The darkness had begun to dissolve into shadowy, tremulous masses. The day is galloping toward me, he thought, and smiled.

There's a problem. I started writing, restraining my momentum. I threw out everything I wrote. I started again, and crossed it all out. The initial concept was good, and perhaps a few of the lines ... But something felt wrong. An urge to burn everything I'd written overtook me. I would have, if I weren't staying at a hotel. I wonder if the need for a rupture with my previous poetry that I've been feeling so strongly over the past few months might be evolving into a personal dilemma. What am I doing? Who am I? What's the sense in all this?

I have to avoid it. It won't get me anywhere.
A dead end.
6:40 am.

The light is coming through the window.
Who am I? What am I doing?

I tore it all up.

7:25 am.

Ten hours later he was awakened by a knock on the door. He stumbled out of bed, fumbling for his glasses. He heard footsteps retreating. The valet had slipped a note from John under the door. He took it to the window to read, then went back to sleep. For some reason he was in Vienna, a city he had never visited. He was following a young man with large feet. He hadn't seen the young man's face. I wonder if the rest of him is large too, he thought. They were walking on the Ringstrasse, a boulevard that seemed to be deserted and lined with bare trees, and every so often one saw wooden posts like those in the ocean, only these were sunk in snow. The young man's shoes were black and shiny. They arrived at a large church whose imposing turrets pierced the sky. Now the bells will start ringing all at once and bring the turrets crashing down, he thought. But there was complete silence and he felt gripped by vertigo, as if he were seeing everything from above, the dome, the turrets, the parapets, the bell tower, and hundreds of meters farther down, two tiny specks in the empty churchyard: himself standing rigidly behind the young man. Only when the young man turned toward him, revealing his face, a face that had now been erased, did he remember something odd about John's note and suddenly jump out of bed. He dressed hurriedly and went down to the lobby. The concierge hadn't seen John go out. His shift had begun at one. At one on the dot, he stressed. But the gentleman wasn't in his room, either—the maid who went up to clean had found it empty. And the room key was in its wooden cubicle. It had been there when the concierge arrived.

The clock at the desk read 6:15 pm. John's key hung like a lonely yellow tooth.

He left the hotel. He went as far as the corner of Rue Auber and stopped. The sun burned his back. He read the note again:

> *You think you're an island, a continent all to yourself. The rest of us are all tiny pieces, just dots on a map. Be well, my dear brother. But don't ask for whom the bell tolls*

John must have written it that morning, still upset by their conversation the night before. He recognized the reference to the poem by John Donne. No man is an island entire of itself, etc.

He remembered his brother's pale face as they climbed the stairs behind the valet, his gaze pleading. He had asked him not to speak to anyone. To keep it a secret. Could he be serious? About a governess in Mansoura?

He was probably worrying for no reason. John was even-tempered, he hadn't shown the odd behavior Pavlos had—or even Aristides, their third brother. Yes, Aristides, too, in his way. But he'd never doubted John. He always reacted calmly, even in moments of crisis. Rational from youth, with artistic tendencies, to be sure, but steady as a rock.

What was he thinking, writing a note like that?

The sun burned pitilessly. He searched for some shade where he could take cover. In the stifling glare, his brother's careful handwriting, the nearly manic attention paid to the letters' alignment, the even spacing between the words, all foreshadowed something unpleasant, irrevocable. And why had he left the period off of the final sentence? In such a fastidious note it couldn't be an oversight, it had to be intentional. He read it again, for the fifth time.

The last phrase set off an alarm in him: don't ask for whom the bell tolls. Donne's poem ended similarly: "and therefore never send to know for whom the bell tolls; it tolls for thee." We're all stuck like tiny pieces to a map. Each of us is a speck of land, a clot of dirt. When someone dies, don't ask who, for it's as if you're dying yourself. The more he reread it, the more worry gnawed at him. The morbid contrast of the black letters on the white card. Perhaps his brother wasn't the rock he imagined. There had, in the past, been indications of oversensitivity. Was it possible that, rattled by his own hostile response to the revelation about his feelings, those base feelings, his brother had decided … If something of that sort had happened, the guilt will lie with me, he thought. *Be well, my dear brother.* That greeting in the middle of the note struck him as hypocritical—a veiled threat that revealed itself with the tolling of the bell. But how could that be? Perhaps he himself had gone a bit mad, from exhaustion and the hollow emotions of the last few days. He was probably being absurd. Yet while his worry may have been unwarranted, and his suspicion seemed unlikely, each passing minute seemed to make room for his doubts, which swelled, incorporating small details that became new evidence. His doubts ceased to be doubts, as scenes from the previous night ran with unbearable precision through his mind, his references to the red kerchief, his own insistence on digging at his brother's discomfort with all his questions, the two of them climbing the stairs behind the valet with the lantern, a moment that now seemed to have lasted hours, the pleading look in John's eyes as he sought an ally in him—his only potential ally in the family—and was proven wrong. He saw John standing there at the head of the stairs, defenseless, exposed to the shadows cast by the trembling flame. But what was he supposed to do? The Fat One was the first thing to come into his head. He had to think of everything, weigh it all, and plan all his movements, which he would perform like an automaton before finally collapsing. Before allowing himself to collapse.

I should cross myself and say I believe, he told himself. I should say my belief is unshakable. Lord, please. He turned and headed back to the hotel under the blazing sun.

Dear Lord, please.

John was standing at the hotel entrance in his white straw hat.

"Ha, ha … *La grasse matinée*," John called from a distance. Then he started to talk about his long, lovely walk as far as Sacré-Coeur, how he decided to go to Passage Jouffroy on his way back, taking a shortcut through Rue du Faubourg-Montmartre, and how he'd just written their mother a letter full of details about Mardaras and Madame that were sure to entertain her, how despite their late night he was in fine fettle today.

They went into the hotel.

He should have been flooded with joy but he was enraged.

He led the way into the salon and bumped into a chair, tipping it over. John bent over behind him and set it back in its place.

He went over to the window and sat.

He tossed the crumpled note onto the table.

"Have you gone entirely insane?" he asked.

John watched him, smiling.

"You scared me."

"How do you mean?" the other wondered. He picked up the note, smoothed it on his knees. "It's by John Donne, you must have realized. I think it expresses our differences quite simply, how you view the world … You must admit, your way of seeing things is rather different from how mere mortals think."

"You're the mere mortal?" he spat through clenched teeth. "You?" he repeated, raising his voice.

But he already felt empty, tired, indifferent.

"You don't take criticism well. You're a continent unto yourself," John began, waving to get the waiter's attention so they could order.

He was in no mood to be dragged into a battle of words. Nor to explain to his brother how worried he had been. Those ten minutes of panic, perhaps more than ten. He would only make himself ridiculous. Besides, it would give John the upper hand. He felt as deflated as a punctured sack, and all that remained was a thorn, a thick little thorn in his side—the suspicion that, rather than bring them together, this trip had pushed them apart.

They ordered cheese sandwiches and iced tea. It was too late for lunch, and John was already thinking up a schedule for the rest of the day, their last in Paris.

"As for the letter I wrote to our mother, I signed on your behalf, too. And I finished our shopping at Passage Jouffroy, I took the list with me. We're all set."

New guests were arriving at the hotel. Their silhouettes hurried past, reflected in the plate glass, disappearing as in a puppet theater.

He was almost certain it had been the young dancer behind that closed door last night. With a woman. He had caught the tone of his voice. Expressionless, neutral. Their embraces had calmed the woman's anger. How long had he sat there? On his knees with his ear to the door. He had lost all sense of time. What on earth am I doing here? he'd wondered. How did I sink so low? It was nearly dawn. He'd known he should leave before someone saw him. But the taste of danger increased his longing.

"I'll be right back," he said and stood.

There was a gold cage with engraved bars on the reception desk.

"The St. Petersburg Ballet," he began, gazing past the concierge's shoulder.

"They left this morning."

"What was their next destination?"

The concierge didn't answer right away. He bent over the guest book and flipped through it.

"Where were they headed?" he repeated.

"To Venice."

Inside the cage was a white cat.

So he was gone. He'd be on the train by now, crossing the Apennines. That hideous woman would be nestled by his side, perhaps even holding his hand. Scenes from the previous night passed through his mind—and for a moment he felt like laughing, but then a band tightened around his chest. Yet another missed assignation, yet another trajectory interrupted midway.

John was studying their Coty guidebook. Every so often he jotted a note in the margin.

"Don't make any plans that involve me," he said as he sat down. "I'm not about to venture out into that furnace until the sun goes down."

It had surely been the young man behind that door. How could it not have been? He'd recognized the voice. Immature, awkward. Frightened or apologetic at times—but only early on, as the quarrel unfolded. Later, when the woman began to emit those disgusting roars, rather than sighs, when things in the bed heated up and he, too, had caught fire, body to body with that damned door, fooling himself, hoping for something, but what? Waiting for something, but what? Telling himself, just a few minutes more and I'll go back to my room—then there had been other sounds, virile, brutish. Oh, if it were me in that bed with you now, he thought. What pleasure I'd give you. How you would scorn her caresses afterward, her vomitous sighs. You'd never go back to that woman.

His knees sent pinpricks up his body and at times he felt as if snakes were slithering over his back. The nape of his neck had seized up. How did I sink so low? he thought again. How humiliating. Up against a stranger's door, pricking his ears for pants, moans, divine and profane sounds, enflamed by fear, the flesh of his earlobe against the keyhole, his eyelids drooping or perhaps shut altogether to intensify his concentration, the stubble growing on his face, his stinking body, the acrid scent of his sweat. For a long while he heard nothing. A dragging sound from some other floor, a guest searching for a candle or a chamber pot in the dark, then not even that, no sound at all, the entire hotel sunk in sleep and he all alone at the edge of the world. Perhaps the young dancer and the woman had fallen asleep, exhausted by their lovemaking. He felt the need to let go, to shake free of this terrible absorption. Every so often his mind would run elsewhere, to a line, always the same line. He could feel its contours, its atmosphere, but there were no words. The image of an old man in a window. Not so very old. Standing in a window, sunk in recollections. A man who worshipped erotic pleasure. For whom arousal was sacred. Nonsense. He couldn't concentrate. He needed to get up and leave. Right away. Yet every time he was about to leave he would hear something, or think he heard something, the slightest creak that kept him where he was. *Tsik.* Silence. *Tsik.* His whole life trying to fit itself into a *tsik.* Liquid glimmers passed under his eyelids. His eyes hurt. He tried to imagine them in bed. He banished the woman and put himself in her place with the young man. The night's wick burned. At some point he had kissed the door. He had reached the point of actually kissing the door.

"I don't know if you noticed," John said, "but yesterday Mardaras was flirting with Madame in quite a particular way. A very vulgar way, I might add."

I don't give a damn, he thought.

"He was stroking her knee under the table."

He opened his mouth to laugh. The image of the cat in the cage that he'd seen at the reception desk came to mind. It was white, yet not white. Hairless, entirely bald. All that remained was its skin.

"Will you explain why you were so upset by the lines from Donne?" John asked.

It was obvious there was something else on his mind, something he'd been preparing himself to say for a while, but still hesitated.

The governess. Not just now.

"About what you said yesterday on the stairs," he began.

John coughed.

I beat you to it, he thought.

"Let me think about it, I need a little time," he murmured. He closed his eyes. He was at the edge of something crucial, important. A vague shape was beginning to form. A line from the night before. He needed to look over all his papers, his notes. He needed to stop feeling such doubt. The past few days had undone him. Don't ask for whom the bell tolls. It tolls for thee.

It wasn't John's fault for writing the note, he was the idiot who had imagined his brother could take such a desperate step. Paris has wrecked me, he thought. He drained the rest of his tea, picked up his hat, and stood. He'd forgotten something in his room, he said, and would be back in a moment.

The room was neat, neutral, white. On entering he was surprised at how impersonal it looked now that the maid had tidied up, and as he opened the wardrobe door and groped blindly with one hand in his open suitcase, he felt as if he were trespassing upon an uninhabited space. How empty it was, how silent. Table bare, basin wiped clean. The maid had pulled the curtains back and the sun fell abruptly onto the bed like a jet of dust in which tiny specks hovered. He stared at the light for a long while in surprise. Those specks, which didn't exist, were visible. Entirely discernable. Sitting with his back to the mirror he observed how each speck glinted and disappeared or rather faded in a gush of illuminated dust. He could feel heat rising off the bed where a large yellow disc of light painted the sheets. That sensation of warmth made him feel sick to his stomach. He tilted his head back and looked at the ceiling. Shadows danced over the plaster molding. If he watched for too long, he was sure to feel dizzy.

6:40 a.m. to 7:30 a.m.

What had happened during that time?

7:45 a.m. at the latest.
Or 8:00 a.m.
It couldn't have been any later.

What had he been doing for all that time?

Where had he put his papers?

6:40 a.m. to 8:00 a.m.

The game of chase on the ceiling continued.

Shade and shadows.

He lit a cigarette and tried to clear his mind of the scenes from the previous night. He remembered the precise moment. 6:40 a.m. He knew what time it was because he had stopped writing, glanced at his watch, and decided he simply couldn't keep at it, there was no sense in going entirely without sleep, the poem simply didn't want to come out, he'd started at a good pace but it kept resisting, so it was better just to read over what he had written, paying particular attention to the words he'd crossed out—sometimes there was a little diamond beneath those lines that he had to dig back up, a slip of a word that needed to be gathered close with devotion—and then try to sleep. Light was filtering in through the window. A dry, colorless light that presaged a day of unbearable heat. He felt disappointed. Irreme-diably disappointed. Damned adjectives, he thought. Damned rhyme. Earlier the thought had crossed his mind that his dif-ficulty writing might in fact not be about writing. Perhaps it wasn't that his talent was still raw, unrefined. Perhaps the issue lay with him, some internal obstacle. The great need for rup-ture in his poetry he had felt so strongly in recent months, the reckless urge to break the rules—though he wasn't yet ready, he knew he wasn't ready—to shake free of lyricism and elegance, to banish all influences from other poets and movements, to become a movement of his own, may in the end have reflected a need for rupture in his life, with what his life had been thus far. Rupture with the rules, with social conventions. He faced an enormous dilemma. The familiar dilemma. How could someone who lived a conventional, conservative, mediocre life write important poetry? How could he speak of great passions, heroic ages? But that was wrong. He shouldn't confuse the two. If he did, anything he wrote would be doomed from the start. Yet how could one separate them? He recalled his papers spread over the dressing table. A dozen lined pages covered in smudges. Corrections, crossed-out lines. A few crumpled sheets on the floor by his feet. That dilemma wasn't merely a source of deep discontent, it had imprisoned him. He knew from experience that if he could puzzle out the cause of some displeasure it would bring him relief. Of course the problem wouldn't cease to exist. But he would at least escape its clutches for a while. For a while. A mediocre life, he thought. Constrained by prohibitions and boring obligations. Those stairs at the Third Circle of Irrigation. That suffocating dining room. Sirens' calls from the street outside—and he irresolute, indecisive, sitting across the table from his mother, a jar of quince spoon sweet between them whose thick glass refracted the dying light of the afternoon. Perhaps his mind would clear if he tried to express these hesitations. At least it would help when the problem presented itself again, the next time he fell prey to the same doubts. At least there was that, he decided, pulling out a clean sheet of paper. He'd written down his thoughts and noted the time. 6:40 a.m. What had he done next? Where had he put his papers? He never left them out in plain sight. Even if he was sick he would get out of bed and stow them away. The thought that someone might come in and read what he had written ... Particularly the thought that someone's eye might fall on an incomplete line, a half-finished poem, would make him jump up even out of the grave.

Where had he put his papers?

He stubbed out his cigarette and stood. He started to search the room again. In the cupboard he found the loofah glove, still wet. Another detail from the previous night that he had to ignore, since it would only distract him. It would pull him back into mazes, erotic associations, those shameful scenes before the closed door. He tried to concentrate. To banish the dancer, the hideous woman, the governess. To banish the naked bodies wrestling on the unkempt bed. He had to skip over the entire night, which kept sucking him in like a tornado, and arrive at his room as it had been that morning. The same room where he now sat. It was 6:40. Day had broken. Light was coming in through the window. He had taken note of that. He was sure of it because that was precisely when he stopped writing and looked at his watch. I have to go to sleep, he'd thought. His gaze had fallen for a moment on the smudged papers, his chicken-scratch, the notes at the bottom of the page, the dozen alternates for an adjective. Damned adjectives. Damned similes. At his feet lay other pages, crumpled, torn. The ones that weren't worth keeping.

At any rate.

By 6:40 he had written whatever he was going to write.

No matter how he strived, how he wracked his brain, he couldn't remember where he had put his papers. Somewhere the maid wouldn't find them ... As if the maid would care one whit for a few crossed-out lines. Written in Greek, no less! He searched the nightstand again, the dresser, the wardrobe. He pulled out all the drawers. He emptied his suitcases, his trunk.

He got down on all fours and checked under the bed. He rolled back the rug. He kicked the leg of the dressing table and yanked at the mattress hard enough to topple it onto the floor. He watched entranced as the yellow disk of sunlight sank onto the warped boards beneath.

He lit another cigarette, realizing it was impossible for him to isolate the morning, to divorce it from the preceding night. After all, it was the consequence of that night. What he had written was still hidden within the night itself. There had been a tiny hair … And now everything hung by a hair's breadth. A hair, he chortled. Yesterday, in front of the closed door. When his longing for the young dancer had reached a peak of ecstasy, when the smallest detail might become, had in fact become, a symbol worthy of worship.

Hair, hair's breadth, horsefeathers, horseplay. At least I haven't lost my sense of humor, he thought. Then, with a jolt like a formidable swimmer diving into the water, his body inscrutably, almost furtively, like a jaguar's limbs, gathering energy for the next movement that would suddenly emerge, a word leaped out. *Abandon.* A word from Plutarch that had appeared out of nowhere the previous night. Just before he returned to his room. He had still been kneeling in front of the closed door. *Abandon.*

It was probably from the *Life of Antony.* Or the *Life of Alcibiades.* Probably. He wasn't sure. He'd reread them both recently—he kept the volume tucked into his desk at work, beneath the records of the Third Circle of Irrigation. There was a particular passage in the *Life of Antony* that had impressed him deeply. The description of that dramatic scene on the night before Caesar's armies entered besieged Alexandria. During dinner, Antony orders his slaves to serve him lavishly since the next day he may no longer be their master, they may be attending someone else. His companions protest, tears in their eyes. He brushes off their protestations, as if drunk on the idea of death. Yes, that was the passage. Later, around midnight, a miraculous phenomenon takes place that Plutarch describes further on in his text. The city is sunk in silence, in apprehension and dejection over what will soon transpire. Suddenly a strain of otherworldly music was heard. *All at once harmonious sounds from myriad instruments were heard, and the shouting of a crowd …* Melodies, the leaping of satyrs, the sound of instruments. Bacchic cries. The hum of an invisible crowd passing through the city. As it approaches the city walls, the noise becomes deafening, then suddenly stops.

Something shiny caught his eye down low. The knob of the dressing table drawer. How had he not thought of it earlier? That's where his papers must be. He rifled through it with one hand and pulled out a scrap of soap, a black comb, a wrinkled paper wrapper. Nothing.

He pulled the entire drawer out of the dressing table. At the very back was a list of expenses and a few pieces of paper, carefully folded. The letter to Pericles Anastasiadis that he had forgotten to mail. Now it was too late. It would arrive after he did. *Abandon.* The Alexandrians who heard the music that night interpreted it as a sign from the gods. They said Dionysus and his procession had crossed the city and entered the enemy camp, abandoning Antony. *The god abandons Antony.* Abandons the man whom, a few years earlier upon his entrance into Ephesus, the crowds had celebrated as Dionysus himself, the women dressed as Bacchae, the men as Satyrs. What did the hair have to do with all that? Somehow it had led him to the word. The hair called forth the word, *abandon*. A tiny hair strategically placed on the soft testicle of a young Russian dancer. Despite his irritation, he couldn't help but register the ridiculousness of the situation, and smiled bitterly.

He took off his glasses and rubbed his eyes.

Then he leaned out the window and craned his neck, trying to catch sight of all the things he couldn't see. Buildings lacking outlines. A blur. Down on the street lampposts leaned, the figures of passersby merged like stains on the sidewalk. A well that swallowed up all shapes. There was nothing clear, nothing certain.

He put on his glasses. He stood before the mirror and looked at himself.

The face of a fool.

That was the only certainty.

And then he remembered. He'd torn it all up. Everything he wrote that morning, every single line. He'd even torn up the note in which he recorded his doubts. When the maid had come by earlier on her rounds, she must have gathered the torn sheets of paper and threw them out. But wait a minute … His other writings? They hadn't been at the bottom of the suitcase when he looked. What had he done with them? The revisions of older poems, the lines he had written over the course of the trip. Each evening he added any new pages to the stack at the bottom of the small suitcase. Were those now in tatters, too? An image came to mind, brief but enough to verify this fear: he standing in the middle of the room, just before getting into bed, torn pages scattered at his feet, washed by an unexpected calm, a sense of absolute peace.

He paced swiftly through the room. He went back to the mirror and looked at himself again. He sat down on the edge of the bed frame. The light had dimmed. With a finger he stroked the naked boards.

Abandon.

He tried to remember.

The word had stuck to that tiny hair.

The hair held the word, was its guard.

But who am I kidding? he thought.

Who am I kidding?

He pulled his watch out of his vest. 8:35 p.m. The precise time when he realized he had torn up his papers, had destroyed them all. I need to remember this, he decided. He lay down on his back on the mattress he had pushed to the floor. The ceiling was sweetly shaded, brushed with dark purple shadows. I'm better now, he thought, because I've been forsaken, and in fact he did feel better. For a moment he thought he was falling asleep and that a fly was buzzing in the room. It circled his face, humming, fluttered its wings at his eyelids and ears, approached his nose, landed on his left nostril. It was extremely annoying. He didn't feel like opening his eyes, like waking up just to shoo it off, so the fly slipped into his dream, or rather his dream was sucked up by the fly, the dream became an enormous fly standing against the light, licking its feet. A gigantic black fly. Stuck to the windowsill with six legs and voracious eyes. The strange thing was that only he could see it. Behind him his mother was passing out lemonade to the other children. The maid brought a tray holding a cake blazing with candles. It was his birthday. He heard them calling him. His heart pounded. He was very happy but deep down also sad. Great joy always brought him a feeling of distress. He had blown out the candles, forgotten the fly. The others sang "Happy Birthday." Then he ran off with the other children to play hide and seek in the garden. When it got dark they were called inside. In the drawing room a fat boy, who must have been older, blond, covered in freckles, appeared before him carrying his old teddy bear. "You still play with these?" he taunted. "Look at what Costakis plays with," he shrilled. "You're a baby, a baby!" The children gathered around him. "Give it to me," he said, "if my mother sees you'll be in trouble." "Why?" the round little boy asked. "Because it's very valuable." He told them how his teddy bear had been officially baptized at the church with candles and candied almonds. That the archbishop himself had dipped it in the baptismal font and afterward they gave little gold crosses to all the guests. Soon after he heard the child asking his mother if it was true that the teddy bear had been baptized. The Fat One in her imperial glow had laughed and answered that no, it was a lie. Then her tone changed. "Turn around and look at me," she told him sternly. "Turn around this instant!" She stood tall and imposing in her lavish yellow frills. Still beautiful. He had seen the other children pushing to get close to her, hanging from her lips, excited by the scolding that would follow. "I don't want you telling lies again. Do you hear?" his mother shouted. "Enough with your fantasies. The next time I'll make you drink castor oil." Then she left the room. His face burned. Sobs shook inside his chest, but he held them in and managed not to cry. He walked off as slowly as he could. In the next room he stopped before the big black fly. "And if I tell them you're here?" he asked. The fly was as big as an owl. As big as a jungle beast. "If I tell them that whatever I think up, whatever I imagine really does exist?" Again he felt that bothersome fluttering on his nose, his ear, his eyelid, and at the same time heard a hollow, rhythmic beat. He opened his eyes. The fly had landed on his mouth. He shooed it with his hand. It had grown dark. Someone was knocking on the door.

"What's wrong with you? What on earth happened in here?" John stuck his head through the doorway, took a few steps into the room and then backed out again. He said that Mardaras was there and eager to tell them about the surprise he'd been saving, but he wanted both of them there at once. "What happened in here?" he asked again.

"I'll explain, I'll tell you later," he said, closing the door.

The rest unfolded quickly. John suddenly felt sick to his stomach. Then he developed a fever. The fever receded almost immediately but left him feeling weak. Mardaras was waiting with a fresh flower on his lapel. He had saved a surprise for their final evening. A fantastic surprise that he had managed to arrange thanks to well-connected friends. John was lying in bed with a cold compress on his forehead. "You go," he said, "don't miss it, I'll wait up for you to tell me all about it afterward." Before they left, he bent to say goodbye and as he approached his brother's pillow he was already regretting what he was about to say. "About our conversation yesterday on the stairs … I'll try, I'll speak to mother." What had come over him? He would certainly break his promise: not only would he not intervene regarding the governess, but he would fight that vile romance, do whatever he could to break it up.

John smiled.

"I knew the line by Donne would help," he said.

A stylish calèche was waiting for them on the corner of Rue Auber. They set off. Mardaras was quiet. Two black, half-blood horses pulled the carriage, which was shaped like a gondola, airy and shiny, gilded figures carved into the lacquer finish. The spokes of the wheels were painted vermillion, the harnesses polished to a gleam. On each side a bronze oval lantern shone. Never before had he ridden in such a smart, aristocratic conveyance. Carriages like this didn't circulate anymore. On their left the grand Opéra slid slowly by in a hazy glow, the statues on its dome lingering in the eye even after the building itself was no longer visible—the wings of Harmony like a golden stamp on the summer night. On Boulevard des Italiens a few passersby stopped to watch the carriage go by. The coachman, who earlier had jumped down to unfold the running board so they could climb in, hadn't spoken a word. His dark blue silk livery with wide piping was tucked into the cuffs of his boots; his top hat was pulled low, hiding his face.

It was very pleasant to ride in such a luxurious vehicle, a different experience altogether. Its interior was padded with red leather; there were velvet pillows everywhere, as in an Ottoman parlor; the doors were dressed with fine, glossy satin; the seats were comfortable. He looked outside. They were passing Café Riche. Le Tout-Paris. The crème de la crème of Paris luxuriating in dainty indolence. A few heads turned toward them, aperitifs in hand. And then Maison Dorée with its gilded trim, and in those famed private rooms, the flowing champagne and illicit passions, quenched far from prying eyes. Poor John, whom he had let hope that they would dine there. Another broken promise, though his brother's sudden indisposition had let him off the hook.

Just then an orchestra was playing on an outdoor stage, a jaunty tune with a slightly melancholy twist that reminded him of something. The comparison with Alexandria was beyond obvious. And entirely at the latter's expense. Suddenly he was gripped by a hunger for Paris. A craving for lights, boulevards. It was their last night. A propulsive force ran deep within him, a longing for shows, walks, restaurants, well-dressed, haughty crowds, but above all lights, lights. Who knows when or if I'll come here again, he thought. And right away he wondered: Who knows whether I would be a better poet if I lived here. Whether writing would come more easily to him, whether the lines would roll over the page naturally and artlessly, rather than his spitting blood for every word. Whether he would gain recognition more easily, perhaps even make a name for himself. Whether he would be invited to the best salons, sending his regrets at the last minute. Alexandria constrained him, limited his horizons. If he lived in Paris, if he were successful in Paris, surely his fame would spread quickly. But would he be a better poet? He thought of the hairless cat at the hotel reception, curled into a corner of the cage, naked in its own skin, defenseless.

"To be honest, I'm glad it's just us two tonight," Mardaras said.

The same thought had occurred to him.

"Without John," his companion stressed.

They would have to cross all of north Paris and then out through the Porte de Saint-Ouen. There the Zone began. At that point the coachman would have to jump down and close the top of the carriage and fasten it with hooks. It was a dangerous area, the kind of place that housed generations of rubbish pickers and rag and bone men. But not only. The entire Parisian underworld had hideouts there—whenever they were being pursued, they took refuge in its shacks and huts. A ragtag mob of thieves, pickpockets, cutthroats. How naïve were they, including not a few writers, who maintained that the *zoniers* were poor, harmless beggars. A tragic mistake. Those poor beggars robbed carriages, took people hostage. They knew how to make bodies disappear.

The other day an entire gang of them had tried to rob Mardaras. They had thrown rocks, sticks, branches into a deserted stretch of road to force the coachman to stop. He himself hadn't seen what transpired, he was too rattled to watch, and it had all happened so quickly. Luckily the coachman whipped the horses and they'd been off like lightning.

Nonsense, he thought. Mardaras's usual exaggerations. They were passing through a poor, dimly lit neighborhood. The movement on the street had died down. The horses' trotting hooves rang out clearly against the cobblestones. Rhythmic, staccato. Such impressive horses. Jet-black with white stars on their chests. He could have watched them for hours, cantering in perfect synchrony, strong muscles clearly outlined, packed with energy, eyes wide, nostrils flaring as they sniffed the night air. It was true, he felt more at ease without John there. Freer, perhaps? His brother's indisposition seemed to have arisen at precisely the right moment.

His curly hair resting on a velvet cushion, Mardaras was saying how sensible John was—in his opinion, perhaps too sensible. Incurably reasonable, if he could be permitted such an expression. He, on the contrary, seemed more open, less conventional. Though he was the younger of the two, he had the air of someone who was comfortable in different social situations—a man of the world, to put it one way. Reasonable, but a bit *fantaisiste*.

"You see," he continued, "the Ark is the anti-mimesis of reason."

"What do you mean?" he broke in. The compliments, the comparisons to John, had begun to annoy him.

"Mimesis, anti-mimesis," Mardaras replied, as if that explained everything. He craned his neck, trying to make out the face of the silent coachman, who was sitting erect, his body as stiff as if he had swallowed a walking stick, and launched into a speech about the Ark's coachmen, an extremely exclusive group who had all taken a vow of silence, though rumor had it that noblemen looking for a bit of amusement sometimes bribed one of them into letting them take his place. This one might be the Marquise de Sayner, or baron so-and-so.

"He's quite elegant and haughty."

"Indeed," he agreed.

They were driving through a district of warehouses. Figures lurked in the dark, or perhaps it was just his imagination, as the carriage was moving very quickly. The breeze hit his face, the horses' manes fluttered. Mardaras murmured in a conspiratorial tone that he had heard something quite unbelievable. He didn't know if he should mention it, but nevertheless, at any rate, he would tell him. A reliable source had revealed to him that Oscar Wilde had been seen at the Ark about a year earlier. But how could it be? Wilde had been released only a month ago from the prison in Reading, where he'd been held for the previous two years. The information shocked him, kept him up all night. Was he brought to the Ark in chains? Was Lord Douglas with him? Unless he had some way of sneaking out of prison whenever he liked, and then crossing the English Channel … He was quite entertained by the idea, given that Wilde was the first preacher of anti-mimesis. The high priest of anti-mimesis, as one article had called him. He had followers in Paris, too, a few harebrained young poets who adopted anything foreign that came their way. Moréas certainly wasn't moved by these theories of mimesis and anti-mimesis, for him they were simply British idiosyncrasies, like kippers, puffed up to camouflage the absence of an important body of work, and the only reason the English were tricked into liking kippers was that they'd never tasted a lovely coq au vin. Undoubtedly, though, the Ark suited Oscar Wilde perfectly. Wouldn't it be extraordinary if they were to see him there? A divine coincidence.

He said nothing. He wasn't terribly familiar with the work of Oscar Wilde, so his information was incomplete. The horses were moving even faster now, hooves clattering on the pavement, the coachman now on his feet, driving upright, his shadow swaying in the darkness. Mardaras's voice had begun to lull him to sleep. He was talking about two distinguished Englishmen who dressed in women's clothing, Boulton and Park, he'd heard that they, too, had been to the Ark, one of them had asked people to call him Stella—they were now likely in prison themselves, or one of the two had died, Mardaras wasn't sure—at any rate if the story was true, if they had really visited the place, it would be the perfect vindication of the Ark, the pinnacle of anti-mimesis, in which art imitated life—because if you'd seen those manly women in a painting you would have thought them the creation of some sick inspiration, though in fact they emerged from life itself—all works of art try to take their mold from life, try to imitate reality, and therefore never spring fully formed from the artist's imagination.

"I really don't understand what you're saying," he interrupted. "That's mimesis in its classical sense, as defined by Aristotle."

"Do you think so?" Mardaras hesitated.

They were approaching the walls of Paris. He saw a long line of fortifications like the corpse of a whale.

"Whereas Wilde seems to have claimed the opposite."

"Which is to say?"

"That the work of art inspires life. That life imitates art, something like that."

Mardaras laughed. "Perhaps. Either way, Moréas is still correct. English peculiarities."

It wasn't worth spoiling his mood. Soon they would be arriving at the Ark. He was very impatient, the place had attracted his curiosity—though the rumors likely surpassed reality. And he didn't expect it to offer the sorts of pleasures he himself sought. But it was the *parfait divertissement* for this final evening in Paris. Later, back at the hotel, as he sat on the edge of John's bed, his brother eager to hear all the details of the *aventure*, they would be able to regain their former complicity.

"Though you and Oscar Wilde do have something in common," Mardaras began again. He was speaking entirely of their poetry, under no circumstance did he wish to be misunderstood. He suspected that the high priest of anti-mimesis had influenced him in some way, in some covert manner, for there was something in his poems that reminded him of Wilde—they were both skeptics—which he could say because he had a nose for poetry the way others have a nose for wine, and besides, he'd met all the poets, knew all the movements. Thanks to his connection with Moréas, of course—but again, he didn't wish to be misunderstood.

"I mailed an envelope to Moréas two months ago. Did he receive it? Did he read the poems I sent?" he asked. The saliva in his mouth had dried up.

The envelope from Alexandria had arrived after Moréas's

departure. Sadly. But he needn't worry, Mardaras himself was responsible for his correspondence. He could assure him that the envelope would reach its intended recipient—besides, he had given it strict priority when organizing the incoming mail.

What was the use of such an annoying conversation? The question was, who had written that note. Moréas, of course. This unpaid secretary was simply so careless that he didn't notice the envelope had already been opened.

The area they were traveling through seemed abandoned. A buffer zone. The only sound was of the horses trotting, and the whip, which whistled through the air. Here and there doors gaped in skeletal buildings. He noticed something shining, a dull glow rising sideways out of the ruins. A bit farther on, the moon appeared abruptly through a cracked window.

They were crossing through the city walls. A cart had been stopped for inspection at the gate. A villager had gotten out and was gesticulating. There were low bushes ahead of them, decapitated trees—then a moat forty meters deep.

Suddenly he noticed a quick motion. The coachman's shadow jumped down into the darkness. They heard an awful whinny, and the carriage shook. The coachman reappeared astride the horse on the left. The beast began to rise onto its hind legs, and the coachman flattened himself against its body, clinging to its mane.

"What is that madman doing?" Mardaras shouted, then cried: "We're entering the Zone!"

They were moving fast. To the left and right, ahead and behind, a forest of rubbish. Mounds of abandoned things: boards, rags, old furniture, broken windows. The road, if it could be called a road, ran alongside a canal of oily, stagnant water, and then started up an incline. Their speed decreased. The horses moved forward with difficulty, sluggishly, hooves sinking into the mud. Soon they were racing again. Now they were passing a field of watermelons, or at least he seemed to see a few oblong melons, and between them rows of sacks that were human bodies. They entered a shantytown. Scattered fires blazed on posts. An old woman lay in an overturned cupboard, blissfully smoking a pipe, her eyes sealed shut. Nestled beside her, in her petticoats, two small children threw fleeting glances, like birds, at the passing carriage.

"He didn't put the top up on the carriage, so I'd wager—" The sound of the horses' hooves drowned out Mardaras's voice. He inched closer, leaned toward him. "Can I ask you a question?" Mardaras said. He paused, opened his mouth to speak, then seemed to change his mind. A small fire was burning outside a tavern, some shapes swayed, bellies trailing in the dirt, and for a moment the weak flames illuminated a large man sitting on the ground, half naked, his thick lips sweaty, an expression of listless malevolence under his cap.

"Do you see the Benakis family often?" he heard his neighbor ask.

What a question.

"Fairly often," he answered.

He looked at the moon which was now high above them. It seemed to be moving quickly toward them with some urgent request as the carriage sped on, approaching it in turn. And yet it was motionless. Deathly pale. Like the face of a chloroformed sick man on a table who can no longer ask for help.

"A remarkable family. Or so I found when I visited Alexandria."

Mardaras inched even closer.

"I believe they had three daughters. Their second daughter …"

"Penelope?"

"An exquisite young lady. Perhaps you've seen her lately?"

Mardaras had slid even closer. He felt those eyes boring into him, expectant. So he, too, has loved, he thought. Even this idiot with the silly carnation in his buttonhole had been pierced by those arrows. What was the use in telling him, then, that Penelope Benakis had married two years earlier?

"Not in some time," he replied.

Mardaras looked away and sighed. A minute later he returned with gusto to the issue of the poems, telling him not to worry. He wanted to assure him, etc., etc. It would be the first envelope to greet Moréas's hands on his return. Mardaras always read his correspondence first, even when Moréas was in Paris, since he received so many letters from young poets seeking his opinion, some of whom were clearly insane, madmen from the provinces. Moréas didn't have time for every upstart around, and had asked him to read the poems and write a synopsis, a few words expressing his opinion on the work of each poet, and then arrange them in order of importance.

"He must have great confidence in your judgment," he murmured.

"Complete."

He couldn't let it pass.

He had to say something.

At least a word or two.

He looked outside. The moon had grown suddenly larger and he noticed that a piece was missing as it slid down, hurriedly skimming past the scattered clouds. He wondered what he would say, what on earth he could say. He needed to find some comment that was both caustic and ambiguous, that would put this idiotic fool in his place without revealing how distraught he had been. He tried to shape a phrase in his mind, but couldn't find the right words, he needed to calm himself first, calm down, he thought, calm down, as the carriage pitched forward with a bang before leaping into the air as if another vehicle had rammed into it. The carriage jumped forward and they were thrown backward. Bareback on the horse, the coachman spurred it frantically. The wheels groaned.

They were moving ever more quickly. The entire wasteland of rubbish sped by. There was no time for him to see anything but the coachman's thighs gripping the beast's flanks and his head in its top hat burrowed in the ebony mane. The horses seemed alarmed, hindquarters quivering. He, however, now felt composed though his fingers were crushed from his tight grip on the doorknob. Once again he mulled over those four words: *Weak expression Poor artistry.* The four words that had poisoned his stay in Paris. Mardaras had written them. It was his criticism. Mardaras, who was now gripping his collar and clinging to him, eyes shut. A hollow din rose from the horses' sparking, galloping hooves. And yet I feel magnificent, he thought. The wind whipped against his face and he flared his nostrils, breathing deeply. Before them, an impenetrable darkness. The moon had gone into hiding. I feel fine, I'm alive, he kept thinking to himself. An unknown force had taken him under its wing. The carriage flew. The entire landscape flew. He thought: The black horses gallop through the night, manes hissing, moon in hiding. *Noir dans le noir.* I'm alive. I tore up all my writing. *Abandon.*

The carriage stopped with a jolt. They were in a clearing amid dense foliage. The coachman dropped the reins and jumped down. He said something, whistling the phrase through his teeth, or perhaps he said nothing at all. Then he walked off, limping, without even turning their way.

An oil lantern hanging from a branch offered a dim illumination. Mardaras tugged at his sleeve.

"Let's go, we must be close, quickly …"

There was a thump. A bird fell at his feet. It unfolded its wings, righted itself and flew off. Another thump. Another bird from the sky. This one alive, too. It flapped its wings uncertainly and disappeared. Two more birds fell at once with a whistling sound.

"Quickly," said Mardaras, "there are guards."

What would you like me to tell you about the Ark? he would ask years later. He'd be well known, highly regarded, the young would hang on his words. Then he would fall silent for a moment.

From the outside it looked like a farmhouse. A graceless building in the middle of nowhere surrounded by wild grasses. Ducks, rabbits, geese wandered freely among open coops. Roosters crowed, donkeys brayed. An army of chicks trailed behind each hen. Shortly before, in that clearing where the birds had fallen from above, two young men had slid out from behind the tall trees and introduced themselves as pigeon keepers. They were worried, a dozen or so pigeons were still missing, some had been gone since morning—they kept their gaze trained upward in search of little black specks stuck in the fabric of the sky. Then, as they were talking with Mardaras, who had recovered from his panic in the carriage and again assumed his familiar, pompous air, they all suddenly heard an otherworldly drone, and soon another bird came into view, nearly crashing into them. It landed on the ground, its chest pulsing like a runner's on reaching the finish line.

Was it true? Had such things really happened?

The birds falling from the sky. The valet or steward in the cobwebbed wig who took their names at the entrance. There was no password—that had been yet another fabrication, Mardaras had said he'd memorized them all, only it was forbidden to reveal them. A maidservant dashed out from behind the valet, shoulders bare, hair loose. He turned and saw her running barefoot toward the coops. Until you went inside, it was impossible to comprehend the size of the place, how enormous the Ark was, and how rambling its architecture. The entrance hall was imposing and somewhat peculiar, a jumble of styles. Crystal chandeliers, expensive but mismatched furniture, hunting trophies on the walls. Two men in long capes were playing cards behind a folding screen in the vestibule. The windows were entirely covered with black silk curtains whose purple tassels trailed on the floor. Scattered sculptures, samovars, a life-sized porcelain dog. Valets in red livery. Waiters with silver trays of champagne.

Clusters of guests strolled up and down the large hall as if out for a walk in the countryside. The lighting was dim. One man lay on the rug, gripping a pocket watch with a gold fob tightly to his chest—he appeared to be unconscious yet wore an enigmatic smile. People passed by, some stopped to look, but no one paid much attention. He entered the hall beside Mardaras, who scanned the scene, impatient to find a familiar face. He took a glass of champagne from a tray and drained it. His hand shook. He could still feel the effects of the fervor that had washed over him earlier in the carriage—the strange euphoria at the thought of having torn up his writings. An inexplicable euphoria. Illogical. Under normal circumstances he would be a wreck, in despair. The revelation as to who had written the note had come as a relief, but that wasn't why. As soon as he'd found out, he pictured himself standing that morning in his hotel room, torn papers scattered on the floor at his feet as the first colorless light of day came in through the window—how calm he had been, how utterly calm, master of the situation. The image thrilled him deeply, excited his emotions, awoke a sense of freedom as they sped faster and faster through the night and the truncated moon slid down through the sky, staggering, falling, vanishing. At some point, when he had time, he would have to sit and consider it all. A waiter passed by and again he reached toward the tray. The bubbly liquid cooled his throat. Try to understand, he told himself. That insane ride through pitch darkness. How much joy had flooded him when he could see nothing at all before him. He was racing through the night. Free, moving forward blindly.

"Let's go, let's go," Mardaras said impatiently. They could now hear a faint tuning of instruments amid the voices and laughter, repeating itself incessantly, interrupted every so often by nasal trills like a ferret's whine, only to begin again, sad, monotonous. There was an arch at the back of the room, an unshapely construction supported by two brick pillars where twin red alcoves hosted white statuettes. They went closer. An orchestra sat on a platform flanked by marble columns, playing instruments that seemed rather antiquated. They stopped to listen. The plaster dome over the orchestra was painted to resemble the sky, deep blue streaked with stringy clouds, with a little angel in the corner gripping the edge as if shaking out a tablecloth. The tuning continued, insistent, repetitive, piercing him in the gut. What's my relationship to music? he wondered. No matter how hard he tried, he didn't enjoy it. Music didn't interest him. He could live without it.

But I couldn't live without the voices in the street, he thought. Without the shouts, the sighs, the whispered words. At times he was moved by vulgar, popular songs. Those sentimental songs in which the singer's voice seems to trail away during the refrain, the kinds of songs you heard only in disreputable establishments. Not that he would ever admit as much to the fashionable people around him. The opera, what a nightmare. How he suffered at the opera. How often he had feigned interest, squirming in his chair as his mind flailed about, seeking relief in some other topic, trying to seize on some event, whatever came to mind, as the Fat One sat beside him, emitting murmurs of admiration.

Someone addressed him. He turned and saw a very stiff young man wearing a dark tuxedo and an icy gaze. Mardaras, still at his side, gave a slight bow and introduced them. Oh, but they had already met. Where? The previous evening, at Le Rat Mort with Madame de. On hearing the name Madame de, Mardaras gave a start and bowed again.

"Tell me about your last profound thought," the young man said. His lips moved rapidly under his blond mustache, which was waxed and twisted into two little hooks.

The comte de Losange.

"Call me Edmond," he said.

A bit later, when Mardaras vanished for a few minutes, Edmond asked again what his last profound thought had been.

"How on earth to get out of here," he said, smiling.

The reply seemed to please the comte. Mardaras appeared again and conversation turned to the war. The unfortunate war. Turks armed with German rifles against hapless Greeks with carbines left over from the revolution. Thermopylae and Smolenskis. Larissa. Long-suffering Larissa, which fell without a fight on Easter Sunday. Black '97. There had been no dyeing of Easter eggs this year, in any house. According to Mardaras, whoever dyed eggs was considered a traitor worthy of execution. One of the men asked him something. About Palaio Faliro, which Edmond had recently visited as representative of, or hanger-on to, the envoy of the Loan Committee.

"I've never been to Greece," he replied.

Mardaras looked at him, stunned.

"That explains everything," he said.

What am I doing here with these people, with all these ghosts? he wondered. He would have liked to return to the hotel, he was in a mood to write. All these people, these theatrical figures, what did they matter? But while he found the Ark rather disappointing, his mood was still fine. He wanted to hold on to the euphoria of the carriage ride. Surely he could squeeze a few words out of that insane journey. Perhaps an entire line. It had been a lovely night, but he'd had his fill. Enough, he thought.

Two women were headed toward them, giggling behind gauzy black veils that hid their faces. Their blooming gigot sleeves fluttered. They looked like courtesans. The comte de Losange hurried over to greet them, and he noticed the comte's slight limp. A suspicion passed through his mind, though there was no way to prove it.

A conversation began about a performance he hadn't seen at the Grand Guignol. Mardaras was trying to drag him into a neighboring room, and he followed without much interest. In a low-ceilinged salon, thick with smoke, a few middle-aged men were playing whist with furrowed brows. He stood in the doorway. He had no desire for the French to strip him of all he was worth. Seeing his expression, Mardaras smiled. Apparently he had another ace up his sleeve: there was a hamam in the Ark, too, dug into the rocks, where he would witness scenes that the next day would seem like a dream. The hamam offered the loftiest of experiences, and the most depraved. Eunuchs in bathrobes played violins, society ladies dressed as odalisques posed in tableaux vivants. Was he ready for something of the sort? Could he handle it?

Another nice bit of gossip to bring back to Alexandria, he thought. All his friends and acquaintances would be eager to hear all the details. They continued down a corridor with walls stained by damp, then descended a few steps. The ceiling dripped, hurricane lamps flickered. They seemed to be splashing around in water. They had probably passed into a neighboring building. It was as if they were walking along a path in the countryside with protruding stones and weeds, only there were walls on either side. They went down some more stairs. It was terribly hot. They entered a brightly-lit room. At one end stood a door with a porthole window. Behind a long table were three servants in fezzes and red starched robes who were taking people's walking sticks, gloves, and top hats. A waiter passed by with a tray and he took a little glass of liqueur with a silver base, then reached out his left hand and took another. He must have downed five or six in a row, walking aimlessly this way and that, trying to delay.

Mardaras couldn't wait any longer.

"We have to go into the changing rooms," he announced, flushed.

That's too much, he thought. He went to the door and peered through the round window. All steam and haze, nothing visible.

He turned to Mardaras and explained that he needed to return to the hotel, tomorrow would be a long day, they had an early departure and he hadn't yet finished packing. In any case, he would be extremely indebted if Mardaras would find him a carriage quickly. Mardaras pretended not to have heard, but merely looked at him blankly. Am I drunk, or is he? he wondered.

"I've had enough anti-mimesis for one evening," he added, trying to be clever. It was a mistake.

"No amount is ever enough," Mardaras finally spoke. "There's one more thing you need to see before I let you leave," he continued, slowly pulling his watch from his waistcoat pocket. "Come, it's time." He turned and left the room.

Back along the same route. The grassy path. The corridor with the stagnant water. The steps. As they climbed, his desire to write intensified, though he also knew he was now entirely drunk. It was hot. He was sweating. The damp on the wall reminded him of a mural depicting scissors and fingernail clippings. He despised fingernails. The way you cut them and they kept growing, then you cut them again and a week later they were again too long. Clinging to the flesh beneath, which was as tender and defenseless as a sheared sheep, they grew and grew, while the fingers remained the same, enduring unawares the tough carapace that grew relentlessly longer. If there were such a thing as natural selection, if Darwin's theories were correct, why on earth did humans still have fingernails? Why hadn't they disappeared, like tails and fur? The walls of that long passageway seemed to be covered in dirty nails engraved on the wall, some sunk into the stone. When he was a boy his mother used to clip his nails close to the flesh, and he always suffered for a long time afterward, he couldn't pick anything up, would wander through the house with clenched fists. And the clippings, those half-moons … Some people kept them as a sort of relic, left or supposedly forgot them on the nightstand or beside the washbasin, yellow half-moons, some soft as rubber, others as unyielding as bone. Once, the maid was dusting the table with quick circular movements, and she saw them, how could she not have seen them, a whole heap, though by all rights there should have been only ten, and while she always dusted carefully, that day she seemed to overlook them, perhaps on purpose, and the cloth in her hand swept past them several times, then moved in another direction, increasing his agony, until with an absentminded motion—but was it truly absentminded?—she brushed them aside, scattering them on the floor. Nausea flooded him. Now they were lost, invisible, and he might step on them at any moment, if he were to walk there barefoot. And then there were cuticles, those pointy scarabs that sprouted between flesh and nail.

They waited in line before a doorway concealed by heavy yellow curtains, where a small crowd had gathered. They entered a long, narrow, unadorned space that looked like a schoolroom, with desks arranged in a semicircle. A valet led them to their places. He heard applause. A small old man appeared and bowed deeply. The applause grew louder. Someone dressed as a high-ranking military officer ushered two women into the room. One was wearing a nightgown. "The madwomen from Salpêtrière," Mardaras whispered in his ear. The small old man began to speak in a resonant voice, but Mardaras also kept whispering to him, in a state of terrible excitement, unfortunately he hadn't been able to attend any of the hysterical séances in Salpêtrière, and after Charcot, the great Charcot, left, they had been banned from the hospital, so now the séances took place at the Ark under conditions of utter secrecy, the old man was Charcot's successor, and the phenomenon was entirely unique, had upended all medical theories. Nobody no-one, he thought.

One of the women was entirely listless, but the one wearing the nightgown began to tremble. "The queen of hysteria," some-one called. "The goddess of hysteria." Which was the goddess and which the queen? A servant struck a leather rod against a copper tray with a shiny curved lip, and it rang in his mind with a fluid sound that snuffed out all others. Bong. He craned his neck to get a better view. *Bong. Bong.* Sound, anti-sound. On the third bong one of the women collapsed in a heap, and the officer caught her in the air just in time. The old man pranced with mincing little steps toward the other woman, carrying a large, forked magnet which he displayed to the audience as he approached, walking on tiptoe as if attempting some crime. He lifted the magnet with a theatrical gesture, then passed it slowly before the body of the sick woman. The audience leaned back, then forward. Some sighed. The woman began to laugh, first gently, then with hilarity, then to cackle. It was a revolting laugh. The old man waved the magnet over her belly in insistent circles. Everyone in the room held their breath. *Bong.* The laughter sud-denly ceased. The woman leaped in place and arched her body backward into a bridge. *Bong.* Another leap and the woman stood upright again. Another bong. Nobody no-one, he thought. Each strike of the rod was discernable, each resulting clang of the tray distinct. The sound of the strike was entirely clear—yet at the same time it caused a prolonged echo that came in waves, the murmur of a chant echoing in his skull until it suddenly died out, leaving him unprepared, uncertain, experiencing that emptiness, that absence of sound, as something almost tangible. What was strange was that he felt as if the echo existed only for him, as if only he could hear it. Only him. Each *bong* brought a new beginning. Condemned from the start. Or perhaps it was the sound that inexorably followed? Either way, the result was the same. The sound carried its echo within. Mimesis contained anti-mimesis.

The hair held the word.

It was its guard.

I've lost it, too, I've drunk so much my own mind is ringing like a bell, he thought, still in a fine mood.

A valet approached and handed a card to Mardaras. He read it and gave a start in his seat, then turned toward him in agitation. Madame de was at the Ark, too, and was waiting for him at the entrance. She had come on her own in search of the boy with the pigeons, it was unheard of, entirely unheard of. He had to rush to her aid. He would be back as soon as possible. But just in case … He would arrange for a carriage to be waiting for him at the door. Another five minutes, he decided. The woman in the nightdress was holding the officer's arm and they were strolling up and down, she dallying, miming a fashionable walk. The other woman had fallen unconscious on one of the desks.

Nobody no-one. Why was that stuck in his head? Cavafy was a nonentity at first but thanks to his hard work. Thanks to his hard work what? Thanks to his hard work and persistence Cavafy became what he became. Nobody no-one.

Nullitas. Nonentity. He felt as if he were hovering just above the crowd, weaving gently between the heads in the audience. Some held lorgnettes up to their eyes. Luckily he didn't feel dizzy. You're nottheworstnorthebest, he thought. This era was notthebestnortheworst. The words had stuck together. It was nottheworstnorthebest of times. He recalled a lighthouse, buoys scattered over the silver waters, a sky streaked with orange. It wasn't a scene from Alexandria, but probably a painting by some romantic who'd worked from memory, beautifying the city with his brush. You're nottheworstnorthebest. Tangled words. Beneath his drunkenness lay a worry that alcohol couldn't dissolve. The idea of his return to Alexandria pressed on his chest.

He stood to leave. The spectacle no longer interested him. *Bong. Bong.* Enough. He wanted to go back to the hotel. Each bong was a new beginning. And yet it arose from something already dead. Glowing, lifeless. He noticed a movement in the second row, a furtive fluttering at one of the desks up front that sent shivers down his body. The crowd was even thicker now, all the seats occupied. A few onlookers had wedged themselves into the narrow corridor and were waving their gaudy fans, waiting for the valet to find them a seat. How would he ever reach the front row? He began to make his way forward, muttering pardon, *excusez-moi*, pushing, stepping on shoes and frills, knowing it was a mistake, he would never make it. He would never make it. It couldn't be. He was drunk, that was all. He saw that chestnut-brown hair nodding at him again with a shake of the head. Then he saw the profile, those full lips. How could the dancer be here? Perhaps he hadn't left Paris after all. Perhaps the performance in Venice had been canceled. Perhaps he had merely changed hotels. Scenes from behind the closed door came to life. The shortened breath, the cries, the sweet caresses. Wild caresses. Slaps. Naked bodies on an unmade bed. That endless journey to his room, trembling lest he lose the priceless hair. How he had found the strength to rise to his feet, grab hold of the door frame, walk away. How he had found the strength to let go of the hair. *Abandon.* Passionate kisses deep on the mouth.

He bumped directly into a young man with protruding teeth who was sitting next to his very beautiful mother.

It was a hot, oppressive night, the sort where not a leaf stirs. He went outside. He heard the heavy door lock behind him, heard his feet descending the stairs. He took a few steps forward. What would he say if they asked him about the Ark? He turned around to look. A grim farmhouse in the middle of nowhere with a pitched straw roof. Ivy trailed over the worn façade. The pale moon sat on the chimney like a jaunty cap. The windows were covered over with boards nailed crosswise, a detail he hadn't noticed earlier.

What would you like me to tell you about the Ark? he would ask. Then he would fall silent for a moment, knowing that the anticipation would increase his audience's interest. He would look at the faces across from him. Some would be innocent, expectant, a thirst for knowledge shining in their eyes; others would be prematurely arrogant. Lost causes, thick-skinned, indifferent. He would try to concentrate on the first, on those who longed for poetry and truth because for them poetry and truth were the same—he would address himself to those innocents who would soon learn how mistaken they were.

The Ark doesn't exist, he would say.

Of course they would wait for him to go on. An audience of that sort doesn't give in easily. Someone would laugh nervously. Someone else would make a philosophical or perhaps comical comment in hopes of encouraging him to continue, believing it was merely a *trouvaille*, a rhetorical device on the part of the great poet whose aim was to excite his audience's imagination. He would interrupt that last admirer's comment with a piercing glance. The Ark doesn't exist, he would say again, and for the last time. Then he would slowly rise to leave. As he withdrew from the room he would feel all eyes trained on him, would sense their uncomfortable silence, their disappointment. But if they asked him again, he would say the same thing.

The same thing.

There was no carriage waiting for him.

A strange quiet. Hens and ducks nowhere to be seen. He paced up and down, annoyed at himself for trusting Mardaras. He should go back, ask the valet at the entrance to call a carriage, otherwise he might be waiting a long while. He heard a commotion. Muffled voices. Over by the coops two shadows moved. Perhaps it was his coachman drinking with the caretaker. He went closer. There was no one there. Behind the chicken wire the hens seemed to sigh in their sleep. Again that same muffled sound, the growling of some small animal. In the neighboring coop sat three rows of pigeons, as still as statues on their shelves. He saw a body lying on the ground and took a step back. Then he stepped forward again, gluing his face to the chicken wire. "Halt," a voice called. One of the pigeon keepers was running toward him. The other appeared, too, and gave him a sudden shove.

"Let him go," said the first, coming closer. His breath stank.

"Listen to me," he said, and grabbed him by the scruff of his neck. "You see those birds there, see their eggs?"

"Look closely," he said, ramming his head into the cage.

"Do you see those eggs?" he insisted.

He saw a boy whose hands were tied behind his back, a kerchief over his eyes.

"So, listen up. You may want to skin those eggs, but you can't."

"Isn't that right?" the other chortled.

"Eggs don't have skin. Understand?"

His head was thrust forcefully against the chicken wire. The wire cut into his skin and he couldn't breathe.

"Understand? Eggs don't have skin," he whistled.

The boy in the coop shifted. He tried to stand but fell back down. A pigeon flew toward him, fluttered past his face. It was the boy with the melancholy eyes he had seen near Galeries Lafayette.

"Now you say it, so we know you've understood."

A blow hit his ribs. His knees buckled, his body doubled over. The pain was sharp, stabbing. How did I not cry out, he wondered, how did I not make a sound?

One of the pigeon keepers grabbed him by the shoulders and shook him.

"Are you deaf?"

"Speak up."

"Do you see those eggs?"

Behind the chicken wire the boy looked at him with those eyes, which had grown even bigger in the darkness.

Another blow came from the left, landing in his gut. As he

sank to the ground, pain filled his mouth and he felt as if his teeth were swimming in blood.

"Eggs don't have skin," he stammered. His glasses fell in the dirt.

A carriage screeched to a halt. The door opened, someone called to him. He picked up his glasses and ran.

It was the same carriage with the velvet pillows that had brought him and Mardaras to the Ark.

The comte de Losange had a glass of cognac ready in his hand and placed it under his nose. He gestured for the coachman to whip the horses. Then he leaned toward him, saying it was a rare liqueur, aged in oak casks, this barrel, from that year, an irrefutably excellent vintage. The casks were made in a particular village in Limousin, and the wood of the local oak gave it that uniquely bitter scent of vanilla.

"Listen to me," he cut him off, "we have to go back, a child is in danger."

The comte began to laugh.

That laughter astonished him. Still out of breath, he tried to ignore it, and told the comte about the boy with the pigeons who was being held captive at the Ark. They had to return right away, the boy was in danger. He was in a pigeon coop, bound and blindfolded. And the pigeons were very unusual birds, with a special gift. Otherwise why would those two pigeon keepers have attacked him? They had beat him mercilessly—he didn't want even to imagine what might have happened had the comte not appeared.

The comte didn't seem particularly impressed by this speech. It was all a show, in his opinion, a mise en scène to increase the Ark's allure. The men he took to be pigeon keepers must be cheap actors. There was no sense in getting involved. Besides, they couldn't have hit him terribly hard, there wasn't so much as a scratch on him, or a split eyebrow. All he needed was a good dusting off. It had all been a *fantaisie*.

"Commedia dell'arte, if you ask me," the comte concluded, twirling his waxed mustache.

"Just a minute," he said. "There's something you might not know. Those pigeons were involved in the spiritualist encounters at the home of Madame de Filion. That child was their trainer. Suddenly, a month ago, the pigeons disappeared, and the boy with them."

It was the last card in his hand. He described the pigeons' harmonic arrangement during the séances, the seamless communication with the dead, and whatever else he could remember from Madame de's descriptions.

"Madame de," the comte smiled slightly. "Don't make me laugh any harder, it's bad for my stomach. That exquisite old woman invented the whole thing."

There was no point in insisting. Nor in mentioning the skin of the eggs—it would merely offer definitive confirmation of the comte's opinion that the whole scene had been staged. They seemed to be entering Paris. Ant colonies of lights approached in the dark.

They were silent for a while. The events of the evening returned in a jumble to his mind. Every so often he felt little waves of dizziness. He thought of the torn papers on the floor of his hotel room. "Again in the Same City" was safe in Alexandria, thankfully. He hadn't made any significant edits during the trip.

All eleven versions of that poem were in an envelope on his desk. Again in the same city. They must have been approaching the Grands Boulevards. The Saint-Pétersbourg wasn't far. The streets were nearly deserted, the lamps snuffed, faint flickers of gas on the marquees. A few passersby hurriedly chased their shadows. Some caught up with them, and the shadows disappeared only to unfurl a few steps farther down the sidewalk, longer, more threatening.

Paris, the city will follow you, he felt like shouting. Three revelers lurched toward them from the other direction, walking sticks hanging at their sides like useless bayonets. No one would escape. Always in the same city. *And as you've squandered your life in this small corner, you've ruined it all over the world.* Perhaps his moment was finally close at hand, he thought, and abandoned himself for a moment to a foolish dream, the sort of dream a spanked child would have, he knew—how once he was famous, when the Mardarases of the world had acknowledged his talents, they would trail after him wherever he went, and hesitate before addressing him.

The carriage must have turned. They were crossing the Champs-Élysées.

What time was it? He had no idea.

"I'm going to take you somewhere," the comte said.

He had no desire to go anywhere else.

"Somewhere," the comte repeated, smiling to himself. "I won't tell you anything else, you'll see for yourself."

They were passing the Tuileries. Place Vendôme. Palais Royal.

He was entirely certain that the birds he'd seen in the coop were the ones Madame had told him about. As still as statues on the shelves. The image of the boy haunted him. Bound with rope, on the ground amid bird droppings and filth. If he could have kneeled down beside him, he would have tried to relieve his pain. He would have caressed him. Kissed his wounds.

They seemed to be heading east. The horses' shoes rang out rhythmically against the pavement, their hooves practically meeting in the air.

"Can you tell me what erdeon means?" the comte asked.

"Erdeon?"

"It's a Greek word. E-r-d-e-o-n," he spelled it out.

"It doesn't mean anything. There's no such word."

"Strange."

The comte was skeptical. The word had stuck in his head after his trip to Greece. He must have heard it somewhere. Not at the meetings of the Loan Committee, that much was certain. It must have come from one of the wealthy Athenians who had surrounded them like puffed-up turkeys, or perhaps a plebe in a working-class neighborhood during one of their evening outings, a plebe, why not? In Greece—as he'd determined more than once, thanks to his excellent knowledge of ancient Greek—the commoners may have looked like cavemen, but every so often they tossed out a rare, sophisticated word, a refined phrase he hadn't heard before and which made an intense impression on him. "Think a bit more on it," he insisted.

"The word doesn't exist."

The coachman tugged the reins. The black horses slowed, then stopped.

Discovering in a French coachman's eyes the gaze of a young

fellah from the Nile Delta—that's what passed through his mind as the carriage stopped and the coachman came back to lower the running board, then held out a hand to help him down. Deep chestnut eyes, almond-shaped, with a hint of sorrow that wasn't sorrow but ennui, he thought and jumped nimbly out of the carriage, ignoring the outstretched hand. He had always been a keen judge of physiognomies—he and John would place bets, and he enjoyed it greatly. What sort of work do you think he does? Does he come from an aristocratic family, or only nouveau riche? It used to be their favorite game.

The carriage drew off. He and the comte de Losange were alone on the sidewalk.

In the distance he could make out the Hôtel-Dieu.

Before them was a little building with a sign reading *Cabinets d'aisance*.

"You go in first."

"I'm not in that sort of need," he said.

"It's not what you think."

The comte disappeared into the *pissotière*.

Two men emerged looking nonplussed, straightening their clothes. One inhaled deeply, sniffing the air. They strode off in opposite directions, then seemed to remember they were together, came back, and lit cigarettes. From their heavy accents he could tell they were from the provinces.

"Not much happening tonight."

"Just wait."

"Remember when we first came to Paris? That's what you told me, wait."

"I said the same things back then, eh? How the time passed."

"Life is a weekend."

"It sped by, didn't it?"

The glowing tips of their cigarettes lit their misty faces—they must have been just a step before middle age—and though they spoke calmly, the stance of their bodies, the way one awaited the other's reaction, betrayed an uncertainty in their relationship and at the same time a stifling intensity, directed somewhere else, toward some other spot. Now and then they threw him sideways glances.

"Back when it was still Saturday night ... You know how it seemed to me then? Like gold coins rang in my ears wherever I went. Then it was Sunday morning and the ringing was gone. Nothing. Silence."

"From Sunday afternoon on it's all downhill."

"And where are we now? Sunday afternoon."

Life is a weekend. He missed the rest of the conversation.

"What are you doing out here?" The comte gestured for him to come inside.

The stench was unbearable.

Five urinals in a row, emptying into a grimy trough full of secretions and filth.

"Read the sign on the wall," the comte whispered.

"Ne pas déposer de croûtons de pain dans les urinoirs."

"Come over here," he said. They hid in the shadows at the back of the *pissotière*.

They heard footsteps. The comte gestured for him to keep silent.

One of the men from the provinces rushed in. He stood uneasily, scanning the space with his eyes, perhaps wanting to make sure they were gone, since he hadn't seen them come back outside. He fell to his knees and plunged his hand into the trough. As he groped around, the urine overflowed into the drain, and with his head turned toward the door of the *pissotière* to make sure no one was coming, he began to pull at a long string. There was a baguette tied to one end. It was dark, and he wasn't sure what was happening. The baguette appeared to be wrapped in a net. The man disappeared.

Beside him the comte, completely cool and unperturbed, again motioned for him to keep quiet.

A ray of opaline light from the streetlamp slipped in through a hole someone had made between the tiles, and as it fell on a mirror on the opposite wall, it seemed to him that a strange landscape was taking shape, in which the *pissotière* was depicted upside-down, the trough hovering above the urinals.

Erdeon. I'm erdeon, he thought.

He swirled the word around in his mouth and decided he liked it. For some reason the word was connected in his mind with the skin of eggs. No such word existed, that much was certain.

A young man came inside, unbuttoned his pants, and began to urinate. From his vantage point, he could see the man's penis poking robustly out of his underwear, thick, dark, ringed with heavy creases.

He buttoned up again and left.

One of the men from the provinces appeared right away out of nowhere, approaching like a bird of prey. He grabbed the baguette out of the trough, tore the netting around it, opened his mouth wide, and pressed the bread with his hands so as to lodge it under the roof of his mouth. Just then the second man appeared, eyes glistening in the opal ray of light. It wasn't drunkenness, but some other, strange desire. He unbuttoned his pants with spasmodic movements and urinated on the baguette, which the first man held out like an offering as he continued to urinate, a stream that seemed never to end.

He felt flushed. His heart beat irregularly. He needed to calm down. By now he had become accustomed to that unbearable stench, perhaps it even excited him. The comte at his side was watching with an icy gaze. He wracked his brains, tried to think of something, anything, to get some distance from the sight, quickly, before his perturbation betrayed him, before he was humiliated. He needed to think of something unpleasant … the furless cat at the hotel reception. But instead of the cat, he saw pulsating before him the member of that boy at his school in Liverpool, the strong stream of his urine, and his member, thick and white, with those same creases.

It was the second man's turn to urinate. The other kneeled before him. Now all he could see was the urinating man's back, the shoulders hunched, then thrown back, then hunched again.

He looked at the shimmering ray of light. It cut through the *pissotière* like a taut cord, directing its energy at the upside-down landscape on the wall, where a filthy trough hung over urinals now partially obscured by the men's shadows—a grotesque scene created by that very ray of light, by its opaline glints, even if, in the end, that destination seemed inevitable. It all meant something but he was too confused to figure out what. At least he had managed to calm himself. He was once again in control. At least there was that.

Erdeon, he thought.

What a pity the word didn't exist.

One of the men was hunched over, buttoning his pants. The other was holding the wet baguette, and as he turned, probably to ask something, the baguette landed in the ray of light—an ordinary, long, white baguette, dripping urine as a punctured pipe drips water. The ray of light was disturbed, and the landscape on the wall vanished.

Then the two of them fell on the bread together, starting to devour it straight from the lip of the trough. He felt as if he could distinguish the sounds of the chewing, the greedy gulping, short gasps of breath and the smacking of lips and tongues, he saw their hands tearing at the bread, and then the panting intensified, the smacking ceased and the only sound resembled a death rattle. Beside him the comte was nodding his head, sniffing slightly as if in approval.

A passage from Plutarch came to mind, on the rules of the feast. Whether it was fitting for philosophical questions to be discussed over a meal. It must have been from the *Symposium of the Seven Sages*. There was another passage that staged a discussion about an animal carcass from which the best and worst part was to be removed—the tongue. As obscene as it was, he thought, there was also something sacred about that feast in the *pissotière*. The men's elation was almost religious. They might have been bowing down before the profaned bread as if in some sort of purification ritual. A preparation for Holy Communion. Body and blood. He remembered that afternoon in Constantinople, in the remote church by the vinegar shops, with the young apprentice he had followed. How they had knelt there in the bare pews, under the humble dome, distant from each other yet also close. He remembered the flickering flames of the candles, the unbearable silence, the incense, the austere figures of saints on the blackened iconostasis. The dark pulpit like the mouth of a whale. The symbols of faith had increased his desire, without a doubt. Perhaps pleasure and faith weren't so distant from each other after all. Perhaps, he thought, they belonged to the same sphere, a higher sphere that only a select few could approach, inaccessible to the crude and ignorant. It required a stance that was aesthetic and ethical at once—a vantage point from which sacred reverence and erotic excitement no longer belonged to opposing worlds.

The feast had ended. A cloudy ecstasy was etched into the men's expressions as they clumsily buttoned their overcoats, fingers fumbling at buttonholes. They were wearing long, loose overcoats, out of keeping with the season. Though not so strange, he realized, when he noticed that one of the men had a massive erection. They shoved the remains of the sopping baguette in their pockets and left.

"Do you want to stay here on your own for a while? There will be more to see soon enough," the comte said.

He didn't answer. He was still agitated. He hastened to follow the comte outside.

THE HYMN TO THE TINY HAIR

There are days and days. Glorious days that pass in a single breath and quiet days when nothing happens at all. Mornings when everything seems possible, planned by a heavenly hand, and others when you wake with a rancid taste in your mouth, when the abominations of the previous night rise before you once more, ghosts of a carnival, as in Seleucia when they brought Crassus's severed head to the table, dripping blood, Bacchae dancing wildly in celebration of Surena's victory, or when mournful messengers arrived in that Greek colony, or other carefree mornings that sour before you've realized it, day darkening into night, as when Julian received the oracle from Delphi, *Tell the emperor ... Phoebus no longer has his house, nor his mantic bay, nor his prophetic spring*, a pseudo-oracle that the Christians invented seven centuries later, or then again when some remarkable, unforgettable era unexpectedly springs to life, days of triumph under a golden sun, days that will soon be extinguished, like the cloudless day on which the Pythia warned Nero to fear the number seventy-three, and Nero went ahead and plundered the oracle's copper statues, thinking he had plenty of time, since he was only thirty years old, or when suddenly near midnight a strain of music sounds ... When entirely unexpectedly, on that terrible night in Alexandria that Plutarch describes, the sounds of instruments were heard, melodies and ululations in the deathly calm, an invisible procession crossing the city, and people said it was Dionysus the double god, of life and Hades both, of light and of darkness, headed for the walls with his entourage, Dionysus leaving, abandoning Antony, or … Or. Or a night like the previous night whose mad flame slowly consumed the wick, his wick, and he waited and waited for the blast, the enormous crack of the explosion. But no blast came. There was no explosion. He stood in his room wearing a clean shirt. Washed, combed. He had managed to wake up in time. His luggage was ready, padlocked shut. Soon the valet would be there to take them downstairs.

He looked at his watch. Another half an hour.

In that labyrinth that was and was not, he thought back over the Ark, and his mind slipped to another image, at an outdoor market late in the afternoon, in some other part of the world, where a crowd had gathered, everyone waiting, even the shortest, the oldest, the blind and the crippled, dozens pushing and shoving around a choking cloud of smoke that suddenly flared, scorching hats and tailcoats. What on earth are they waiting for? he wondered.

Half an hour. Not a bad title for a poem.

And those people in the caves, where had that image come from? Those creatures in caves, not yet people, hunchbacked, half ape, hairy, wrapped in sheepskins. Hewing, grinding. How they slowly stand erect. A crowd of erdeons. Mornings of stone on which the smallest movement is a feat. The first light trembles, dimly illuminating these figures, knees still bent, shadows on the wall, a hairy arm groping for some support, they stagger, stumble, manage to stand, dragging a foot bit by bit over the ground, then the other foot, a slight movement as they steady themselves, arms outstretched, balancing their unwieldy wings, slowly, slowly, a bit farther, a bit more, they rise. Homo erectus.

Homo erectus.

It was no different from an important work of art, he realized with surprise at that very moment. The same leap. The slightest leap that brought you to your feet. A magical movement that conceals all the effort behind it, all the failed attempts, the sadness and rage, days and nights crawling on all fours through the cave, while inside a voice keeps telling you to stand, that you can stand, until with a little jump there you are up on two feet as if it were the simplest thing. As when the technique has been mastered, when the poet's talent is eclipsed by the quality of the poem and what remains is pleasure, the certainty that what you're reading is something extraordinary.

The tiny hair, he thought.

Abandon.

His gaze fell on the bed. He looked at the creases in the sheets, the mussed covers, the pillows, and remembered every detail of his languor, how these past few days he had writhed and rolled over that bed, and then sat on its edge, unhappy, irresolute. His mind felt light, empty. Like a diver slipping into the water with no preconceptions, curious as to what he'll discover, a coral, a battered shoe, some ancient warrior's javelin.

> *He who saw the lights of Infinity*
> *And knows when they appear when they fade*

Lines by Callimachus, a leisurely flow. *How the sun darkens and the stars invent new paths as the hours turn … Erotic sadness wears you deeply down, and desire bitterly shakes your heart …*

After all, he thought, Berenice's lock, a blonde braid, inspired those exquisite lines. And it had become a star, too. *Oh, that I could be a royal lock again, and Orion would shine beside Aquarius.*

Who knew where Berenice's star shone in the celestial dome. He'd never looked for it. *At night the gods crush me, hide me, but when day breaks …* If a lock of hair could inspire Callimachus, he thought again. And if a tiny hair could beget such agitation, so many associations and images, and sweep him up to such an extent that he had knelt and kissed a stranger's door. That particular hair and no other, springing from the soft testicle of a young Russian dancer, distinct from the others, slightly rougher or longer, tickling your palm, enflaming your desire … *since it established the trophies of eros …* its memory stroking your face like a breeze, becoming a breath of creativity … *and I for these works rise dancing into the stars …* and accompanies you on the narrow, untrodden path of Art, that tiny hair.

"Hairs and horsefeathers," he said out loud and felt like laughing.

He thought he'd heard someone knocking on the door but there was no one there. He glanced down the empty corridor and went back into the room. The train to Marseille would be leaving soon. John might already be waiting in the lobby.

There are days and days, he considered. And there will be others. Days and nights when a person wonders, what am I doing here? How did I end up like this? Days when the world we knew has vanished and the new world hasn't yet arrived.

He stood up again. That must be the valet coming for the luggage.

"Good morning, sir."

Before him stood a boy with sandy hair, very slight, with something like a birthmark on his face. From his vantage point, the mark on the boy's cheek looked like an island, an unexplored island, a stretch of dry land that spread even wider when the boy smiled and his small, sad eyes lit up.

ACKNOWLEDGEMENTS

When I started writing this book, I never imagined how many years it would take me to finish it, or how many people I would involve in the process in one way or another. Or even how many times I would have to leave, carrying photocopies, manuscripts, and books, going somewhere else, with the hope that that "elsewhere" would be better than where I was.

Thanks are due, above all, to two people who helped me throughout the writing of this novel: Paul Vangelisti and Dimitris Daskalopoulos.

My deepest gratitude as well to Professor Ioannis Metaxas, president of the Cavafy Archive at the Onassis Foundation, and to Theodoros Chiotis, project manager of the archive.

I also thank the friends and acquaintances who helped in various ways and who eased or made more enjoyable the bleak bits of the journey. They are: François Perez, Eva Stefani, Panayotis Makris, Béatrice Wilmos, Manolis Savvides, Evelyn Toynton, Vicente Fernández Gonzalez, Anaid Donabedian, Anton Shammas, Lena Pasternak, Panayiotis Sotiropoulos, Catherine Velissaris, Eglal Errera, Achmy Halley, Maria Rousaki, Kostas Kasolas, Vana Solomonidou, Caterina Carpinato, Diana Haas, Despina Provata, Andreas Dimopoulos, Ellen Evjen, Nikos Papafilippou, Katerina Schina, and Markellos, who read 153 different versions of the last paragraph. Vasileios Filippatos for the days in Alexandria. Michel D. who patiently supported me through the years of writing this book. The one and only Toula Kontou everywhere and always. And finally, the most lively of all sources of inspiration: the man who shouted, "I'm erdeon," naked from the stage.

For the gift of time, peace, and a beautiful place in which to write, I thank: Villa Marguerite Yourcenar, Civitella Ranieri Foundation, Maison des écrivains et des traducteurs étrangers à Saint-Nazaire, Rockefeller Foundation Bellagio Center, Bogliasco Foundation, Instituto Sacatar in Brazil, the House of Literature on Paros, and the Baltic Center for Writers and Translators.

ERSI SOTIROPOULOS has written fifteen books of fiction and poetry. Her work has been translated into many languages, and has been twice awarded Greece's National Book Prize as well as her country's Book Critics' Award and the Athens Academy Prize. *What's Left of the Night* won the Prix Méditerranée Étranger 2017 in France.

KAREN EMMERICH has published a dozen book-length translations of modern Greek poetry and prose. She has received the Best Translated Book Award for her translation of Eleni Vakalo's *Before Lyricism*. She teaches comparative literature at Princeton.

THE LAST WEYNFELDT BY MARTIN SUTER

Adrian Weynfeldt is an art expert in an international auction house, a bachelor in his mid-fifties living in a grand Zurich apartment filled with costly paintings and antiques. Always correct and well-mannered, he's given up on love until one night—entirely out of character for him—Weynfeldt decides to take home a ravishing but unaccountable young woman and gets embroiled in an art forgery scheme that threatens his buttoned up existence. This refined page-turner moves behind elegant bourgeois facades into darker recesses of the heart.

THE MADELEINE PROJECT BY CLARA BEAUDOUX

A young woman moves into a Paris apartment and discovers a storage room filled with the belongings of the previous owner, a certain Madeleine who died in her late nineties, and whose treasured possessions nobody seems to want. In an audacious act of journalism driven by personal curiosity and humane tenderness, Clara Beaudoux embarks on *The Madeleine Project*, documenting what she finds on Twitter with text and photographs, introducing the world to an unsung 20th century figure.

A VERY FRENCH CHRISTMAS

A continuation of the very popular Very Christmas Series, this collection brings together the best French Christmas stories of all time in an elegant and vibrant collection featuring classics by Guy de Maupassant and Alphonse Daudet, plus stories by the esteemed twentieth century author Irène Némirovsky and contemporary writers Dominique Fabre and Jean-Philippe Blondel. With a holiday spirit conveyed through sparkling Paris streets, opulent feasts, wandering orphans, flickering desire, and more than a little wine, this collection proves that the French have mastered Christmas.

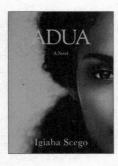

ADUA BY IGIABA SCEGO

Adua, an immigrant from Somalia to Italy, has lived in Rome for nearly forty years. She came seeking freedom from a strict father and an oppressive regime, but her dreams of film stardom ended in shame. Now that the civil war in Somalia is over, her homeland calls her. She must decide whether to return and reclaim her inheritance, but also how to take charge of her own story and build a future.

IF VENICE DIES BY SALVATORE SETTIS

Internationally renowned art historian Salvatore Settis ignites a new debate about the Pearl of the Adriatic and cultural patrimony at large. In this fiery blend of history and cultural analysis, Settis argues that "hit-and-run" visitors are turning Venice and other landmark urban settings into shopping malls and theme parks. This is a passionate plea to secure the soul of Venice, written with consummate authority, wide-ranging erudition and élan.

A VERY RUSSIAN CHRISTMAS

This is Russian Christmas celebrated in supreme pleasure and pain by the greatest of writers, from Dostoevsky and Tolstoy to Chekhov and Teffi. The dozen stories in this collection will satisfy every reader, and with their wit, humor, and tenderness, packed full of sentimental songs, footmen, whirling winds, solitary nights, snow drifts, and hopeful children, the collection proves that Nobody Does Christmas Like the Russians.

THE MADONNA OF NOTRE DAME
BY ALEXIS RAGOUGNEAU

Fifty thousand people jam into Notre Dame Cathedral to celebrate the Feast of the Assumption. The next morning, a beautiful young woman clothed in white kneels at prayer in a cathedral side chapel. But when someone accidentally bumps against her, her body collapses. She has been murdered. This thrilling novel illuminates shadowy corners of the world's most famous cathedral, shedding light on good and evil with suspense, compassion and wry humor.

THE YEAR OF THE COMET BY SERGEI LEBEDEV

A story of a Russian boyhood and coming of age as the Soviet Union is on the brink of collapse. Lebedev depicts a vast empire coming apart at the seams, transforming a very public moment into something tender and personal, and writes with stunning beauty and shattering insight about childhood and the growing consciousness of a boy in the world.

MOVING THE PALACE BY CHARIF MAJDALANI

A young Lebanese adventurer explores the wilds of Africa, encountering an eccentric English colonel in Sudan and enlisting in his service. In this lush chronicle of far-flung adventure, the military recruit crosses paths with a compatriot who has dismantled a sumptuous palace and is transporting it across the continent on a camel caravan. This is a captivating modern-day Odyssey in the tradition of Bruce Chatwin and Paul Theroux.

THE 6:41 TO PARIS BY JEAN-PHILIPPE BLONDEL

Cécile, a stylish 47-year-old, has spent the weekend visiting her parents outside Paris. By Monday morning, she's exhausted. These trips back home are stressful and she settles into a train compartment with an empty seat beside her. But it's soon occupied by a man she recognizes as Philippe Leduc, with whom she had a passionate affair that ended in her brutal humiliation 30 years ago. In the fraught hour and a half that ensues, Cécile and Philippe hurtle towards the French capital in a psychological thriller about the pain and promise of past romance.

ON THE RUN WITH MARY BY JONATHAN BARROW

Shining moments of tender beauty punctuate this story of a youth on the run after escaping from an elite English boarding school. At London's Euston Station, the narrator meets a talking dachshund named Mary and together they're off on escapades through posh Mayfair streets and jaunts in a Rolls-Royce. But the youth soon realizes that the seemingly sweet dog is a handful; an alcoholic, nymphomaniac, drug-addicted mess who can't stay out of pubs or off the dance floor. *On the Run with Mary* mirrors the horrors and the joys of the terrible 20th century.

OBLIVION BY SERGEI LEBEDEV

In one of the first 21st century Russian novels to probe the legacy of the Soviet prison camp system, a young man travels to the vast wastelands of the Far North to uncover the truth about a shadowy neighbor who saved his life, and whom he knows only as Grandfather II. Emerging from today's Russia, where the ills of the past are being forcefully erased from public memory, this masterful novel represents an epic literary attempt to rescue history from the brink of oblivion.

THE LAST SUPPER BY KLAUS WIVEL

Alarmed by the oppression of 7.5 million Christians in the Middle East, journalist Klaus Wivel traveled to Iraq, Lebanon, Egypt, and the Palestinian territories to learn about their fate. He found a minority under threat of death and humiliation, desperate in the face of rising Islamic extremism and without hope their situation will improve. An unsettling account of a severely beleaguered religious group living, so it seems, on borrowed time. Wivel asks, Why have we not done more to protect these people?

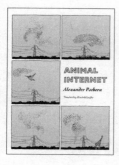

GUYS LIKE ME BY DOMINIQUE FABRE

Dominique Fabre, born in Paris and a life-long resident of the city, exposes the shadowy, anonymous lives of many who inhabit the French capital. In this quiet, subdued tale, a middle-aged office worker, divorced and alienated from his only son, meets up with two childhood friends who are similarly adrift. He's looking for a second act to his mournful life, seeking the harbor of love and a true connection with his son. Set in palpably real Paris streets that feel miles away from the City of Light, a stirring novel of regret and absence, yet not without a glimmer of hope.

ANIMAL INTERNET BY ALEXANDER PSCHERA

Some 50,000 creatures around the globe—including whales, leopards, flamingoes, bats and snails—are being equipped with digital tracking devices. The data gathered and studied by major scientific institutes about their behavior will warn us about tsunamis, earthquakes and volcanic eruptions, but also radically transform our relationship to the natural world. Contrary to pessimistic fears, author Alexander Pschera sees the Internet as creating a historic opportunity for a new dialogue between man and nature.

KILLING AUNTIE BY ANDRZEJ BURSA

A young university student named Jurek, with no particular ambitions or talents, finds himself with nothing to do. After his doting aunt asks the young man to perform a small chore, he decides to kill her for no good reason other than, perhaps, boredom. This short comedic masterpiece combines elements of Dostoevsky, Sartre, Kafka, and Heller, coming together to produce an unforgettable tale of murder and—just maybe—redemption.

I CALLED HIM NECKTIE BY **MILENA MICHIKO FLAŠAR**
Twenty-year-old Taguchi Hiro has spent the last two years
of his life living as a hikikomori—a shut-in who never
leaves his room and has no human interaction—in his parents' home in Tokyo. As Hiro tentatively decides to reenter
the world, he spends his days observing life from a park
bench. Gradually he makes friends with Ohara Tetsu, a
salaryman who has lost his job. The two discover in their
sadness a common bond. This beautiful novel is moving,
unforgettable, and full of surprises.

WHO IS MARTHA? BY **MARJANA GAPONENKO**
In this rollicking novel, 96-year-old ornithologist Luka
Levadski foregoes treatment for lung cancer and moves
from Ukraine to Vienna to make a grand exit in a luxury
suite at the Hotel Imperial. He reflects on his past while
indulging in Viennese cakes and savoring music in a gilded
concert hall. Levadski was born in 1914, the same year that
Martha—the last of the now-extinct passenger pigeons—
died. Levadski himself has an acute sense of being the last
of a species. This gloriously written tale mixes piquant wit
with lofty musings about life, friendship, aging and death.

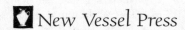 New Vessel Press

*To purchase these books and for a full listing
of New Vessel Press titles, visit our website at
www.newvesselpress.com*